QUEST of FATE

DAVID WILDE

DO not believe in anything simply because you have heard it.

DO not believe in anything simply because it is spoken and rumoured by many.

AuthorHouse™
1663 Liberty Drive
Bloomington, IN 47403
www.authorhouse.com
Phone: 1-800-839-8640

Published by AuthorHouse 06/15/2012

ISBN: 978-1-4685-8645-9 (sc)
ISBN: 978-1-4685-8646-6 (e)

I dedicate this book to my lovely wife, without her love and support I wouldn't have penned QUEST OF FATE.
I love her as I always have and always will.

INGREDIENTS:

- Take a regular suburban couple.
- Add a generous amount of love - pain – betrayal and death then mix with intrigue and the unexpected.
- Simmer stirring constantly while turning up the heat.

You now have the recipe for:
QUEST OF FATE by David Wilde.

"CAUTION TAKE CARE" THE RESULT MAY BE TOO HOT TO HANDLE.

CHAPTER ONE

It was five past seven pm when Elaine Jessop arrived at her Chelsea apartment building. She was in a jubilant mood because earlier that day she had been promoted to be personal assistant to the Managing Director John Ford. She had been John Ford's secretary at "World gems incorporated"—A renowned International diamond handling and distribution company—for the last three years.

The date was Friday the eighteenth of July two thousand and six. She cheerfully greeted the Concierge as he opened the door for her. On entering the lobby she bid good evening to the duty security officer then took the lift to her penthouse apartment. Her mood changed to disappointment though when she entered the apartment to find it was empty.

She was expecting her husband Clifford to be home and she was eager to share her good news. It wasn't unusual for Clifford to be late home because he held a high profile position with HM Customs and Immigration, however that day he said he would be home early.

His position as investigative officer often kept him late due to him having to respond immediately when circumstances called for it, as was the case that day.

He was about to leave his office when he received a call to sanction and oversee an interception of an unidentified craft inside British waters. The boat was being shadowed by the Coastguard and Clifford was the only officer on duty that could supervise such exercises.

Elaine kicked off her shoes, she was angry because she had planned to take Clifford out for a celebratory dinner and a bottle of champagne. They didn't go out very often because of the irregular hours their respective job's incurred.

She checked the house phone for messages but there were none so she decided to celebrate on her own. She opened an expensive bottle of wine they were saving for a special occasion, figuring this to be just that, she poured a glass and took it and the bottle into their lavish bathroom and placed them on the side of the Jacuzzi and lit some scented candles. She turned the Jacuzzi on and removing her clothes climbed into the bubbly water. Adding scented oils she lay back, sighing with pleasure as the foaming water engulfed her tired body.

Whether it was the effects of the wine or the warm relaxing foam she wasn't sure, but she felt herself drifting away as her body relaxed. However she was abruptly brought back down to earth by Clifford, saying: 'Room for one more?' This made her jump, she forgot for a moment where she was and started to thrash about, soaking Clifford's trousers and drenching the floor. However she soon recovered, and said: 'Oh hello, I didn't hear you come in, what are you doing creeping up on me like that? You made me jump.'

'I noticed.' He replied. He leant over and kissed her on the forehead and apologised for being late, now that she had relaxed a little she forgave him. She told him to go and pour himself a drink and she would join him in a minute.

She stepped out of the warm soothing foam and glanced at the full length mirror, admiring her figure any woman would envy, she threw on a robe and joined Clifford in the lounge. He had poured her a brandy and she told him: 'I was very angry when I came home and you weren't here, I was dying to tell you my special news and you spoiled it.' He kissed her on the cheek and asked: 'Well what is this special news? That's got you so worked up.' Excitedly she told him about the promotion and he congratulated her, she could tell though that he had something else on his mind and asked: 'Is anything wrong Cliff? You look troubled.' He told her it had just been a long day and the operation didn't go too well. She asked: 'Oh why was that?'

'Well we stopped an unidentified boat that had entered British waters which was carrying almost a million pounds worth of crack cocaine aboard. Two of the perpetrators had guns and were killed in a shoot out with armed Coastguard officers, another jumped overboard and they couldn't find him.

While all this was going on I was watching the stern and I spotted a hinged seat which had a storage space beneath and the seat was partly raised. I took it upon myself to check it out and in the process I detected a movement from beneath the lid. I cautiously moved closer pointing my gun and called out: "ARMED OFFICER COME OUT SLOWLY AND SHOW YOUR HANDS."

Nothing happened at first but after a second or so the lid slowly lifted and a man began climbing out. That is when I froze and my heart stopped because the man was actually my brother Sam. Well actually as you know he's my half brother but I haven't seen him for about fifteen years. Understandably I was stunned but I pulled myself together and asked him what the hell he was doing there, he was just about to answer when I heard a movement coming from below the wheelhouse. Not thinking rationally I told Sam to duck back down and close the lid, stupidly I threw him my card and told him to call me when it was safe. Knowing his shady history though I should have guessed he was up to no good.'

'What the hell were you thinking Clifford? A man in your position as well, you do realise that this could end your career as well as mine not to mention the legal consequences? If and when he does call, tell him to disappear back to wherever he came from and wash your hands of him.'

'Yes darling of course I will, it was just the shock of seeing him after all these years, don't worry I will send him packing.'

'Glad to hear it now go and get the take away menus and let's pick some supper.' They chose a Tai meal and Clifford phoned the order in.

While they were waiting for their meals Clifford's mobile rang, he looked at the caller display but didn't recognise the number, however he accepted the call and was horrified to discover it was Sam. Clifford mouthed the words: "It's him—Sam." Elaine gestured to him by running her finger from one side of her throat to the other indicating he should end the call. Clifford began telling Sam that he had made a mistake by not reporting him but Sam cut in saying: 'I'm in trouble Cliff I need your help, please? I'm desperate I must see you tonight.' Clifford told him to hold on. He told Elaine what Sam had said but she just reminded him of what he had promised earlier. Clifford replied: 'I'm sorry Elaine but he is family and he's in trouble and needs my help the least I can do is hear him out. I am going to see him.' Elaine was furious and snarled: 'What about the food it will be here soon?' Clifford told her to have hers and he would warm his up when he got back.

Elaine reacted angrily she got up from the couch saying: 'Fine you go and ruin my day I hope you and your brother have a wonderful time.' She stormed out of the room slamming the door after her.

Clifford met up with Sam at a pub in town, he found him at the bar with an all but empty beer glass. Clifford sat on a stool beside him and pointing at Sam's glass asked if he wanted another, Sam said he would have a pint of lager. Clifford ordered the lager and an orange juice for himself. The barman brought the drinks and Clifford asked Sam: 'What the hell is going on Sam?' This had better be good, you have started a domestic and argue is something we never do so, out with it.' Sam replied hesitantly: 'Well I come out of prison five months ago .... Clifford raised his eyes to the ceiling and gave that "here we go again look" but Sam came back at him saying: 'Oh yes that's right still the same old Sam, well I'm not actually, I was in jail because I was set up. It all started when a bloke I used to do a few jobs for asked me if I wanted to earn some serious money, I jumped at it because I was on my uppers and needed cash fast to pay my rent. He told me He and two other guys planned to rob a security truck that was delivering a month's wages to a large supermarket. As it was a bonus month there was expected to be around a half a million on board and I would have got an even share. I had a mate who worked for the security company that provided the truck and the guards he was supposed to tell me the time and date of the delivery, and said he would arrange it so he would be on the van. However he got cold feet when he found out who was fronting the job so he just gave me the time and date in here one night, and that is when he told me he was getting out and disappearing because he was terrified of what the boss would do. Who incidentally is a mean vicious swine who would murder his grandmother for a few quid.'

The first part of the plan went well, my part was to walk out in front of the truck as it slowed down to turn into the supermarket's rear entrance, pretending to trip and fall, then as the truck braked the other two ran out with shotguns and pointed them at the drivers cab. That is when it all went pear shaped. The driver didn't respond he just sat there looking at them with the engine running. The boss shouted that if they didn't get out they would open fire. Again the driver ignored him but this time he put the truck in gear and started moving towards the three of us, I got up quick but fell backwards hitting my head on the curb, the driver then headed straight for the other two. They opened fire shooting at the windshield but it was only superficially damaged, the driver then drove faster at them and realising the robbery was foiled they threw down their guns and legged it.

By this time a crowd had gathered over the road and as they ran away the pig in charge shouted out loud: "Sorry boss you are on your own now." Two men that were watching noticed that I wasn't armed so they leapt on me holding me down until the old bill came. When I was interviewed I wouldn't give up the others involved so I got ten years, I got out after six years for good behaviour though.'

Clifford listened stunned at what he heard, he thought for a bit then said: 'Ok but you said you were in trouble now. What's that all about?'

'Well when I got out the guy who ran the job was waiting outside the gates in his car, he offered to give me a lift and buy me a meal, I accepted because the food was atrocious in side but, I wish I hadn't because once I had eaten he leaned over the table and told me that I owed him and the other guy, they reckoned I should have known about the truck's toughened windshield. I tried to reason with him but he just said that he didn't care and I had to make up for the money they should have got, He said that I had six months to find half a million quid or I was dead. I believed him as well, as I said he is ruthless and does not let anyone get away with anything.'

'Ok I get that but, how does the boat enter calculations?'

'Well just before I was released a guy was brought in and he befriended me, he was in for armed robbery and a man was killed, he was forty five so he knew he would not be getting out much before he was sixty, if then. One day in the exercise yard we got talking and I told him what I was in for and that I was getting out the next week, that's when he told me of the boat and the drugs. He said He knew the runners and they had dropped him in it in a similar manner that I had, so he decided to tell me about the run today. He told me they were meeting up with a boat outside our waters, it had a large hoard of heroine aboard and they were supposed to deliver it to some big drug baron. He told me how to find the boat and how I could get on board without being seen, he said that if I got my hands on the drugs I was to contact him in jail and he would arrange a deal with some people outside and I would be very rich. That meant I could then get that moron off my back and disappear, however you lot had to come along and well, you know the rest.'

'I don't know, you have pulled some pranks in your time Sam but you have reached new heights with this one, robbing drug smugglers, Not very smart was it Sam, how in hell did you hope to pull it off?'

'To be honest I had no idea what I was going to do, I didn't even have a gun, I had to try something though I was desperate can't you see that?'

'Yes but, there is desperate and there is stupid, guess what category you come under?'

'Very funny, anyway how about you and that smart missus of yours I bet you are worth a bob or two, you could help me out, you wouldn't miss half a million.' As Sam was saying that Clifford was taking a sip of his drink and almost choked, he then asked: 'What planet are you from? I couldn't find that sort of money and even if I could there is no way on earth I would hand a penny of it over to you, if you remember you walked out on your family years ago and didn't give anyone of us a second thought, you didn't even come to your poor mother's funeral.'

'I couldn't I was busy anyway you lot wouldn't have wanted me there.'

'That maybe so but you could at least have sent some flowers.'

'Look enough of the tear jerking, are you going to help me or not?'

Not! 'Now if that's all, l I have a home to go to.'

'Lucky you, you were ranting on about family ties just then, well where's yours? However if that is your answer, then fine you'll be sorry though.'

Clifford finished his drink and offered Sam fifty pounds but Sam told him to stuff it pushing him to one side and storming out of the pub.

Clifford sat on his stool trying to take in the situation. He ordered another drink and sat thinking while he drinking it. He looked at his watch and seeing it was ten past eleven he decided he should go home.

Clifford arrived home at eleven thirty and the apartment was in darkness, he quietly crept into the bedroom, he saw that Elaine was asleep but as he was undressing she said: 'You managed to drag yourself away from him then?'

'Don't be like that Elaine; if it is any consolation I think we have seen the last of him.'

'Well as you have woken me up you may as well tell me all about it.'

'You were right to try and stop me seeing him darling, do you know what? He only wanted me to give him a half a million pounds?'

What! 'Where on earth did he think you were going to get that sort of money from, what did he want it for?' Clifford went on to tell her Sam's story, she listened dismayed then she said: 'Hang on I know it's late but I think we need a drink.' Elaine put on her dressing gown and went to the drinks cabinet in the lounge and poured two brandies, on her return to the bedroom she remarked: 'Well my instincts were spot on you are well rid of him darling.'

CHAPTER TWO

Two weeks later Thursday the thirty first of July Clifford arrived back in his office at eight thirty pm after a long tiring raid on a warehouse in the dockland. There was an E-Mail on his computer from Sally his secretary, it read: "Police called, you need to contact a Detective Chief Superintendant Lewis at Chelsea Police station ASAP". Clifford looked at his watch and was amazed it was so late he sighed and called the number. When the phone was answered Clifford gave his name and said he was returning a call from DCS Lewis, the sergeant asked him to hold the line. A few seconds went by before another male voice came on the line saying: 'Good evening DCS Lewis speaking.' Clifford said he was returning his call.

'Oh yes hello Mr Jessop. Tell me Sir, are you related to a Samuel Peter Jessop?'

'Yes I am he's my half brother, what is this about, is he in trouble again?'

'Well actually I have some very disturbing news for you Sir, your brother was discovered in Stones Park earlier today, I am sorry to tell you he has passed away.'

Oh my God! 'What happened, how did he die?'

'I'm afraid he was murdered sir, I am sorry to give you this news over the phone but we have been trying to contact you all day, your secretary said she couldn't tell me when you would return.'

'Yes that's correct I have only just arrived back in my office. Murdered you say, how? Why?'

'We have no idea who murdered him sir, or why, we were hoping you could shed some light, the Pathologist is positive it is murder though. There was no ID on him just your business card we identified him by his finger prints from his police record. When was the last time you had any contact with him sir?'

'A couple of weeks ago, he called me on my mobile out of the blue, the first time I have heard from him in fifteen years actually.'

'Did he seem troubled to you at all?'

'Well yes he said he was in trouble and needed to see me urgently, I met him in a pub in town, he said he needed a large sum of money.'

'Which pub was that sir?'

'The Spinners it's on the corner of Oakwood Street.'

'Yes I know it, exactly how much money was he after and did you give it to him?'

'No I didn't, he wanted a half a million pounds. Look how was he killed, did he suffer?'

'That is a lot of money. I know this has been a shock but would you mind if we continue this down here at the station? We need a formal identification anyway then we can continue in my office.'

'Yes of course, I'll just call my wife and let her know and I will be straight down. Where do I have to go?' Lewis told him to go to the front desk and the sergeant would call him. Clifford hung up stunned at what he had just heard, he was trembling as he called Elaine, she too was obviously shocked, she asked if he wanted her to go with him, Clifford said he appreciated the gesture but he would be fine and would call her when he was on his way home.

On his arrival at the station Clifford approached the front desk and a Sergeant asked if he could be of assistance. Clifford told him who he was and why he was there, the sergeant called DCS Lewis who told him to escort Clifford to the viewing room and He would meet him there.

DCS Lewis was waiting in the corridor outside the viewing room, he shook Clifford's hand and thanking the sergeant he gestured with his hand for Clifford to walk into the room, he told Clifford: 'May I offer my condolences Mr Jessop, I will make this the least upsetting as possible so if you would go to the small window we can get started.'

Clifford went to the window which had a black curtain on the other side of it. Lewis closed the door, the light dimmed and the curtain was drawn back.

The window looked out into a brightly lit room and a trolley stood on the other side of the window with a white sheet covering it. Clifford knew it was Sam's body and became anxious which he found strange as he was used to seeing bodies while in the process of his job.

Lewis stood behind Clifford and asked: 'Mr Jessop if you are ready then the morgue assistant will reveal the face of the body for you to see, if it is Samuel Jessop then please state the fact clearly.

The sheet was pulled down revealing just the face, Clifford froze when he saw that it was in fact Sam he was amazed at how peaceful he appeared.

After pulling himself together he said: 'Yes that is Samuel James Jessop'. DCS Lewis thanked Clifford and asked if he wished to stay a while to say goodbye but Clifford declined and the curtain was closed.

Lewis opened the door and invited Clifford to follow him and led him to his office. He asked if he would like a cup of tea, Clifford said he would prefer a strong black coffee. The DCS pushed a button on his phone and a male voice answered, Lewis asked for a tea for himself and Clifford's coffee. Lewis then said: 'I am sorry I had to put you through that ordeal Mr Jessop but it is essential I'm afraid. If you feel up to it I would like to ask you a few questions.' Clifford said he didn't mind so Lewis asked him: 'On the phone you said Sam was in trouble could you elaborate on that for me?'

'Well he was very scared, apparently the boss of the gang that was with him on the failed wages snatch had been harassing Sam since he got out of jail, he reckoned Sam owed them for the failed wages robbery saying it was his fault but, Sam said this guy set him up by running away shouting something like: "You're the boss".

'Yes I read the file. Was he—the boss?'

'You're kidding he couldn't of ordered a coffee, He said the guy told him he would die if he didn't get the money, I suppose that's What's happened, maybe if I had treated him better.'

'Don't reproach yourself Mr Jessop that sort of people never think like you or I, they probably would have killed him anyway even if you had given him the money.'

'How was he killed?'

'The pathologist report states that there was blunt force trauma to the back of his head caused by a blunt instrument, he was found face down on the edge of the pond his face in the water, I'm sorry but it seems that he was probably unconscious and most probably drowned although it is highly unlikely he would have known anything about it. SOCCO found scuff marks in the grass near the scene which suggests he was attacked then staggered before falling unconscious.'

'How awful he was no saint but he didn't deserve to die like that, I suppose I will have to arrange a funeral not that many people will attend. When will the body be released?'

'Not for a while I'm afraid, we haven't received the full post mortem report as yet and there are several other tests to be carried out, you will be notified when we are finished. By the way did he mention to you the names of his two accomplices in the robbery attempt?'

'No he was stupidly loyal to them.'

'More scared than loyal I suspect Sir, now just one more thing Mr Jessop, we have Sam's photo from his records have we your permission to release it to the media and around other forces? Someone may just recognise him from the park and maybe give us some information.'

'Yes by all means, now if that is all? I would like to get home to my wife.'

'Yes of course Mr Jessop and please accept my condolences once more.'

They said their goodbyes and Clifford left the office.

Clifford got home just after midnight, Elaine was on the sofa reading when he came into the lounge she put the book down and asked him: 'How did it go darling? You are as white as a sheet, here sit down I'll get you a drink.' Clifford declined the drink but said he would love a nice cup of tea. Elaine went and put the kettle on and returned to the lounge, she sat next to him and took his hand, she said: 'Now then tell me all about it?'

'It was horrible Elaine he was hit on the head and left to drown in a pond.'

Oh my! 'Poor Sam I know I said I hoped we would never see him again but I would never wish that on anyone.'

'Of course you wouldn't darling, I see a lot of bad things in my job but you never anticipate that happening to someone close to you.' Elaine agreed and then went to make Clifford's cup of tea, she returned with a tray of tea and biscuits and sitting back down she asked: 'Do they know who killed him—you didn't say anything about finding him on that boat did you?'

'No I didn't I'm surprised though seeing I was so shocked, no I just said that he called me out of the blue asking for money and told them what he told me. They don't know who killed him but it doesn't take much guessing. They are putting his picture out to the media. Hoping someone saw him in the Park.'

'I don't mean any disrespect by this darling but at least our careers are safe.'

'True now where's that tea?'

The following Monday Superintendant Lewis received a phone call from the Pathologist, he told Lewis: 'My original findings were correct, death was by drowning. The head wound was caused by a blow with a smooth round object like a metal pipe or a bottle, there were traces of some sort of drug in his system but I am waiting on Toxicology to get back to me. Lewis thanked him and then called his Detective Chief Inspector Martin Deacon-Lewis's assistant—bringing him up to date with the news on Sam's death, Deacon remarked: 'That doesn't give us much Gov, there was nothing found at the scene resembling a pipe or a bottle but, I'll send a team back to have a more thorough look around the area. He then said: 'I read your E-mail regarding your chat with the victim's brother did he say how his brother happened to have his card especially as they weren't supposed to have seen each other for so long?'

No! 'I have been pondering over that one myself though, I think we need to have another word with Mr Jessop, you go Martin it is possible he didn't think about it because I admit I didn't I'll put my hand up to that one.' Deacon chuckled saying: 'Well I won't tell anyone if you don't.' Lewis just said: 'Go on off you go don't milk it.'

Deacon hung up and called the Jessop's apartment but no one answered, he assumed Clifford was at work so he called Clifford's office number and asked to speak to him. Clifford's secretary answered and Deacon told her who he was and that he needed to talk to Clifford, she buzzed Clifford and he told sally to tell Deacon he could come to his office at one o'clock that afternoon. Clifford panicked a little thinking that they may have found out about the boat incident, however he continued on with his work.

At five past one Sally buzzed him to say Deacon had arrived, He told her to send him in. Deacon knocked the door and Clifford shouted for him to go in. Once he had introduced himself Clifford said: 'Sit down can I get you a coffee or tea?'

'No thank you I won't keep you long Mr Jessop I just wish to clear something up. Can you tell me how your brother came to have your card on him? After all you have had no contact with each other for some time that is correct is it not?' Clifford paused not knowing quite what to say, after a few moments he said: 'Sorry Inspector, yes that's right we haven't, its fifteen years to be exact. I was wondering myself how he could have obtained it I can only think he has picked it up from the office somehow.' Deacon replied saying that he found that hard to believe because security was like fort Knox. Clifford asked Deacon if he minded hanging on for a minute, he said he didn't and Clifford called Sally in, he asked her if anyone had been looking for him recently, she thought and said that to her knowledge there hadn't she then said: 'I will call security in case they have someone on record.' Security told her that apart from expected and official visitors no one else had been checked in. She relayed this information to Clifford and DCI Deacon. Clifford assured Deacon that no one could get into the building undetected especially his brother who was no super criminal because as Deacon himself had remarked the place was like a fortress. Deacon thanked Clifford and apologised for taking up his time and left still none the wiser how Sam ended up with Clifford's card.

After Deacon had gone, Clifford called his wife at work and told her in a shaky voice: 'I think the Police suspect me of something.'

'Suspect you of what? You're not making sense, now calm down and tell me what you mean.'

'Well an inspector deacon has just been here he wanted to know how Sam got my card, I told him I had no idea but I got the impression he didn't believe me, I don't know maybe I'm just being paranoid, sorry I bothered you darling I know you are very busy, forget it I will see you this evening.'

'Very well darling but I am never too busy to talk to you, I love you see you later.'

When DCI Deacon returned to the station he went straight to Lewis's office, he sat down and said: 'That man is definitely hiding something but, I just can't put my finger on it, I will though.' Lewis replied: 'I have no doubt about that Martin, incidentally while you were out the post mortem results came in. He was a user there were needle marks between both big toes and there was low class heroine in his system. Ben is carrying out more tests, furthermore the men you sent back to the scene found an empty wine bottle in the gutter of the bandstand roof, forensics are testing that at this moment so we may get a break.'

CHAPTER THREE

While eating their dinner that evening Clifford asked Elaine: 'Should I go to the nursing home and see Sam's uncle to let him know what's happened? He is his last remaining living relative after all, actually he's his father's brother, trouble is he is ninety three now and as you know he has Parkinson's disease. Admitted he was never very close to Sam like most of the family because of his wild way's but then he may wish to bury the hatchet "not the best choice of words I dare say" and he may wish to come to the funeral.' Elaine said that he should at least tell him then his conscious would be clear, it would then be up to his uncle to decide. She added: 'Obviously the nursing home would have to give their blessing because he may well be too ill to attend.'

Meanwhile the Pathologist called Lewis and told him there was blood and tissue on the bottle matching the victim's but there were no prints. He said he would be in touch if he found anything else. Lewis called Deacon with the news and he remarked that it looked like they were professionals. Lewis agreed, he then said he was going home and Deacon should too. Deacon said he had some paperwork to finish up then he would. Lewis hung up then called Clifford to say that they had found the murder weapon, he continued: 'Were you aware your brother took drugs?'

'No but I'm not surprised, I just wish I had given him a chance years ago maybe he would still be alive.'

'Well unfortunately that is something you will never know, now have a nice weekend Mr Jessop.' Clifford said goodbye and put the receiver down and told Elaine what Lewis had told him.

After dinner that evening Clifford went to the nursing home, he pressed the door bell and a nurse opened the door wearing a blue uniform and a white cap, she asked how she could help, Clifford said: 'Hello my name is Clifford Jessop I wish to speak to my Uncle Clive Jessop he is a resident here.' The nurse invited him in and said: 'Please take a seat Mr Jessop and I will fetch someone who can help you.' Clifford sat on a seat in the foyer and the nurse disappeared down the corridor. A few minutes later another nurse arrived dressed in a dark blue uniform with white cap and dark blue belt, she introduced herself as Senior Nurse Jo Henderson and asked Clifford to follow her. She led him to an office and closed the door. She asked if he had seen his uncle recently, Clifford looked down at his lap saying: 'I am ashamed to say no I haven't, time goes by so fast, in fact the last time I saw him was last Christmas. I am coming to see him next week though because it his birthday, unfortunately something has happened and I need to talk to him now.'

'There's no need to be ashamed Mr Jessop we all live busy lives and that is why people like your uncle are placed in homes like ours so they can get the help they need and their loved ones can get on with their lives. It is hard for families to allot the time and care that your uncle and many others like him require. Now you say you have something important to discuss with him. Are you able to tell me the details?'

Clifford told Nurse Henderson what he wanted to discuss with his uncle including wanting Clive to attend the funeral. She listened and then said: My word! 'I am so sorry Mr Jessop. As far as the funeral is concerned that would depend how he is on the day, you see he has good and bad days, more bad days than good lately. When is the funeral?'

'I can't say at present the Police won't release the body yet they are still doing tests.'

'Well we would have to play it by ear at the time we would send a nurse with him in any case as he is permanently in a wheelchair these days?'

'Yes he was at Christmas. Sam and his uncle weren't that close, He was a wild boy in his youth and walked out on us when he was seventeen, our mother never got over it and she died six months later so I don't know how he will react.'

'Well let's go and find out, he is in the common room, I'll take you to his room and bring him along so you can talk to him without being interrupted.'

When the nurse arrived with Clive he was leaning over one side of the wheelchair, he was shaking badly and Clifford noticed he was thinner in the face. He could not get over how his health had deteriorated since Christmas.

The nurse put the brakes on the wheelchair and straightened Clive up in the chair. She said she would leave them alone to talk and pointed to a bell on the wall telling Clifford to push it when he was ready to leave.

Clifford pulled up a chair and sat facing his uncle, he took his wrinkled hands in his and said quietly: 'Hello uncle it's Clifford.' There was no response from Clive so Clifford tried again, he kneeled in front of him and asked: 'Do you recognise me? I saw you at Christmas I had Elaine with me.' Clive seemed to react a little at the sound of Elaine's name so Clifford continued: 'Yes that's right Elaine. Uncle I have some bad news, Sam your nephew has passed away.' There was no more response from Clive so Clifford stood up and pressed the bell. A few minutes later nurse Henderson appeared and Clifford told her: 'I'm afraid he hasn't responded to me, I thought he was going to when I mentioned my wife's name Elaine but that was it.'

'I must admit I didn't think you would get far he has not been well for so long. The doctor has seen him and has increased his medication for his Parkinson's. Would you like me to break the news to him when he is a bit more responsive?'

'I don't know I feel it is my place to do it but then I could be at work when he is well enough so, yes please but I will be back to see him and not just for his birthday.'

'That's fine Mr Jessop, I am very sorry for your loss and don't worry I will be very sensitive when I tell Clive. Goodbye for now Mr Jessop.'

CHAPTER FOUR

Just over two months went by with no further developments in Sam's murder. It was Wednesday the seventh of October. Clifford left work relatively early and got home at five thirty. He knew Elaine was going to be late as she had to attend a meeting with her boss and a very important new client.

Clifford was very angry that Police hadn't yet released Sam's body for burial, while he was waiting for Elaine he decided to ring the station. He had tried on several occasions during the last two months to persuade the Police to let him bury Sam but was stonewalled each time. This time though he was not in the mood to be fobbed off. He called the station giving his name then asked to speak to DCS Lewis who was just leaving to go home but took the call but, he was soon to regret it. As soon as he came on the line Clifford went straight for the juggler saying: 'Clifford Jessop here, I take it you have gotten no further with my Brother's murder.'

'No Mr Jessop we haven't, we've had no response to our appeal via the media or the press. No one will admit to having seen him since he was released from jail, he seemed to be a loner whose friends only appeared to be criminals and low life's, I'm sorry Mr Jessop but it is just one of those cases.'

'Just one of those cases eh? Ok but you must have extracted every last ounce of evidence from his body by now so when are you releasing him? I wish to bury him and get some closure.'

'Well as I have told you again and again Mr Jessop it is customary procedure to hold a body during an ongoing investigation so we can't release him yet, I am sorry.'

'Ongoing investigation, this could be "ongoing" past Christmas. Well I am informing you that I am going over your head, I am contacting the Chief Constable and I am sure you will be hearing from him in the near future.'

"Clifford knew the Chief Constable due to his position as a Custom's officer they had also attended the odd charity event supporting Alzheimer's and Parkinson's disease.

Lewis retaliated: 'Threats will not get you anywhere Mr Jessop and Chief Constable Price will not interfere in a still active investigation, so I suggest you wait until we can release the body.' Clifford said no more and hung up. He immediately found the Chief Constables office number and dialled it; the CC's secretary informed Clifford that he had left for the day, Clifford thanked her then located the CC's home number, he called the number and a woman answered: 'Hello Helen price speaking.' Clifford asked to speak to the CC, she enquired who was calling and Clifford told her, she asked him to hold on, a moment later the CC answered: 'Hello Charles Price speaking.' Clifford replied: 'Hello Charles, Clifford Jessop here from Customs and Immigration I am very sorry to bother you at home but I have a personal matter I would like your help with.' The CC replied: 'Hello Clifford it's been a long time. What can I do for you?' Clifford explained the problem and Charles said: 'Yes I heard about your brother, I am sorry for your loss, I'm not sure though what I can do.The superintendant is correct in what he is saying but I can also see your position, three months is a long time to wait to bury your brother. However it is not normal protocol for a Chief Constable to intervene in a case unless there is a serious problem but, the DCS is a fellow Mason so leave it with me and I will do what I can, I'll ring you when I have news. I assume you are still on the same number?'

'Yes Charles I am and thank you.'

'Don't thank me yet, actually Clifford while you are on the phone we are having a little dinner party next Friday to celebrate Helens dreaded fiftieth birthday. Why don't you and your charming wife come along? In fact the superintendant and his wife are coming as well.'

'That sounds nice I am sure I speak for Elaine when I say we would be delighted to come. How is Helen? I don't think she remembered me when she answered the phone earlier.' Charles quipped: 'Well she is nearly fifty you know.' "I heard that." Helen called from the kitchen. Charles laughed and continued: 'I am at a christening this weekend and in the city on Monday so if I haven't before, then I will have a word with Lewis on Friday. Aperitifs are at seven and dinner at eight. Now Clifford if there's nothing more I will bid you goodnight.'

'No nothing Charles and thank you for your time and for the invitation it will be nice to have a little diversion from things, goodbye Charles and thanks again.'

'Ok Clifford, I will tell Helen that you think of her as a little diversion.' They both laughed again and hung up their phones.

While Clifford was talking Elaine had come home, when he hung up she said: 'Hello darling were you taking my name in vain just then?' Clifford answered saying: 'I sure was I have volunteered you as a strip 'a' gram at a dinner party next Friday evening.'

'Oh lord well I hope they all have new batteries in their pacemakers, they will need them when they see my super models body.'

"Yeah right" Clifford replied giving her slim waist a playful squeeze and then poured a glass of wine for them both. Elaine asked: 'Come on then tell me what it's all about.'

'Well I was tired and fed up when I got home so I called that DCS Lewis to give him what for regarding Sam's body, they still have no more evidence but still refuse to release Sam's body. I told him I was going to contact the Chief Constable and I did, that was who I was talking to, he is going to have a word but can't promise it will help. Obviously you heard the bit about the party, Helen is fifty next Friday and they are having a small dinner party and he invited us, unfortunately Lewis and his wife will be there too.'

'That sounds wonderful, now I'll have to go shopping for a new gown. I am glad that Lewis is going to get a boot up the proverbial though, right I am going to make dinner why don't you go and have nice soak in the Jacuzzi?'

Friday morning Clifford took the lift down to the car park, climbing into his car he drove out of the garage and took a left turn onto the street, as he did so he noticed a black BMW sports car parked on the same side of the road but, He paid no attention to it other than having to manoeuvre around it.All of the windows were dark tinted which prevented him from seeing in the car and He drove on ignoring it. However as he approached the turn off to the Customs building car park he glanced in the rear view mirror and he noticed what he assumed was the same car, it was about four car lengths behind him. Clifford slowed down and made his turn then stopped and watched in his rear view mirror, the BMW drew level with the entrance of the car park and stopped, it stayed there for a couple of seconds then sped off with screeching tyres, Clifford leapt out of his car and rushed to the road but the car had gone.

Clifford entered his office calling good morning to his secretary whose office was adjacent to his. It was separated by just a plate glass window. She saw him arrive and acknowledged his greeting.After he had hung his coat up she tapped on the frame of the door. She was standing there with the morning mail under her left arm and a cup of coffee in the other hand. She entered and handed him his coffee and placed the mail on his desk

Clifford returned the Good morning and sipping his coffee he asked her: 'Sally; would you get Chief Superintendant Lewis on the phone and put him straight through to me?'

A couple of minutes later his phone rang, he answered it and it was Lewis, he said:'Good morning Superintendant.' Lewis replied:'God morning Mr Jessop what can I do for you today?' Clifford sensed a hint of sarcasm in Lewis's voice but ignored it, he answered: 'I am not sure but I think I am being followed.' Lewis was quiet for a moment then said: 'What gives you that idea then sir?' Clifford went through the incident with the BMW and the DCS paused again before saying: 'Is this the first time you have noticed the car?'

'Yes but it doesn't mean it is the first time it has followed me.'

'No it doesn't but I am not sure what you require of me.'

'I would have thought that was obvious Superintendant, have someone watch the area around my apartment building and this one.'

'I'm sorry there is insufficient evidence to tie up my men, it just seems to be a coincidence. Are you sure it was the same car even?'

'Not exactly but it seems too coincidental to me and if it was then it may be connected to my brother's murder and you have no new leads. Whatever your view I am requesting this as an official of the government.'

'Yes well, you do like getting the big guns out to get your own way Mr Jessop but, I am very sorry I still need to have something other than one encounter with a strange car, by all means though don't hesitate to call if something else happens, now goodbye Mr Jessop.'

Clifford was furious and slammed the phone down and blasted out: "Dam that man". Sally looked up and Caught Clifford's eye, she pointed to her cup and Clifford nodded his head and blew her a kiss. Minutes later she brought him his coffee, he thanked her and asked her to close the door behind her when she left.

He began opening the day's mail and noticed a large brown envelope addressed to him in person with the words "private" at the top. It was written in pen which was odd because all mail was usually typed. He called Sally on the intercom and asked her to come in, she entered his office and Clifford pointed to the envelope and asked: 'Do you know anything about this, did it come with the normal mail?' Sally answered: 'No sir it was on your desk when I brought the other mail in. Why is there something wrong?'

'I hope not but will you contact security and ask if anyone left it with them or did they let anyone in this morning.' Sally returned to her office and called security, they said that no one left it with them and no one had been signed in that morning. Sally related this to Clifford and he said: "Hell" 'Ok Sally we will have to call the bomb disposal unit, I can't take any chances.' He told her to call them and alert the emergency marshals and commence evacuation procedure.

The Bomb disposal unit was quickly on the scene, evacuation of the building was efficiently completed with all the staff in their allotted muster points before they arrived. An army land rover arrived first followed by two larger trucks. The land rover was driven by a sergeant, he climbed out of the vehicle and Clifford greeted him. They shook his hands and Clifford said: 'Good morning I am Clifford Jessop, Senior Customs Officer, the building is empty and all the staff are at their muster points.' The sergeant introduced himself as Sergeant Baker and said: 'Very impressive. Now what do we have?' Clifford told him about the envelope and handed him the building floor charts, he had marked off his office. He said to the sergeant: 'It is probably a waste of time and it must sound very petty but I didn't want to chance opening it.'

'Don't worry about being petty, my men and I would prefer all call outs to be false alarms, we would rather you be wary and alive than brave and dead.' Sergeant Baker left Clifford and consulted with his men, then took a large rucksack from the land rover, he chose one man to accompany him and ordered the other to listen to the radio telling him to obey any order he gave. The sergeant advised Clifford to join his staff and then he and his assistant entered the building.

The men climbed the stairs to the fifteenth floor and located Clifford's office, the Sergeant told his man to stay outside. Baker slowly approached the desk and the envelope. He placed his bag on the floor and opened it taking out a small device that detected explosives. He switched it on and slowly passed it backwards and forwards over the envelope. Satisfied there were no explosives in the package he called his man in. Sergeant Baker asked the man to get the Geiger counter from his bag, the man handed the counter to Baker and he repeated the sweep over the envelope. He completed the check and told his man to radio the other men to tell them it was a false alarm. They put the equipment back in their bags and returned downstairs.

By the time they reached the bottom many staff members were already returning to the building. Outside he met up with Clifford and told him: 'Ok sir I checked for explosives and radio activity, the envelope is not booby trapped. Clifford thanked him and the bomb squad left.

CHAPTER FIVE

Clifford returned to his office and once everyone was settled back in their respective workplace's Clifford returned to opening the mail he decided to open the envelope that had caused all the mayhem first. Using his letter opener he opened the envelope and poured the contents out onto his desk and gasped with shock and slumped back in his chair. Sally saw this and after firstly knocking his door she went in and remarked: 'Mr Jessop you are as white as sheet. Whatever is the matter?' He leaned forward and pointed to his desk, there were several large photos of Clifford and Elaine walking or driving in and out of their apartment building and car park. There were also pictures of them coming and going from their respective workplaces. Sally was speechless for a minute then she said: 'What is this about sir, are you and your wife being followed?' By this time Clifford had regained some composure and replied: 'Sally; have you noticed anything suspicious when you have been coming and going like a black BMW parked outside?'

'No I don't think so, nothing that has stood out anyway. Is that why you called the Police today?'

'Yes it was but it was a waste of time the Superintendant doesn't believe me; he just thinks I am paranoid.'

'Well he will be begging your forgiveness when you shove this lot in his face.'

'I'm not sure I will bother, I may just investigate this myself I will probably get further.'

After thinking for a moment he continued: 'Although I suppose I should report it.' Sally agreed and wished him luck. She said she would inform security and tell them to keep a close watch on the front and rear entrances.

Clifford reluctantly called the Police Station, when he asked to speak to Lewis he was told that he was out but DCI Deacon was in his office so Clifford agreed to speak to him. The DCI came on the phone and Clifford told him about the photos, He asked if he knew about the BMW incident that morning and Deacon said that he had but at the moment there was no proof it was related to his brother's death. Clifford replied in an angry tone: 'What do you people want? They aren't going to go around with a great big arrow above their heads pointing and saying: "IT'S ME". What would happen if I said: "There's nothing suspicious there" each time I go out on a Customs raid?'

'There is no need for sarcasm Sir however I will make a note of your call. Would it be possible to bring the photos and envelope in to us, it would be helpful if they weren't handled too much we will want to finger print them?'

'Well if you have time to look at them, heaven forbid though I should interfere with you issuing a parking ticket to someone but hey, yes I will send them in by special courier, however they have been handled by me and the sergeant of the bomb squad.'

'We will take that into account and I will ignore your remarks Mr Jessop it is obvious you have had a traumatic morning. I look forward to receiving the photos, now goodbye Mr Jessop.'

Clifford slammed the receiver down he looked at the clock and it was just twelve noon, he carefully slid the photos back into the envelope and placed that into another and sealed it, writing on it "From Clifford Jessop for DCI Deacon" he then buzzed Sally asking her to arrange a special courier to deliver the envelope to the Police Station, he then said he was going out but she could contact him on his mobile. He had decided he was going to look for the car himself.

He drove out of the car park and took a good look around then headed towards his apartment building. He stopped about fifty yards from the building and switched the engine off. He turned the radio on and slipped in a CD, he then sat back and watched the traffic coming and going. Close to forty minutes went by but there was no sign of the BMW, neither was there a sign of any Police attendance, he decided to give it another ten minutes and then go back to work. A few minutes later his mobile rang, thinking it was connected to work he answered: 'Hello sally.' There was no reply he said hello again and still there was no answer and then the line went dead. A couple of minutes passed and the phone rang again, he looked at the call register but there was no number registered but Clifford decide to take the call anyway, he said hello again and still there was no reply, after a few seconds the line went dead again. He was fed up and unnerved by the calls so decided to return to work. As he started the engine the mobile rang again, he put the car in neutral and answered the phone saying angrily: "LOOK I DONT KNOW WHO YOU ARE BUT STOP CALLING ME, OR I . . . . Before he could continue he heard Sally's voice, she said: 'Are you alright sir?' He stuttered: "Yes, yes I'm sorry sally I thought you were someone else.' Sally replied: 'Obviously sir, sorry for disturbing you but the Coastguard has intercepted a radio conversation from an unknown source. It's in French and the interpreters say that it is in code they are attempting to decode it as we speak. They estimate the vessel is about forty miles inside British waters and heading west. So far they have failed to respond to the coastguards calls to identify themselves. The Coastguard is standing by at Tilbury.'

'Thanks Sally I was just on my way back, please arrange a helicopter to pick me up from the roof helicopter pad.'

Clifford was picked up and whisked off to join the coastguard on their launch, once aboard the skipper ordered the launch to proceed at full ahead. Clifford was welcomed aboard by Chief officer George Taylor. "They knew each from previous operations".

George brought Clifford up to date and said: 'The conversation ended after we requested they identify themselves. Since then there has just been a signal transmitted, although we can't tell where or what kind of vessel it is, it does seem to be at anchor though. Unfortunately the signal died about twenty minutes ago but we feel it was coming from the same co-ordinance as the conversation.' George Taylor unrolled a chart and pointed to the spot the signal last came from saying: 'It's about ten miles east of Southampton, however their launch is out of service so we got the call, the authorities there are standing by.

Clifford suggested that they despatch a chopper to survey the area around the co-ordinance the signal was last detected.

As they sped towards the area the helicopter reported spotting a small craft at the location, it appeared to be anchored. The pilot flew closer and said it was a small rubber sailing dingy with no sail up, there was nobody aboard but there was some blue sheeting in the centre of the craft. The Coastguard officer instructed the pilot to do a twenty five mile circular sweep of the area and report any vessel's they spotted straight back to him.

It took a half hour for the launch to reach the area and locate the dingy. Eventually the launch pulled alongside and dropped anchor. As they did the pilot reported back that there were no vessel's in the sweep zone so Clifford said: 'Well it looks as if whoever they were they've eluded us, anyway let's check this out. Clifford said to George: 'You and I will go aboard and see what we have but I think the launch should move to a safe distance away just in case.

Once the launch was far enough away George and Clifford put on gloves and inspected the sheeting which was a thin piece of plastic, Clifford said: 'I will slowly lift one corner of the sheet and you shine your torch underneath in case there is a booby trap. They repeated this process until they had lifted all four corners. All they could see was a wooden box turned upside down. Clifford and George looked at each other and began slowly lifting the sheet off. Once the sheet was clear of the box Clifford crouched down and cautiously raised one end of the box. As there seemed to be nothing untoward George did the same his end. Eventually the box was lifted right up, beneath it was a diesel generator wired to a marine radio transmitter. George said: 'Well I didn't expect that, I will call the boat back.' While George did that Clifford examined the radio, there was a wire trailing from it and went up the short mast, at the very top was a makeshift antenna constructed from some stiff wire. The generator had run out of diesel which was why they had lost the signal. Clifford showed George what he had found and said: 'They certainly are professionals they bought themselves the necessary time to get far enough away with this little device, that's one up to the bad guys, for the moment. Ok men, hitch the dingy to the launch and let's go home.'

When they were back aboard the launch George radioed Southampton port authorities and reported their find, they said they would put choppers in the air and keep watch on the area and would notify them if they discovered anything.

CHAPTER SIX

It was nearly five past six when Clifford arrived back in his office, he wrote up his report on the computer so Sally could type it up in the morning, he waited a half hour but there was no more news about the mystery boat so he went home. Elaine had only just got home herself when Clifford got in, she could see he was tired so she greeted him with a smile and kissed him saying: 'You look whacked darling sit down and I will pour us both a drink, she poured them both a brandy and sat next to him on the couch. She handed him a glass and put her arm around his neck pulling his head onto her shoulder. Clifford gave a long sigh and felt himself relax a little. After a while he asked her: 'How was your day, do you like being the old boy's PA?' She replied: 'Oh he is a sweetheart, you know he even get's me my coffee. I'm sure he thinks he is the PA.' They both giggled and she added: 'Something odd happened today though, I received two calls on my mobile but when I answered there was no one on the other end. I checked the caller ID but no number was registered.' Clifford sat bolt upright saying: 'You too what time was that? I had the same thing happen to me about one o'clock.' Elaine confirmed that was about the same time she received her two calls so Clifford went on to tell her about the car incident and the photos, plus how Deacon had reacted when he reported it. She listened then said: 'Surely this is all related to Sam, I think we ought to do our own investigating? After all we can't do any worse than those Detective's, we will have to be extremely careful though these people obviously mean business and I am already frightened.'

'And how do you propose we do that?' Clifford asked giving her hand a reassuring squeeze.

'Well we could start by going to that pub where you met Sam.'

'Yeah but the Police have already done that.'

'I know but with their attitude I wouldn't want to be too cooperative and people don't always like talking to cops, so you never know, it's worth a try.'

'Maybe, when were you thinking of going?'

'No time like the present that's if you are up to it, and we can get a takeaway on the way back.'

'Very well I'll go and have a shower and a quick change.'

When Clifford was ready they set off for the pub, they walked in hand in hand. Clifford felt Elaine's hand tremble slightly and gave it a squeeze. They looked around but there were only a handful of customers. When they went to the bar there were three men sitting on stools, two of the men glared at them but the other one was too drunk to notice.

The barman asked what they wanted and Clifford asked for a glass of red wine and an orange juice. When he brought the drinks Elaine showed him Sam's picture and asked if he had ever seen him in the pub. Immediately his mood changed he looked them up and down and asked: 'Are you cops?' Clifford assured him they were not and told him: 'He was my brother he was murdered nearly three months ago and the Police are doing nothing so we are trying to get some answers ourselves. I was in here with him shortly before he was killed and we just wondered if he came in here before that.' The barman threw the picture back at Elaine and said: 'I don't know him and I'm not getting involved with any murder now finish your drinks and get out.' Clifford came right back at him: 'Look if you don't know him then how can you get involved? You seem to be pretty keen to get rid of us what aren't you telling us?' The barman glared at Clifford and went to walk away but then he stopped, turned back and said quietly: 'Well ok, he may have come in once or twice but you didn't hear it from me, I told you I don't want to get involved.' Clifford told him: 'WE don't want to get anyone into trouble, we just want answers, now did he come in on his own?'

'Sometimes, other times he had a small dark haired bloke with him, I'm sure he was an ex con, they used to sit over there .... He pointed to a cubicle with a seat along the back wall and continued .... they always looked like they were plotting something. The other bloke stopped coming in a few weeks ago, actually your guy always seemed skint so the other one bought him pints but when he was on his own he only had a half and made it last all night.'

'When was the last time you saw him here?'

'The night you were in here with him.'

'Would you mind us showing his picture around the other customers?'

'Knock yourself out.' Clifford handed the barman ten pounds for his help and they took Sam's picture and showed it around but they drew a blank so they finished their drinks and left the pub.

They stepped outside and it was raining slightly, they had only walked a few yards towards their car when a voice from behind said: 'Hang on you two.' They looked around and a tall middle aged man was hurrying towards them. Elaine recognised him as one of the men at the bar, he caught them up and he was breathing heavily, panting he said: 'Let's go around the corner out of sight.' When he was happy no one could see them he said: 'I did recognise that guy in the photo but I didn't want to say anything in there, one night I was waiting for a taxi at closing time when he came out of the pub with another guy, and they were having a right old argument, they couldn't see me it was too dark and I was stood in the doorway for shelter. Your brother was calling him all sorts of names I heard him say something like: "Where the hell does he think I can get that sort of money? Anyway it wasn't my fault, just tell that crazy Moron I can't get it and to leave me alone.' HE seemed to be quite timid so I was amazed to hear him speak like that.' Clifford looked at Elaine then asked the man: 'Would you recognise the other guy again?' He said he thought he would so Clifford asked: 'In that case would you be willing to come with us to the Police? I promise we will keep your identity secret.'

'Yeah you may do but the old bill won't, no I want nothing more to do with it.'

'Look they want to clear this case up as much as we do so if they want your information then they will have to agree, anyway leave them to us we have the Chief

Constable on our side, by the way are you known to the Police?'

'No they have nothing on me and that's how I want it to stay.'

'We understand that but you must also understand this info may well lead to catching my brother's killers, please help us?' The man thought for a second then said: 'Alright but I want it in writing from you and the Police that you will keep my identity secret.'

Done! Clifford said holding his hand out to shake the man's hand. He and Elaine were relieved that at last they may have a lead, Clifford asked the man if he would mind waiting a while, he said no so Clifford took his mobile out and called the Police station and asked for DCS Lewis. Lewis came on the phone and said sighing: 'Yes Mr Jessop what can I do for you?' He told Lewis everything the man had told him and asked if he could take him to the station. Lewis hesitated but Clifford reminded him that they still had no further leads and this could well be one thy needed. After a think Lewis agreed and said: 'I suppose it wouldn't do any harm for him to look at some mug shots. Lewis asked the man's name so Clifford said: 'I have just told you I have promised to keep his identity secret otherwise he will not come in.' Lewis replied: 'That is rather unorthodox Mr Jessop but I will go along with it for now.' Clifford asked if they could come in right away and Lewis agreed.

Clifford ended the call and punched the air shouting: "Yes" Elaine asked if he needed her to go with him and the man, Clifford said no if she preferred not to, she said she would rather go home, so Clifford called her a taxi.

When Clifford and the man arrived at the station the desk sergeant called Lewis. Lewis told the Sergeant to send them straight to the "Rogue's gallery" and a constable escorted them to a room, inside another constable was waiting for them, he greeted them with a hand shake and said: 'Good evening gentlemen I am PC Dawkins, which one of you is looking at our files?' Clifford put his hand on the man's back and said: 'He is.' The PC asked their names; Clifford told him his name but said that the man's identity was protected. The PC replied: 'I see sir, sit here please and I will let you get on with it.' The man sat at the table and the PC opened one of six large boxes and took out some folders about two inches thick. He remarked: 'You have a lot to get through would you both like a coffee or tea?' They both asked for black coffee and with that the constable left.

The man counted the files and said: 'We are going to be here all night, there are six here and about fifty pages in each one plus there are at least ten more files in the boxes.' Clifford said that he was in no hurry but if he wanted to look at some tonight and the rest the next day he understood. The man said that he would get it over with there and then as he had no one at home waiting for him. Clifford patted him on the back and said: 'Good man.'

The man proceeded to look at the pictures one by one. When he eventually reached the last picture he said he didn't recognise any one. Clifford suggested he take another look which he did, after finishing his third coffee once he said the man definitely wasn't there. Clifford was disappointed but kept calm, when the PC proceeded to walk them out of the room Clifford asked him: 'Do you have a sketch artist here?' The constable said they did,

Clifford asked him if there was one there at that time of night?' The PC said that there was one as a young woman had been attacked earlier that evening and they needed her to do a sketch of her attacker. Clifford asked: 'Would you contact DCS Lewis and ask if he would allow our friend here to work with the artist?' The Constable went back into the room and called Lewis. When the PC came out he said that the DCS had agreed and he was arranging for the artist to meet them. The PC asked them to follow him along the corridor and up one flight of stairs.

They reached the artists room and he stood up to greet them. Once they were all introduced the artist explained the procedure saying: 'You give me as many details as possible regarding the man's features and then I will sketch it. If anything is not quite right I'll erase or add details as you prefer.

It took nearly an hour to produce a likeness of the man Sam met. Once the artist was finished Clifford thanked him and said: 'Ok my friend let's go and see DCS Lewis.' The PC said he would arrange for someone to escort them to Lewis's office, the PC knocked Lewis's office door and Lewis shouted for him to go in, the PC told Lewis that the two men were waiting to see him and Lewis invited them in.

Lewis invited the two men to sit down and introduced himself to the man then said: 'I know you wish for your identity to remain confidential which is ok for now meanwhile what can will we call you.' Clifford answered saying: 'I k now it's corny but how about MR X?' The man nodded his agreement and Lewis agreed, Clifford then handed Lewis the artist's impression, Lewis studied it for a while and Clifford noticed that he looked disturbed by what he saw. Clifford asked: 'Is there a problem Superintendant?'

'Not a problem as such but I can see why he isn't in rogues gallery, he is one of ours or was.' Clifford pulled his chair closer to the Superintendant's desk and said: 'One of yours, you mean he's Police Officer?'

'Well as I said he was, actually he was a Detective Inspector in the drug squad but every time he discovered a hoard of drugs he would take a small amount out for himself selling it back to the dealers. Unfortunately for him he got too greedy and suspicions grew until a trap was laid and he was caught. He was given the choice of going down for a long stretch or giving up the dealers he was selling to, he could then leave with his pension intact which is what he did. Hang on I'll get the file.' Lewis went out and returned with a thin file, he sat down and opened it. He took out a photo and handed it to Clifford saying: 'There's your man.' Clifford looked at it, and then passed it to Mr X asking: 'Is that's him?' Mr X said it was definitely him. Lewis continued: 'His name is David Malcolm Simpson the last I heard he was working at a local security firm, I don't know if he is still there or even what his job was.' Clifford remarked: 'You could find out though couldn't you?'

'I suppose I could . . . yes. Ok I will chase that up first thing tomorrow.'

'Well, now we are getting somewhere, Sam told me he had a pal who worked for the security firm they tried to rob he was supposed to tell Sam the details of the wagon and be one of the guards but, bailed out because he didn't want to work with the man in charge. It looks now though he has had a change of heart.' Lewis added: 'He may not have had much say in the matter if this guy is as ruthless as his reputation infers.'

'Well you have something to go on now Superintendant.' Lewis typically replied: 'Maybe but MR X here must tell us his name and address. Mr X looked at Clifford and said: 'You said I would remain anonymous.' Lewis told him: 'We do have to have your name on record because we can't go making enquiries on the word of an unnamed source. I would not be able to arrest Simpson even if we find him because the evidence would be classed as hearsay.' Clifford slammed his hand down on the desk and blasted: "You are unbelievable you have had all this time and you have nothing but when you are confronted with solid evidence you just quote red tape. Well if you're not interested then maybe the Chief Constable will be. Come on pal we're finished here.' Clifford and Mr X stood up and turned to leave. Lewis stood up sharply and said: 'Here we go again with the threats I told you it's my investigation, I will look into it and I will let you know if something turns up but, I still need this man's details.'

'No not this time you have had your chance and you're not interested.' With that Clifford shuffled Mr X out of the office with Clifford slamming the door.

Outside Clifford looked at his watch and seeing it had gone midnight he said they should go home. He asked Mr X if he would go back to the DCS with him if he can persuade the CC to agree to him keeping his anonymity.

Mr X replied: 'Why not you seem on the level the way you just handled him in there.' Clifford thanked him and said that he would ring the CC in the morning and meet him back in the pub at twelve thirty.

CHAPTER SEVEN

Clifford didn't sleep very well that night he was seething at Lewis's attitude but he also understood about red tape because of his job as a customs officer, he was relieved though that there seemed to be a little light at the end of the tunnel at last.

He lay tossing and turning until in the end he decided to get up. He looked at the bedside clock and it was only just past five thirty five. Elaine was sleeping peacefully, he carefully got out of bed and went and showered, afterwards he put on his dressing gown and made a pot of coffee, he sat at the kitchen table drinking his coffee mulling over the events of the night before. The next thing he knew he felt a tap on his shoulder. He had fallen asleep at the table and Elaine had woken to find he was missing, she said: 'So I'm not good enough to sleep with anymore.' He asked what the time was; she told him it was ten past eight. Clifford explained that he couldn't sleep and had not wanted to disturb her, then said: 'And yes you are always good enough to sleep with.' He gave her a sly wink and kissed her. He stood up and put his arms around her and gave her another kiss. Elaine laughed and said: 'Go and get dressed while I make breakfast then you will be able call Charles.' He nodded and went up to the bedroom.

It was nine fifteen when Clifford dialled the CC's home number, Helen answered and he said: 'Hello Helen it's Clifford Jessop. Is it possible to speak to Charles?'

'Hello Clifford, I'm sorry I didn't recognise you the other evening hang on I'll fetch him.'

When Charles came on the line he said: 'Hello Clifford I wasn't expecting to hear from you so soon.'

'Yes I'm sorry Charles but there has been a development in Sam's murder.' He took Charles through the events of the night before. Charles listened then said: 'I know it's frustrating and I don't profess to know Lewis's thoughts but he must have his reasons.'

'I can't see what they could be after all he has no leads himself, perhaps he feels embarrassed that I found this witness and not him,'

'I can't say Clifford, what do you want me to do?' Clifford explained that he wanted it in writing from Lewis that Mr X would remain anonymous then he would be willing to give his details, and it would be even more helpful if he, the CC, would give his promise in writing also. Clifford also asked Charles to instruct Lewis to investigate this new evidence.' Charles thought about it then said: 'Alright I will write my authorisation now and I will call the Superintendant and speak to him. I will arrange for my letter to be taken to Lewis later this morning but you will have to contact him yourself and arrange to take your witness in and sort it all out. Now if that is it I have to get ready to go to Buckinghamshire for a Christening, I will have a word about your brother's body when I speak to the DCS. Now goodbye Clifford I look forward to seeing you next Friday.'

'Thank you Charles, I really do appreciate your help.'

Clifford hung up and Elaine said: 'That sounded positive, what did he say?' Clifford told her the gist of the conversation and said: 'Now I have to arrange to take our friend back to see Lewis that could be interesting.'

'You're not kidding I would love to be a fly on the wall.'

'You can come with us if you like.'

'No thank you I can't stand the sight of blood.' They had a laugh then Clifford said: 'I'll wait until after eleven then I will call Lewis and make the arrangements.'

After having a cup of coffee Clifford decided to go out and fetch a news paper and asked if Elaine wanted anything, she said that he could bring some milk back. Clifford walked to the shop which was only five minutes away and as he was walking back he spotted the BMW turning around the corner leading to their car park. He hurried along and reached the corner of their apartment; he sneaked a look but saw nothing so he crept along the side of the building and peaked around the other corner. Clifford was just about to creep along to the entrance of the car park when the car came out and seeing Clifford sped off. He was caught unawares and was unable to get a good look in the car. He went up to his apartment and told Elaine what had just happened. Elaine remarked: 'They are getting very brazen. Why are they watching us? Even if it is surrounding Sam's death I can't see what following us can achieve.' Clifford replied: 'I will let Lewis know when

I see him later. Make sure you stay safe and be careful if you go out.'

At fifteen minutes past eleven on the dot Clifford phoned DCS Lewis. Lewis was expecting the call as the CC had already spoken to him earlier regarding what Clifford and he had discussed earlier that morning. They arranged for Clifford to go in with Mr X at one forty five that afternoon as he was tied up all morning with meetings.

The call was very brief Clifford could tell that the superintendant was not impressed with him going to Charles again. Clifford wasn't worried though he intended pressing Lewis as hard as possible to get Sam's case solved and his body released.

Mr X was at the bar when Clifford entered the pub, it was twelve thirty five. Clifford stood next to him and asked what he was drinking and he asked for a double brandy. Clifford refused saying that he wanted him sober when they saw Lewis. Mr X Said: 'Oh well you can't blame a guy for trying, I'll have another pint then.' Clifford said he would buy him a double brandy after they had seen Lewis. Mr X accepted the deal and Clifford ordered the pint and an orange juice for himself.

Mr X asked Clifford when they were leaving but when Clifford told him one thirty, he moaned that he would have to stretch his pint and make it last for nearly an hour. Clifford told him he should remember his brother was murdered and would not be drinking ever again, Mr X clammed up and stared into his glass.

They left the pub at one thirty to walk the short journey to the station; Clifford kept looking over his shoulder discreetly to check they were not being followed. When they arrived a constable escorted them to the Superintendant's office. DCS Lewis started proceedings saying: 'As you are aware the Chief Constable has agreed that you—Mr X will remain anonymous throughout this investigation. I have his signed letter of confirmation here you may have to reveal your identity though if you are called upon to give evidence in court. However we will do everything we can to protect you.' Mr X said: 'No way.' Clifford then said: 'Wouldn't it be possible for him to give evidence from behind a screen?'

'Possibly but that is a long way off yet. Now I have prepared my letter and I believe that Mr Jessop was preparing one as well.' Lewis placed his and the CC's sealed letters on the desk. Clifford withdrew his from his inside jacket pocket and added it to them. Lewis looked at Mr X and said: 'Now if you would kindly reveal your details I will write them in this file . . . . Lewis showed Mr X the file which was marked—"Confidential to be opened only with the express orders of Detective Superintendant Lewis" and it will be locked in my private safe and only I have the combination.' Mr X hesitated but Clifford assured him that his details would remain a secret between the four of them.

The man still wasn't sure but eventually relented saying: 'Ok but if any of you break the deal I will sue every last one of you.' "Right then, my name is—Graham Arthur Dyson. My address is—Twenty seven St Michaels Drive, Chelsea". Lewis asked for his phone number but Dyson said that he only had a mobile and it was—pay and go—and he wouldn't give the number. DCS Lewis wrote the details down and placed the file immediately in the locked safe. Lewis then said: 'Ok now that is done I can tell you we have been doing some checking and have discovered that Simpson has gone off the radar, he was last seen two day before your brother's death. His estranged wife says that he turned up at her house unexpectedly wanting to see their five year old daughter but it was outside their designated access day. She refused him and he stormed off shouting that she would regret it for the rest of her life. She said he was dishevelled and scruffy. We have issued a nationwide appeal for information and we have posted his details around all other forces. You Mr Jessop will also be pleased to know that I am releasing Sam's body for burial.'

Clifford thanked him then asked: 'Is there any developments regarding the BMW?' Lewis said that there wasn't and Clifford relayed to him the occurrence that morning. Lewis made notes and said he would add it to the file. Clifford then said: 'I am sorry; I went over your head.' Lewis just said: 'Well, we won't dwell on that now.' He thanked Dyson assuring him he will not be contacted unless it was absolutely necessary. Clifford held his hand out and Lewis shook it saying: 'Thank you for coming in and I hope the funeral goes off ok.'

Once outside Clifford thanked Dyson and said he would take him for his brandy. However Dyson said: 'Thanks but I would rather go home if you don't mind. I will take a rain check though.' Clifford asked if he wanted to share a taxi home, Dyson said yes, but asked to be dropped at the end of his road.

Elaine saw immediately when Clifford walked in the door that something had changed, she remarked: 'You look like the cat that got the cream.' Clifford gave Elaine a smile and replied: 'probably because I have, not only has Lewis started investigating the new evidence and vowed to keep our friend's identity a secret. He is also releasing Sam's body.' Putting her arms around his waist and kissing his cheek she said: 'At last you can put him to rest and relax a little. You sit there and I will make a pot of coffee and you can tell me all about it.'

Clifford sat for a while then went into the kitchen and standing behind her he enquired what they were having for dinner. She pretended not to notice so Clifford put his arms around her, he started to nuzzle her neck and ears. While he was nuzzling her right ear with his nose she gave him a playful slap and told him if he carried on she wouldn't cook his dinner, then she said: 'In answer to your question we are having fillet steak, and if you are still hungry I have made a raspberry cheesecake.'

Ooh! 'My favourite, is there anything I can do to help?'

'Yes, Pour me a drink and tell me you love me.'

After dinner they were snuggled up on the couch watching TV, Elaine asked: 'Did the Police say anything about the car following us?' Clifford told her that he reported the incident of that morning but there was no news then. She added: 'The reason I mentioned it is, while you were out I went to buy the steak, when I walked home a black BMW was parked opposite the building. I couldn't see inside the car as the windows were all blackened out so I attempted to cross the road and read the number but it started up and drove off at high speed.'

'That confirms it, someone is watching us.' Clifford got up and went to the lounge window and looked out and said: 'There's nothing out the back.' He went into the bedroom and pulled back the blinds and saw a dark car parked just up from the building entrance but he couldn't be sure it was the BMW. He came back into the lounge and told Elaine: 'There is a car parked opposite the entrance but it is too dark to see if it is the BMW, come on.' Elaine asked where they were going, he told her: 'We'll go down to the car park then we can slip around the side road and sneak a look around the corner and maybe get a better look, we may even get the registration.' Elaine asked: 'Is that wise their obviously dangerous.'

'We won't take any chances I promise but, we have to do something if the Police are to take us serious.'

Elaine agreed and went and fetched their darkest coats, they took the lift down to the car park and made their way along the side of the building and reached the corner. Clifford told Elaine to get behind him as he peered cautiously around the corner. He could see the rear end of the car but not enough to see if it was the BMW or the number. He whispered: 'I'm going closer to get a better look.'

'Be careful darling they could have a gun.' He nodded his acknowledgement and crept out into the street. He crept closer keeping close to the wall using the shrubs that grew alongside the pavement as cover. As he crept closer he was relieved but at the same time disappointed to see that it wasn't the BMW. He turned around and began walking back to Elaine. As he did so to his amazement the BMW passed slowly right past him. He couldn't believe he wasn't seen. Unfortunately he was only able to read part of the number plate although it was enough to see it was a two thousand and one registration.

The car continued towards the corner of the building where Elaine was. She was oblivious to the situation and was getting worried that he was taking so long. She poked her head around the corner looking for Clifford just as the car was approaching and she was spotted, the car instantly sped off screeching its tyres. She wasn't sure what was happening at first but when Clifford came running towards her she realised it must have been the car. As he reached her she ran out hugging him and said: 'I'm sorry darling I fluffed it didn't I?' He told her not to worry she wasn't to know, he told her that he had got part of the number plate and he took out his mobile to call the Police station.

Unfortunately Lewis had gone home but Deacon was on duty, he answered and Clifford informed him of the last few minutes and gave him the part number. Deacon said: 'Ok Mr Jessop, the Super briefed me regarding your meeting with him earlier, I will get the number put through our data base and see what we get.' He thanked Clifford for his call and said he would pass it on to Lewis in the morning.

Elaine and Clifford returned to their apartment, they were chilled to the bone due to the cold damp October night air. Elaine made them both hot chocolate and they waited in their dressing gowns in the warm apartment hoping to hear something following the incident earlier. They waited until after midnight but heard nothing so they went to bed.

It was eleven thirty Sunday morning before they received a call from DCS Lewis HE apologised for the delay and said:'It seems I owe you and your wife an apology Mr Jessop. After your call last evening to DCI Deacon he took the initiative and called your buildings security and asked if there was CCTV outside the front of the building, luckily there is so we sent a car over and collected the tapes. It was checked by our tech team and you will be pleased to know that one camera picked up the car as it passed by the entrance and we were able to make out the full registration. The car was stolen from central London three weeks ago, we have issued an APB and we will watch the area, there is a chance that they won't know they were spotted and come back. I must go now Mr Jessop but we will be in touch should anything turn up.' Clifford hung up the phone and related to Elaine what Lewis said, she remarked: 'At last we seem to be getting the breaks, let's hope we can soon put all this behind us and get on with our lives.'

CHAPTER EIGHT

Elaine was soon to regret being too optimistic about the future, she arrived at work Monday morning and went through the routine of making the coffee and checking the MD's schedule for the day. The mail trolley arrived and she sorted through the letters and packages, she was amazed to discover a thin package addressed to her. Thinking it was a little surprise from Clifford . . . . something he sometimes did . . . . she put it to one side while she took the MD's personal mail to his office. Returning to her desk she set about opening the package addressed to her. She emptied the contents out onto her desk and sat back open mouthed. At that moment the MD arrived, walking past her office and he saw the expression on her face, he poked his head around the door and asked: 'What in heaven's name is wrong Elaine?' She couldn't speak for a minute but then stammered: 'It it's, this'. The MD came to her desk and he also gasped and enquired: 'What is all this Elaine?' Lying on her desk was several photographs of Elaine and Clifford the similar to the ones he had received, there were also pictures of them both entering and leaving their respective office buildings. The MD closed her office door and said: That is our building! Are you in some sort of trouble? What have you gotten yourself into?'

'Nothing Sir, look I should have said something sooner but there has been a car following Clifford and me. We're convinced it is related to his brother's murder. He received pictures like these and we have told the Police. Saturday night it was outside of our apartment again and the CCTV picked the car up and the Police have discovered it was stolen in London.'

The MD replied: 'Well I don't know what to say Elaine obviously I am concerned for you and your husband but I also have concerns for this company, it could well be connected considering what we deal in, look Elaine you go home you are not going to want to be here, I will have a word with our security advisors and the board in the meantime. You go and get some rest. I will call your husband and inform him you have gone home. If you are well enough I will see you tomorrow, don't worry I am sure it will all sort itself out.'

Clifford had only just entered his office when he got John Ford's call, he thanked him and immediately called Elaine's mobile. She answered and he asked how she was, she said that she was ok but wanted him to go home right away. He told her that he had a meeting to go to but he would tell his secretary to reschedule it. She told him not to but to come home directly after. He promised he would and told her that he loved her and he would call DCS Lewis to tell him about the photos.

Elaine left for home and was approaching the apartment building, she was about to turn right into the side road on her way to the car park but, she had to wait for a car that was coming in the other direction. As the car came close Elaine was dumbstruck, the car was a black BMW, she looked at the number plate and it was the same car, as the cars drew level the two driver's windows were directly opposite each other. Pushing the button Elaine put down her window and glared intensely to try and see the driver but was unable to because of the blackened window. The cars were stationary momentarily but then in a flash the BMW sped off.

Elaine sat motionless then instinctively turned into the car park entrance and reversed out into the street. She sped off in the direction the BMW took. She drove a Mercedes Sports car which was a good match for the BMW but it had a good lead on her. Nevertheless she put her foot down and was soon approaching a "T junction" just before that on the right was a taxi rank so she pulled up level with the rear car and wound her nearside window down. The driver wound his down as well, she asked if the BMW had come that way, he said that it had and it was driving so fast he contacted the Police to report it. She asked which way it went and he told her it turned right onto the road to town. Elaine was in a quandary as there was two turnings off that road . . . . one led to a trading estate and the other a municipal rubbish tip, thinking it over she concluded it was more likely the car would head for town as there were a number of multi story car parks the car could hide in.

She drove on and reached the outskirts of the town and set about checking all the open car parks first, unsuccessful she then tried the two multi story parks in that area but drew blanks in both.

She pulled over and parked her car, she used her mobile to call Clifford but his mobile was switched off, she assumed he was still at his meeting. She decided that there was nothing for it but to go home.

Elaine entered the foyer of the apartment building and the Security officer attracted her attention. She walked over and said: 'Hello Jim, how are you?' He said he was well and said: 'A telephone engineer has been to your apartment and he has sorted the problem.'

'Excuse me, what engineer?''What problem? Are you sure it was our apartment?'

'Positive, Mr Jessop phoned just after nine o'clock this morning to say he had forgotten to tell me earlier and to let the guy sign your key out, look there's his signature he arrived at nine ten and left at nine fifty five.'

'Yes I can see that Jim but we have not had a problem with our phone in fact we hardly use it, we use our mobiles mostly. Ok, look Mr Jessop will be home soon we will clear this up then.' She thanked Jim and took the lift to the apartment, when she reached the door she was surprised to find it was slightly open so she decided not to go in, she returned to the lift and went back down and told Jim, he said: 'Ok I'll come and have a look, I have to call the Police though it is procedure but I can do that on the move.' He used his mobile and called the Police, just as they reached the lift Clifford called Elaine; he could hear that she was flustered and asked 'What's the problem are you alright?'

'No not really I have had a hell of a morning and now I find our apartment has been broken into.'

'Broken into, how did they get past Jim?' She told him about phone engineer and Clifford informed her: 'I didn't phone security, there's nothing wrong with our phone, let me speak to Jim.' Elaine passed over her phone so that Clifford could speak to Jim and HE explained, Clifford replied: 'you have been tricked Jim, I never phoned you.'

'I am sorry Mr Jessop, the actual words were: "We have a problem with our phone but I forgot to tell you on my way out, you can let him have our spare key but be sure he sign's it out." The guy even had the phone companies ID badge.' Clifford told Jim not to worry and asked to speak to Elaine. He said to Elaine: 'Have you been up to the apartment?' She said that she was just going with Jim when he phoned, Clifford said he was just parking the car and to wait for him.

Clifford arrived in the foyer and kissed Elaine then spoke to Jim and told him: 'I have called the Police they should be here soon they said not to go up until they arrived.' Clifford asked if Jim had seen the man's face but he said that he didn't actually take a lot of notice not knowing he was an imposter, he was wearing a blue base ball cap though.

As they were talking Elaine spotted blue flashing lights outside in the street and moments later four Police officers and one sergeant appeared in the foyer. Jim greeted them and briefed them as to the situation he then introduced the Sergeant to the Jessop's.

The sergeant shook their hands and said: 'Good morning, Sergeant Paul Ashford at your service. I and one of the officer's will go up to your apartment and I will call down here when we have surveyed the situation. I'll post the other two officers at the buildings front and rear entrances just in case.' Clifford acknowledged the sergeant and asked if he required the apartment keys, He said he did so he could check the locks, then he and the PC proceeded to the lift.

Jim let Clifford and Elaine go around and observe the monitor's from his side of the desk although he advised that they would only be able to see up to the point the police enter the apartment.

They watched as the two Policemen exited the lift and proceeded towards the apartment door, advising his officer to draw his baton the sergeant did the same, indicating with his hand that they should stand at each side of the doorway. Once in position the sergeant put his finger to his lips indicating they should stay silent. The sergeant using the tips of his gloved hand gingerly pushed the door a little further open and peered around the door into the small hallway. Against the left hand wall was a hall table on which there was a telephone and two porcelain figurines, there was a small drawer lying upside down on the carpet with some of the contents were spilled out.

He beckoned the PC to follow him as he advanced even further into the apartment. The lounge door was wide open and they could see that the room had been ransacked, furniture was either upside down or dislodged from their usual positions, drawers and cupboards had been turned out and their contents scattered around the apartment.

The sergeant announced loudly: "POLICE OFFICER'S STAY EXACTLY WHERE YOU ARE WE ARE COMING IN". There was no response so they cautiously edged further in. It soon became clear that no one was in the lounge so they continued to check the rest of the apartment and were soon satisfied that it was clear.

Clifford and Elaine watched intently waiting for some kind of sign or message from the officers and Elaine asked mainly to herself: 'What is taking them so long?' Clifford answered though: 'They have to be certain that there is no one inside, they will notify us as soon as they are satisfied that it is safe.'

That happened at that moment, the sergeant called Jim on the internal line informing that the situation was secure. The sergeant asked to speak to Clifford, Jim handed him the receiver and the sergeant advised him: 'Mr Jessop the apartment is clear but I am afraid there is a mess . . . . Clifford cut in: 'Mess? What sort of mess?' The sergeant continued . . . . the apartment has been turned over and the contents are scattered everywhere. Elaine could see by Clifford's expression all was not well and asked: 'What's wrong Clifford tell me?' Clifford asked the sergeant to hold on and he told her that the place had been messed up. Tear's started to roll down her cheeks and Clifford put his arm around her comforting her, she asked him: 'What have they done to our home? What have we done to deserve all this?'

'I don't know darling let me finish talking to Sergeant Ashford and maybe we can go up and see.' He apologised to the sergeant, HE replied: 'Don't apologise sir it is a very upsetting situation, unfortunately though you will not be able to return to the apartment until scenes of crime have processed it, I am calling them in now sir and they will advise you further. I will also notify the investigative officers at Chelsea central.' Clifford thanked him and hung up, he told his wife what the sergeant revealed to him and Elaine sobbed. Jim interrupted saying: 'Excuse me Mr and Mrs Jessop but while you were talking I have run the internal CCTV tapes back from this morning and I have images of the man, the sergeant ought to see this as well sir. Is it ok if I call him down?'

'Yes certainly, please do.' Jim contacted the sergeant who said he would be straight down but asked Jim to send one of the other officer's up. Jim obliged and soon after the sergeant joined them.

Jim started the playback and it showed the man entering the foyer, he looked around then approached Jim's desk. He wore gloves and a blue baseball cap and carried a silver coloured case similar to the type engineers carry. Once he had shown his ID badge Jim issued the key and the man went to the lift.

Jim then pointed to the second monitor and they watched as he slowly exited the lift and approached the apartment door. Firstly he tried the door handle to see if the door was unlocked, finding it locked he put one of the key's in the lock but it wouldn't fit. The sergeant asked why the key didn't fit as there was only one door. Jim explained that there were two keys on the ring and he must have tried the entrance key to the building. They continued watching as the man used the other key and opened the door, the sergeant remarked to the Jessop's: 'I notice that you have no security alarm system in the apartment.' Clifford sheepishly replied: 'Yes I know, you are right, we keep talking about it but that is as far as it's gone, with the security down here it's never seemed urgent.' The Sergeant looked at both of them and said: 'No doubt you will have a change of heart now sir.' Clifford just nodded then looked at Elaine and lifted his eyes to the ceiling.

Jim fast forwarded the tape to point the man appeared back at the door from inside the apartment, Jim remarked: 'Now this is where it gets interesting.' The man came out into the hallway with his case, he turned to pull the door shut and the case fell open and something fell out onto the floor, Jim paused the tape and the sergeant looked closer and enquired: 'Is that a laptop?' Clifford looked closer and said: 'Yes it is, that's mine.' Jim restarted the tape and they watched as the man stooped to gather the laptop up but the case tilted and more items fell out including another laptop and files. Clifford said: 'Hey that's your laptop Elaine.' Elaine panicked and said that she had files connected with her work on it, Clifford remarked that he also had important files on his. Sergeant Ashford asked why they didn't have their laptops with them at work, Clifford said that it was not the one he uses for confidential work he had that one with him but this one had notes that he edits and downloads onto memory sticks, he then enters them into his main computer. Elaine said hers had meetings, minutes and future appointments etc on hers and she too had another one which she also had with her.

The sergeant nodded and asked Jim to continue with the tape. When the man dived down attempting to prevent the remaining contents of the case from spilling out, the peak of his cap hit the door frame and came off. Clifford gasped and pointed at the screen and said excitedly: 'That's Simpson the ex DI Sam met at the pub.' Elaine asked if he was sure and he said: 'Absolutely, Lewis showed me his picture, run the tape on Jim.'

They continued to watch as Simpson grabbed his cap and hurriedly put it back on his head then grab the items from the floor, shoving them back in his case he entered the lift and arrived back down on the ground floor. He approached Jim's desk and handed him the keys and signed them back in, he then walked calmly out of the building. Apart the mishap at the apartment door, Simpson kept his head down preventing the internal cameras from picking his face up.

The sergeant said well done to Jim then Clifford said: 'Jim; does the camera outside see both ways up the street?' Jim said it did and Clifford asked if they could watch that one, Jim said unfortunately that one was on a timer and couldn't be removed before six am in the morning, Clifford asked when it was ready would he hand that one, and the one they had just watched over to the Police. Jim agreed but said he would have to obtain consent from the security manager. Jim called his Manager there and then, and HE gave his permission.

With this arranged Sergeant Ashford called the Jessop's aside and said that he would take them up to the apartment to see if they are missing anything other than the laptops and also what files Simpson had taken.

They and the Sergeant went up to the apartment, HE told them they would have to wear protective suits to prevent contaminating any evidence, he also asked them not to touch anything. When Elaine walked into the hallway and saw drawer contents on the floor she was upset but when she entered the lounge she burst into tears and grabbed Clifford's arm saying: 'Oh Cliff how can anyone do this to someone's home, look at it, everything is ruined.' Clifford comforted her as best he could and told her that he would look to see what was missing and she should sit on the chair in the hall. She agreed and Clifford began the traumatic task of checking through the carnage. When he emerged back out to Elaine he told her it looked worse than it was, nothing was damaged but as well as the laptops

Simpson had taken credit card receipts and details of their finances.

The sergeant asked if there was somewhere they could stay that night and Clifford said they would book into a hotel, Elaine asked when they would be able return to the apartment and was told not before the following afternoon if then, he said that they could take whatever clothes they required for the night. Clifford gathered up what they needed and then thanked the sergeant and bid the officers goodnight.

Clifford and Elaine returned to the foyer and spoke to Jim thanking him for his help and to ask him to ensure the apartment was locked up securely when the Police have finished. Jim said he would be off duty at ten that evening but he would ensure that the night guy would carry out his request. Clifford said goodnight and assured him that he would speak to Jim's boss and put in a good word for him. Jim thanked him and said goodnight.

When Clifford and Elaine walked outside they both took a deep breath, Clifford said he was calling Lewis on his mobile and would she call a hotel on hers and book them in.

Lewis answered and told Clifford that he had been informed of the situation. He asked if they were both alright, Clifford told him that Elaine was very upset but that was only to be expected. Lewis agreed and asked if anything was missing, Clifford briefed him on what they saw on the tape and he said: 'Ok Mr Jessop you go and get yourself sorted out and we will talk tomorrow when scenes of crime have made their report, I will call you.

CHAPTER NINE

Elaine and Clifford booked into the Berkley hotel, not far from their apartment block. Following a restless night for both of them they arose early. After breakfast they went into town, Clifford suggested Elaine looked for an outfit to wear to the dinner party as it may take her mind off recent events. Elaine wasn't going to pass up an offer like that so they visited various stores and boutiques; eventually she found a trouser suit they both agreed was perfect and it fitted perfectly.

Elaine was redressing after trying on the outfit when Clifford received a call on his mobile from DCS Lewis to say the apartment had been cleared for them to return home. Elaine reappeared from the fitting room and went to pay for the outfit. Clifford standing behind her said: 'You'll be able to try it on properly when we get home.' She didn't catch on at first but as she was signing the credit card slip it dawned on her what he meant. She asked: 'Are you saying we can go home?' Clifford said that they could and she gave a little "yelp" of delight, the assistant gave her an odd look, Clifford just said: 'There's nothing to worry about we don't let her out very often.' The assistant gave a half grin then placed the outfit into a bag and handed it to Elaine. As Elaine turned to walk away she swiped Clifford on the back with the bag then with a happy grin looped her arm through his and said: 'Let's go home?'

In the car Clifford said that he was going to the funeral directors on the way home, Elaine said that was a good Idea and he could pay his last respects to Sam at the same time. At the funeral home Clifford made the funeral arrangements and opted for an internment as it was a family tradition, all of his family were buried in the same church yard and he wanted Sam buried there as well. Clifford and Elaine then visited the Chapel of rest to see Sam. Elaine agreed with Clifford that he did look calm and restful.

When they left the Chapel Clifford suggested they should go and have some lunch as they would be so busy tidying up the apartment later they may not have time to eat properly.

After lunch they returned to the apartment building, Jim the security guard greeted them and Clifford asked if their keys had been returned by the Police. Jim assured him that they had and that he had double checked the apartment was secure. Clifford thanked him and signed for the keys and they went up to the apartment. Elaine again became upset at seeing their belongings scattered all around but at least she was back home and she was determined not to let it get to her.

It took a long time to sort the mess out but once the apartment was straight Clifford called DCS Lewis to inform him that there was nothing else taken apart from the items that he originally reported. Lewis advised Clifford that he had posted two men outside the building's entrance with Simpson's picture in case someone recognised him from the morning before. Clifford told Lewis: 'Yes my wife and I were approached when we came in. Oh and by the way I thought I ought to notify you, I have made funeral arrangements for my brother for two pm next Monday.' Lewis acknowledged the Clifford then informed him that it was usual to place plain clothes officers at funerals of this nature in case the murderer or murderers should show up. HE asked if Clifford had any objections, which he didn't.

Lewis was talking to Clifford when DCI Deacon knocked Lewis's open door and said: 'Sorry to interrupt but I heard Mr Jessop's name, I have the preliminary forensic report from the apartment.' He handed it to Lewis and he read it out aloud to Clifford: "There were no finger prints found but there was skin tissue on the door frame where Simpson knocked his head, which tests confirmed they definitely came from him". Lewis remarked: 'Well there's no surprises there, the CCTV tapes weren't much help either. They showed him leaving the building and walk up the street then he slipped down an alley between two shops which led to a small car park but there were no CCTV cameras in that area.' Lewis said he would be in touch if anything new turned up. They bid each other goodbye and ended the call.

Clifford gave Elaine a rundown of the conversation, she shrugged her shoulders and as Lewis had said: 'No surprise there, now I am going to do some cheese on toast and then you ought to go and see Clive.'

Clifford arrived at the nursing home and was met by a different Nurse than his first visit, she asked him to wait while she fetched the senior nurse. He was glad to see that it was Senior Nurse Henderson. She greeted him and suggested they go to her office, once they were sat down she said: 'I am sorry Mr Jessop but Clive is not any better, in fact he is a little worse. I apologise for not contacting you but I haven't been able to bring the subject of your brother up simply because he's not been well enough.' Clifford asked if he could see Clive and she said of course he could but he wouldn't understand anything he said to him. Clifford decided that it would be pointless to disturb him unnecessarily and he would leave him in peace. He told her the date, time and church of the funeral but she didn't hold out much hope that Clive would be well enough to attend, however she promised to inform him if there was any change, Clifford thanked her then said goodnight and went home.

Friday evening they arrived by taxi at the Chief Constable's dinner party. Charles greeted them at the door saying: 'Hello you two I am really glad you were able to come with all you've had to contend with lately.' He handed them both a glass of bucks fizz and guided them in to join the other guests.

Charles took them to see Helen, Elaine handed her a large bouquet of roses wishing her a very happy birthday. Helen kissed Elaine on the cheek and thanked her she then turned to Clifford and said: 'Hello Clifford welcome to my "little diversion". Clifford smiled and looking at Charles said: 'Thanks for that Charles.' Elaine was a little bemused but Charles explained what the joke was and Elaine laughed. Charles then said that he was going back to his door steward duty as there were still two more guests to arrive so Helen introduced the Jessop's to guests they didn't know.

The last guests to arrive were DCS Lewis and his wife after Charles had introduced the Lewis's to other guests he very diplomatically introduced them to Clifford and Elaine. The DCS said: 'Nice to meet you at last, Mrs Jessop.' He then turned to Clifford and said: 'Good to see you again Mr Jessop.' Charles said jokingly: 'Oh yes I forgot you two have already met.' He ambled away with a little grin on his face.

Mrs Lewis asked: 'How do you and Andrew know each other Mr Jessop?'

'Call me Clifford please—actually we met through a case he is currently working on.'

'Oh I see, and please do call me Karen?' Elaine then added: 'Yes and you must call me Elaine.'

Clifford made their excuses then he and Elaine drifted off to mingle. Once clear of the Lewis's he said: 'I hope we are not sitting too close to them or it will be a very strained conversation.' Elaine reminded him: 'Just remember this is Helen's night and we don't want to ruin it for her. DO WE?'

'No darling, of course we don't.'

'Yes well, to quote Del boy—"You know it makes sense". They chuckled mutually, Charles spotted them and came over, he asked: 'Oh yes and what are you two sniggering at, not me I hope?'

'No just a private joke.'

'Well in that case come on we are going in to dinner.'

As they made their way to the dining room Charles escorted Elaine and Clifford escorted Helen. The dining room was adorned by two impressive crystal chandeliers over a solid oak dining table covered with a white silk cloth. There was Silver cutlery, bone china side plates, crystal wine glasses and crystal jugs containing iced lemon water, all laid out immaculately.

Clifford gave a sigh of release when he discovered they weren't seated near the Lewis's.

The evening went very well and after midnight when guests began leaving Clifford and Elaine stepped out onto the gravel drive. They were joined by Stephen Judd a high court judge and his wife Mary. "Clifford knew Judd from when giving evidence for the prosecution in cases brought by the Customs office". The judge remarked: 'Lovely evening wasn't it? Elaine answered: 'Yes very, Helen and Charles are well matched.'

'Yes and talking of matches Clifford I hear you and our friend the DCS have been standing up against each other recently, let me just say it won't do him any harm to have someone put him in his place once in a while, well done my boy.'

Soon after the judge and his wife were picked up by their chauffeur, as the judge climbed into his limousine he said to Clifford: "See you in court old boy". As the limousine pulled away Clifford and Elaine's taxi pulled up, but as it arrived Lewis and his wife emerged from the house and Lewis went to climb in the taxi, Clifford stopped him saying: 'I think you will find that one is for us.' Lewis asked the driver who it was for and was told it was for the Jessop's. Lewis stepped back out and apologised, Clifford couldn't resist the opportunity and said: 'you've done a lot of apologising lately Andrew.' Lewis just gave a wry grin and stepped back allowing Clifford and Elaine to climb in.

On the way home Elaine linked arms with Clifford and said grinning: 'A few points scored tonight if I am not mistaking "Husband"? Clifford replied: 'I don't know what you mean "wife".' They both had a chuckle and settled back in their seats recalling the events of the evening.

CHAPTER TEN

On Monday morning Clifford and Elaine drove to the local florist and bought a wreath for Sam's funeral. On returning to the apartment there was a message on their answer machine from Nurse Henderson to say that Clive had bucked up over the weekend and the doctor said he thinks he would be able to attend the funeral. She had managed to talk to him on Sunday and although he said nothing there was a look in eyes that made her think he understood. She said that the Nursing home would arrange transport to take him to the church and a Nurse would attend. Clifford thanked her for her help and gave her the directions to the church, he then said goodbye.

Elaine was happy for Clifford and said: 'At least now there will be a small part of the family there even if Clive is not exactly with it.' Clifford agreed with her and she hugged him.

The funeral was being held at a small village church just outside Surrey close to the old family home and Sam was being buried next to his father. The hearse collected

Sam from the Chapel and a funeral car collected Clifford and Elaine from the apartment.

The hearse reached the cemetery at the same moment as the Jessop's. The vicar appeared outside of the church entrance and welcomed them he told Clifford that his uncle was inside the church in his wheelchair. Clifford looked around and spotted the plain clothes Police officers dotted around the area, and then with Elaine entered the church for the service.

Clifford sat in an outside pew in the front row facing the altar where Sam's coffin stood. Elaine sat next to him and Clive and his Nurse were next to Clifford in the aisle.

Clifford said hello to Clive he responded with a weak smile, he looked at Clifford and mouthed something though very quietly. Clifford could not understand him so the Nurse knelt down and asked Clive what he had said, he repeated the words and she told Clifford she thought he said "Sam". Clifford leaned closer to him and said: 'Yes Sam, he has passed away.' There was no reaction from Clive this time so Clifford didn't push Clive he was just pleased to see him a little lucid.

The vicar walked to the front of the altar and began the service, as he did so the door opened and Clifford looked around, a stranger had entered and was sitting right at the back, he wore a brown baseball hat with the peak pulled down and his head bent forward. Clifford watched for a moment or two then assuming it was probably another plain clothed officer he looked back to the front.

The Vicar began the service with a hymn during which the door opened again, Clifford waited until they all finished singing then took another look around. DCI

Deacon had come in and was sitting in the row opposite the stranger who seemed fidgety, this unnerved Clifford a little but he turned his head back to the front. The service concluded and Elaine took Clifford's hand as they followed Clive and the nurse up the aisle, Clifford noticed that Deacon and the stranger were gone.

Outside Lewis was waiting with Deacon who greeted them saying: 'Good afternoon Mr and Mrs Jessop I hope we are not intruding on this sad day but as I indicated to you we find a lot of the time the culprit's can't resist coming to admire their dirty work.'

Clifford remarked: 'That is the first time I've ever heard a funeral called "Dirty work".

'So sorry not the best choice of words I must say, what I mean is they like to make sure they were successful.'

'Yes I got your drift Superintendant and are there any "culprit's" I mean?'

'We're not sure, there was a guy sitting at the back but he left just after DCI Deacon sat down, he followed him out but he had disappeared. A couple of our boys are looking around for him unfortunately though there are various directions he could have gone and the DCI didn't get a good look at his face.'

While they were talking Sam's coffin was carried out towards the awaiting grave and Clifford said to the officers: 'I'm sorry gentlemen but we are going to bury my brother now and it is family only at the graveside.' The Detective's acknowledged Clifford's wishes and stood to one side to let them pass.

The burial service commenced and Clive seemed to be aware of what was happening, Clifford noticed this and he thought to himself that over the years he would have gone through this a few times so perhaps there were a few memories floating back. After the burial service Elaine told her husband to have some time with Sam and she asked the Nurse to leave Clive with Clifford. Clifford knelt down and handed Clive a few flowers and kept some for himself, he threw the flowers onto Sam's coffin and to Clifford's surprise Clive attempted to throw his but not having much strength they just fell to the graveside, Clifford picked them up and dropped them in for him he then put his arm around his shoulders and said: 'Come on then uncle let's get you home for some tea.'

Clifford wheeled Clive to catch up with the others and he asked the Nurse: 'Would it be alright if we took Clive back with us and give him some tea? 'We'll take him back to the home later and of course you can join us if you wish.' She said that she would have to call the home and get their advice. She made the call and the Senior Nurse asked how Clive had been, the Nurse told her Clive had coped very well so she said yes but not for too long as he had to be back for his evening medication. She agreed to let the nurse accompany him and asked her to send the home's transport back.

This cheered Clifford up a little, however Elaine could see that he was still upset so she took his hand and asked: 'Are you alright darling?' He replied: 'Yes I'm alright but I couldn't have coped without you, thank you for coming. Sam was no angel but he was family and then seeing my parent's graves, it's just been very upsetting.'

'Ok let's go home it will be nice for you having Clive to tea.'

They thanked the vicar and nodded their acknowledgement at the two detectives who had appeared from their vantage point. They walked to their car with Clive and the nurse, as they did so Clifford spotted the Black BMW parked at the top of the lane under some trees. He tightened his grip on Elaine's hand and said quietly: 'Don't look but that BMW is parked up there.'—"Indicating the direction with his eyes and head".

Clifford opened the car door with the remote control and Elaine climbed in he then turned to the Nurse saying: 'I see the home transport is still here, I'm sorry but we have a situation and there's a change of plan, will you please take Clive back to the home I will call and explain to them later?' She nodded and wheeled Clive away. Clifford then leaned into his car and said to Elaine: 'I am going back into the graveyard and alerting Lewis.'

He walked slowly back towards the DCS who with Deacon was just about to leave the churchyard. Clifford walked up to them and held out his hand to Lewis pretending to shake his, when Lewis came closer and held his hand out Clifford shook it saying quietly: 'The BMW is at the top of the lane.' Lewis responded saying: 'Alright Mr Jessop look casual and go back to your car but don't drive off yet give me time to get backup, I will call you on your mobile.' The DCS then said loudly: 'Goodbye Mr Jessop we will be in touch.' Once in their car Lewis told Deacon: 'Drive off but not too fast, Lewis then called the local station for backup.

While they were waiting for the call from Lewis, Elaine and Clifford kept an eye on the BMW. A few minutes passed then the call came through, Lewis asked Clifford to turn the car around and drive normally he said that he and

Deacon would be waiting in a lay by just past the bend in the road but Clifford was to just drive on past.

Lewis and Deacon were in an unmarked car and they had stopped in the lay by which was hidden from view just beyond a tight bend. Clifford calmly started the car and turning it around he drove off watching in the rear view mirror for any movement from the suspect car. Just before he approached the tight bend he looked again and the BMW had pulled out but was keeping a safe distance away. Clifford cried out: 'Bingo they have taken the bait.' He continued at a leisurely pace and reached the bend, he had no idea where or when something would happen so he just kept driving.

They passed by where the detective's were waiting but didn't acknowledge them. He continued on while watching the mirror but Elaine told him to keep his eyes on the road and she would keep watch. She continued watching out of the rear window and saw the BMW appear around the bend driving straight past Lewis's car. As it passed the DCS told deacon to let it get about fifty yards away then pull out and follow it.

He called Clifford's mobile which Elaine answered, He asked Clifford to gradually slow up. Clifford complied and the BMW loomed closer. Lewis told Deacon to drive a little faster and they got within twenty yards of the suspects car, at that moment they received confirmation backup was arriving so Lewis directed them to converge onto the exit of the lane.

The DCS then contacted Elaine suggesting that Clifford slow down and brake hard just before the end of the lane, Clifford complied and the BMW stopped.

Lewis and Deacon were right behind and raced up to the BMW's offside ramming into the driver's door caving it in. The DCI leapt out and ran around to the BMW's nearside door, as he reached the other side the front passenger door opened and a leg appeared from the car. Using his foot Deacon forcefully kicked against the door jamming the leg and there was a cry of pain. Deacon then pulled the door open and grabbed the male suspect's arm and pulled him from the vehicle. Lewis managed to climb across to the driver's side and jumped out running to assist Deacon but, finding he had control of the situation HE checked to make sure there were no other occupants. Satisfied there wasn't he aided Deacon and they forced the man against the car and handcuffed him. Lewis then called for the backup vehicles to come to the scene.

Clifford by this time had got out of his car telling Elaine to stay put. He walked towards the scene as a patrol car arrived and Lewis bundled the suspect into the rear seat. Clifford ran over to the car and started banging on the rear door window shouting: 'Who are you? Why are you following us? Did you kill my brother?' Lewis linked his arm through Clifford's saying: 'Now come on Mr Jessop this is not helping, let us do our job after all you've been criticising us enough. We will take him to the local nick and officially arrest him; we will then make arrangements to have him transferred to Chelsea where we can question him properly. Elaine then appeared and said sternly: 'Stop this Clifford we have waited to get this creep now let the DCS take him to jail.'

Clifford walked away angrily, eventually though he calmed down and apologised for the outburst. Lewis assured him that it was understandable and explained that only the Police or a legal representative can speak to a suspect before he has been arrested and charged. He suggested he and Elaine return to Chelsea Police station and wait for him there.

At the local nick the prisoner was officially arrested then charged with stalking and infringement of privacy. The suspect refused to give any personal details so he was put in a holding cell awaiting transfer to Chelsea.

At Chelsea He was booked in and taken to a holding cell, beforehand though he was asked if he knew a solicitor he would prefer to represent him and he said yes and gave Lewis the phone number, Lewis asked him his name so he could give it to the Solicitor but the suspect said:' He won't need it just tell him it's one of "DT's" men.' Lewis shrugged his shoulders and made the call but there was no answer and it went to voicemail. He made several more attempts leaving messages each time, after thirty minutes though he notified the prisoner that He would have to make do with a duty Solicitor until the other man made contact.

Afterwards Lewis met up with the Jessop's at reception and asked if he could have a quick word, he took them into a small room containing a table and four chairs and invited them to sit, he then asked: 'Do either of you recognise the prisoner? Maybe one of you caught a glimpse of him on one of the occasion he followed you.' Clifford and Elaine both looked at each other then said they hadn't seen the driver because the windows in the BMW were too blacked out. He then asked: 'So there's no way of knowing if it was him every time?'

'No there may have of been several drivers.' replied Elaine

'In that case then there's no point in an identity parade.' They apologised for not being more helpful, Lewis said it wasn't their fault and that they may as well go home promising that if the prisoner gave them anything useful he would be in touch. Clifford added: 'I'd just like to say sorry for my earlier criticism's, I was just upset at not being able to put Sam to rest.'

'There is no need to be sorry Mr Jessop I understand thank goodness we all have broad shoulders in this job.' Lewis and Clifford shook hands and said their goodbyes.

CHAPTER ELEVEN

The interview of the prisoner commenced at seven twenty pm, the solicitor had arrived and had been talking to the prisoner in his cell then they were then escorted to an interview room. Once they were settled Lewis and Deacon entered the room and sat on the opposite side of the table, a constable stood guard by the door.

Lewis and Deacon both had case files in front of them and they each sieved through the papers taking their time in an attempt to unnerve the prisoner, finally when they decided they were ready Lewis switched on the tape machine and stated: "Commencement of interview of unnamed suspect, the time is seven twenty, the date is Monday the eighteenth of October, two thousand and six. Present are Detective Chief Superintendant Lewis and Chief Inspector Deacon, also present is the prisoner and his legal representative and Police constable Cole."

Lewis spoke first, he asked the suspect: 'What is your name?' He remained silent so Lewis announced: "For the tape the prisoner refuses to answer." He then continued, asking: 'Do you know why you were apprehended today?'

There was still no reply and again Lewis noted this for the tape.

Deacon took Sam's picture from his file and laid it on the table in front of the man and asked if he knew him, saying: 'He was murdered approximately three months ago and you were at his funeral today.' He still refused to speak so Lewis pulled the Jessop's pictures out and showed them to him, saying: 'You have been following these two people for over two weeks, can you tell us why?' Again he stayed silent.

After Lewis had noted the silence for the tape he said: 'Ok chummy have it your way, we will soon have your fingerprints and DNA results back then we will know who you are, you are bound to be known to us, it's obvious you are not in this on your own but if you continue to be uncooperative then you will take the fall, there's car theft and stalking for starters then of course there's the murder, and I wouldn't be surprised if you are not wanted for other crimes as well but, still it's up to you.' Take him back to his cell constable.'

Lewis was about to announce the suspension of the interview and Deacon had stood up closing his files when the man suddenly blurted out: 'Ok ok you win.' Deacon sat down again and Lewis sat back in his chair, He then asked: 'Ok then what have you got to tell us?' The suspect leaned over and whispered to his solicitor who nodded, the man paused then said: 'Alright yes I have been following these people and I did know Sam but I had nothing to do with his murder but, I do know why he was killed.'

Lewis shuffled his chair closer to the table and remarked: 'Ok now you have my attention, go on.'

'Well a few years ago the guy who paid me to follow that couple "Darren Thomas" organised a raid on a cash delivery van but it ended in disaster, Sam went down for it because Thomas dropped him in it at the scene. When Sam came out of jail Thomas tried forcing him to get a large bundle of money to fund some big job or other Thomas had planned. He said Sam owed him for screwing the raid up, it wasn't his fault but Thomas is a mean son of a bitch. Sam was killed because he failed to deliver the cash.'

'Right now we are getting somewhere, who else was with Sam on the wages job?'

'I don't know I only know Sam was there because Thomas mentioned him.'

'How about this "big job" do you know what it is and when or where it's taking place? We know Sam was after a half million pounds, that is a lot of money to fund a job so how much is he expecting to get out of it?'

'That I couldn't tell you, Thomas only paid me to steal the car and follow these people then report back to him. I did overhear a phone conversation once though and he mentioned a helicopter and four men but that's it.'

'Well how do the two people you have been following fit in to all of this?'

'Beat's me, I know no more than I've told you.'

'Ok now what about your name, are you ready to tell us that?'

'Well that depends if you are going to give me protection? I'm dead if Thomas find's me.'

'As long as you are prepared to testify in court I am sure something can be arranged.'

The man leaned over and whispered to his solicitor, they whispered to each other then the man said: 'Ok my name is Stuart John Pierce, I am twenty seven years old and I have a flat in Parkway Court—number twelve—that's in Porterhouse lane, East Chelsea. Look you are going to find out any way so I may as well tell you. I have a record for car theft and burglary although that was a long time ago. I now work for Benson's—a packaging company—in the trading estate just outside of town. Thomas threatened to burn the building down and blame me if I didn't do odd jobs for him.'

'Why didn't he recruit YOU for this "big job"?'

'I didn't want any part of it, I told him I'll continue to do odd jobs for him but not to involve me in anything else. Most of his jobs end in disaster so I am better off sticking to what I do. I've blown all that now anyway, I'm going down.'

'Not necessarily keep helping us I am sure we can work out some kind of deal.' Lewis then said: 'Ok gentlemen that's it for now we will speak to you again though Stuart, now the constable will take you back to your cell.'

As Pierce was walking away Lewis said to him: 'I guess you are hungry?' Pierce nodded enthusiastically. Lewis said he would arrange something for him he and then asked: 'By the way Stuart is there someone we can call for you, like a next of kin or someone?' Pierce said he had no family or anyone close so Lewis said: 'Ok then Stuart we'll speak again later.'

Once Stuart had been taken away the Solicitor said to Lewis: 'I am not his official Solicitor he still wants the guy he requested to represent him, I will pass everything on to him when he turns up.'

Deacon and Lewis stayed to discuss the interview, Deacon said: 'I notice you didn't ask about the break in at the Jessop's or if he knew Simpson.'

'No I didn't want to put all my eggs in one basket anyway he didn't seem to know the guys in the wages raid so that takes care of Simpson. I deliberately omitted to ask who the four men are in the "big job" this Thomas is planning, I'm hoping he will volunteer that info later. Check up on this Thomas character he must be in the system somewhere, but not tonight it's been a long hard day so go home, I am going to phone the Jessop's and tell them what we have and I won't be far behind you.' Deacon nodded his head in acknowledgement and stood up saying goodnight.

Clifford and Elaine were at home relaxing, Elaine had remarked to Clifford that despite it being Sam's funeral the day's events had made her a little excited. Clifford said that he hadn't wanted to say so but he was also thinking the same thing, because not only had he laid Sam to rest at last, they may even have his or one of his killers in Jail. Elaine had replied: 'Oh I hope so; we so need to get past all this.'

They were about to go to bed as they had decided to go back to work the next day when DCS Lewis phoned, Clifford answered his call and Lewis told him: 'Mr Jessop, DCS Lewis here I'm sorry for the late call but I thought you would like to know the man we caught today has admitted to following you and your wife although he says—and I am inclined to believe him—that he had nothing to do with Sam's murder. He did know Sam through a nasty piece of work called Darren Thomas, who paid this guy—Stuart Pierce—to follow you both. He was also the boss behind the wages snatch fiasco Sam went down for which ties in with Sam's own story. He says Thomas killed Sam after failing to get you to hand over the money, which apparently was to fund some "big job" Thomas is planning. That also ties in with what "Mr

X"—as we will call him on an open line—told us. Did Sam mention this Thomas guy or anyone called Stuart Pierce?'

'No he wouldn't give any of their names the idiot that he was,'

'Well you can relax now Mr Jessop, I don't expect anyone will be following you anymore, I'll say goodnight and I will let you know if we hear anything else, we are considering giving this guy a deal I'm sure he has more to tell us.' Clifford thanked Lewis for the update and told him that he and Elaine were returning to work in the morning then said goodnight.'

CHAPTER TWELVE

Tuesday evening Elaine left the office at five thirty. She took her usual route home but stopped off at a convenience store to get some bits for dinner, she parked her car at the rear of the store in the car park. She walked back to her car and opened the boot, as she was about to put her shopping in when a man's voice said from behind: 'Mrs Jessop?' Before she could turn around a hand was clamped over her mouth and something was pulled over head and face. She dropped her shopping; and her handbag was snatched from her, the man rifled through the bag and found her mobile, he dropped it on the ground and stamped on it, he then threw her bag across the car park.

Although shocked she managed to stammer: 'TAKE MY BAG I HAVE NOTHING ELSE.' The voice replied: 'WE don't want your money darling we have bigger fish to fry now stop struggling and you won't get harmed.' At that moment two hands were slid beneath her armpits while two more grabbed her ankles. Immediately she was lifted off her feet and she automatically screamed but the voice said roughly: 'I TOLD YOU KEEP QUIET, NOW SHUT UP.' She was petrified, she could tell by the tone of his voice that he meant it so she stopped struggling and kept quiet.

She couldn't see through the head cover but she knew she wasn't carried far before she was manhandled into a vehicle; she wasn't sure but thought it was probably a van as it sounded hollow, and that two doors were slammed shut.

Once inside her legs and hands were tied up, panicking Elaine cried out: 'who are you? What do you want? My husband is a very important man he knows the Chief Constable and DCS Lewis you're in a lot of trouble.' The voice replied mocking her: Ooh I'm trembling! 'What do you say lads, shall we let her go?' There was no reply so he said: 'No I didn't think so.' With that her head cover was pulled up and a gag placed over her mouth, she attempted to look around but it was too dark and the head cover was quickly replaced over her head so she didn't get a look at the men either.

It wasn't long before the engine was started and the vehicle moved off at speed with the wheels skidding on the loose gravel. By now she was trembling in terror not knowing what was in store for her, however she desperately attempted to determine the direction the vehicle was travelling by listening for sounds but, gave up because the vehicle made so much noise, it sounded as if the exhaust was faulty and there was a loud whine from the rear wheels.

It seemed a long journey but eventually they stopped, she heard the doors being yanked open with a crash making her jump and she was pulled out roughly. Elaine struggled but was told that if she continued she would be hurt, convinced that the threat was serious she calmed down. She was carried for a short distance into a building and she could just see a light through the cover, her bonds were removed and the voice said: 'Take her out back and we will let her old man panic for a while before we contact him, by the way I am dealing with that little problem from yesterday that should be sorted by now.'

The voice was referring to Stuart Pierce, DCS Lewis had organised for him to have takeaways delivered to the station because he didn't eat normal meals. At the Police station that day at lunch time, a man arrived at the front desk saying he was Stuart Pierce's official solicitor, he said his name was James McDonald and he was asked to sign in. At the same time Pierce's meal arrived, the desk Sergeant asked a constable to take it down to Pierce but the solicitor interrupted him saying that he was going straight to his cell and he would take the meal if they wished. The sergeant accepted the gesture and McDonald was escorted to the custody area.

The custody sergeant was at his desk and McDonald introduced himself, the sergeant asked McDonald to sign in then escorted him to Pierce's cell. The Sergeant peeked through the spy hole in the door and saw Pierce sitting on his bunk, he unlocked the door and opened it slightly telling Pierce to remain on his bunk, he then opened the door fully. The Sergeant told Pierce that he had a visitor and ushered McDonald inside. McDonald said to pierce: 'Good afternoon Mr Pierce I'm James McDonald your solicitor, I have your lunch.' He handed Pierce his meal and the Sergeant locked the door and returned to his desk.

After fifteen minutes McDonald called out to say he was finished. The Sergeant returned to the cell and peered through the spy hole, he saw the solicitor standing by the door and Pierce was lying on the bunk curled up with his back to the door. The Sergeant was puzzled so he opened the door cautiously, the Solicitor walked towards the door and the Sergeant asked: 'What's up with him?' McDonald replied: 'He's tired he could hardly keep his eyes open he's even left his meal, I'll come back tomorrow.' The Sergeant took another glance at Pierce and remarked: 'Young people today, I don't know.' He and the solicitor walked back to the desk McDonald signed out and the Sergeant ordered a constable to escort him from the building.

When Elaine was out of the van a hand grabbed her arm and was told to start walking, she knew she was being escorted by the man that grabbed her in the car park. She tried concentrating where she was being taken noting there was gravel underfoot, next she was sure she was walking on grass as it felt spongier. Eventually she was pulled to a halt and she heard the sound of a bolt being pulled back, the man said: 'Right in you go.' She was pushed inside a building and the hood was ripped off but, she was unable to see any faces or where she was because a torch was shining in her face and was kept like that until the man was outside, the door was then shut and she heard the door being locked.

Elaine was in some sort of a room but it took a little time for her eyes to become accustomed to the dull light. When she was at last able to look around she saw the room was filthy and damp, there was even mould growing up the walls and on the ceiling, Elaine gave an involuntary shiver.

On the floor was a disgusting filthy mattress with a tatty quilt folded on it, she cringed at the thought of having to sleep on that, imagining all sorts of bugs and insects crawling all over it, not to mention the smell of damp.

There was a dirty wooden chair at a wobbly table these were covered in dust, she tried to blow it off but it was too thick and damp and wouldn't move. She screwed up her eyes and slowly lowered herself onto the chair feeling the coldness creeping through her clothes. She had a rather thick coat on but even that didn't protect her. She started crying wondering how it was going to end and at the atrocious conditions of her tiny prison.

Meanwhile Clifford was surprised but not unduly worried that Elaine wasn't in when he got home, she had been working late since her promotion to PA although she normally called when she knew she would be late, however he knew she would have a lot of work to catch up on having had Monday off for Sam's funeral, he just assumed she had forgotten to notify him this time.

He decided to set about making Dinner although not a gourmet chef he could whisk up the odd lasagne or spaghetti. After about an hour though he began to worry so he called her mobile but the line was dead, now he was really worried. He hung up and called her office number but the call was diverted to her mobile. Panicking he tried the reception desk but the call was answered by security. Clifford explained the reason for his call but the officer said that the offices were empty however he said he would check the register to see what time Elaine signed out. He returned to the phone and told Clifford that she signed out at five thirty; he also told Clifford that he had spun the cameras around the car park and her car wasn't there. Clifford thanked the officer and immediately called the Police. He asked to speak to either DCS Lewis or DCI Deacon, he was told that neither of them was in their office but he could speak to DI Barnes if he wished. Clifford agreed and when DI Barnes came on the line, Clifford explained about Elaine and recent events, the DI said he was aware of the investigation as he was on Lewis's team, He asked Clifford if there were any friends or family Elaine could have visited on the way home but Clifford said no and in any case Elaine would have notified him if she had. The DI then asked for a description of Elaine and the details of her car, Clifford furnished Barnes with the details and the DI said he would put out an APB immediately. He advised Clifford to call all of her friends and the hospitals in the region in case she had been involved in an accident, he also advised Clifford to stay in his apartment in case she came home or he had any further news for him. Clifford asked Barnes to call his mobile first if he does have any news.

Clifford hung up and called all the hospitals in the area but was told no one fitting Elaine's description had been admitted into any of them, he also called her friends as the DCI suggested but was told no one had seen or heard from her.

He then called down to the security desk in the foyer of the apartment building, informing the duty officer of the situation, he then said: 'If my wife does come in please ask her to call my mobile immediately?' He hung up and grabbing his car keys left the apartment and locked the door. He took the lift to the underground car park and rushed to his car and sped out nearly crashing into the barrier as it lifted. He headed towards Elaine's office building, once on the main road he slowed down so he was able to look around more carefully.

When he reached her office building he turned the car around and followed her usual route home straining to look ahead and out of both sides of the car. He arrived back at the apartment building with still no sign of Elaine or her car. As he turned into the slipway down to the car park his mobile rang, he pressed the button on the hands free and said quickly: 'Hello Elaine.' Unfortunately it wasn't her it was DI Barnes, he said: 'No Mr Jessop I'm sorry it's DI Barnes, I take it you haven't heard from her?'

'No I haven't, I have driven over her usual route home but there is no sign of her.'

'Mr Jessop; I don't wish to alarm you but your wife's car has been discovered in a car park at Ken's convenience store in lower lane.' Clifford immediately asked: 'What about Elaine is she there? Is she alright?'

'No she wasn't there Mr Jessop, the boot lid was open and her shopping strewn all around, her handbag was also found a short distance from the car it had been rifled but her credit cards and cash haven't been taken and her mobile was found smashed on the ground.'

'Are you saying someone has taken her then?'

'Yes I'm afraid that seems the likely scenario, there CCTV cameras at the front and inside the store but there are none in the car park and it is unlit. Staff in the store said they saw nothing unusual. We are now waiting for SOCCO and forensics arrive but unfortunately that is all I can tell you for the moment.'

'Right I am coming down there.'

'I do not recommend that sir you will only upset yourself more than you already are and it would be wiser for you to go home just in case she or whoever has taken her, contact's you. DCS Lewis is on his way here and he has asked for a recent photo of your wife, do you know what she was wearing when she left for work this morning?'

'Yes she was wearing a white blouse and black trouser suit with a long grey coat. I'm not sure what shoes she wore though.'

'That's fine thank you Mr Jessop.' If it's ok with you sir we would like to send an officer around to collect the photo ASAP, we would also like to set up some recording equipment to to the apartment's phone lines.

Clifford said that would be ok saying he was going up to the apartment right away. Barnes said he was sorry to be the bearer of such bad news but to be assured everything would be done to secure the safe return of his wife. Clifford thanked him and ended the call.

When he finished talking he parked his car and made his way up to the lobby and the security desk, the duty guard said he hadn't seen his wife so Clifford briefed him on the circumstances, the guard said he was sorry to hear the news about Elaine and that he would contact Clifford if she appeared. Clifford left the lobby and took the lift to his apartment, inside he sieved through Elaine's phone contacts in the hope of finding John Ford's home number, finding the number he called Ford. The MD answered, Clifford apologised for disturbing him at home then explained the reason for the call and asked: 'How did she seem ok at work today John, do you know if she had any visitors or unusual phone calls?'

'I'm so sorry Clifford I don't know quite what to say, yes she seemed ok, in fact she told me about your escapades yesterday and she was optimistic things were getting back to normal.

I wouldn't know about her phone calls and as for visitors I didn't see any but you would be better off talking to Rita our receptionist, her desk is right opposite the entrance to the building and she sees everyone, actually she's gone home, I'll call her for you as she may be worried about telling you especially over the phone, are you at home?'

'Yes and thank you John I am at my wits end wondering what she could be going through.'

'Of course you are Clifford, do you think all this has anything to do with those photo's she received? I have to say I have been worried about her since they arrived.'

'I don't know what to think but it would not be a surprise to me if it was, ok I will hang up now and wait for your call.'

John Ford called Rita, she said Elaine had no unexpected visitors but she couldn't vouch for phone calls because they don't all go through the exchange, especially private calls. John called Clifford and relayed Rita's remarks then said: 'I'm sorry I can't be any more help but please call me when you hear anything, we all love her here and we will be worried for you both.' Clifford thanked him for his words and said goodbye.

CHAPTER THIRTEEN

At two fifteen that afternoon DCI Deacon was called into Lewis's office to go over recent developments, the DCS suggested having another go at Pierce to see if he could tell them anything else, so he and Deacon went down to the cells. They met up with the custody Sergeant and went with him to Pierce's cell. The Sergeant looked through the peephole and revealed that he was still asleep. Lewis asked what he meant by "still asleep". The sergeant explained about the solicitor leaving early because Pierce had fallen asleep. Lewis pushed the Sergeant aside and looked in himself, he immediately ordered the Sergeant to open the door at once. The Sergeant unlocked the door and Lewis rushed into the cell. He prodded Pierce on the shoulder but he was cold and lifeless and it soon became obvious he was dead. The DCS asked the Sergeant angrily: 'WHEN WAS THE LAST TIME HE WAS CHECKED?' The Sergeant shakily said that he had only been on duty since two o'clock and at handover he was told that Pierce was sleeping. The daily log report stated that he was asleep when the solicitor left at twelve thirty five and he was the last person in his cell. It also stated that he was checked and still asleep at one thirty.

Lewis used his mobile and called the duty Pathologist then told the Sergeant to get out of his sight. He closed the cell door and posted two constables outside with strict instructions not to let anyone in the cell except for the Pathologist, then returned to his office with Deacon trailing behind him.

Deacon knew not to say anything when the DCS was in this sort of mood so he stopped off and collected two coffees and took them to Lewis's office, he handed one to Lewis and He took it without a thank you, Lewis placed it on his desk and suddenly shouted: "SHIT! I JUST DO NOT BELIEVE THIS HAS HAPPENED". He took a sip of his coffee and a little calmer he continued: 'I now have to report this to the Chief Constable and there is bound to be an internal enquiry. Find out who let the solicitor in and where he came from and get the CCTV from the cell area? Oh and by the way thanks for the coffee.' Deacon just said: 'Yes Gov right away.'

Deacon went down to the front desk and asked who signed the solicitor in and who actually called him. The duty Sergeant looked in the log and saw that it was the Sergeant on the morning shift that signed McDonald in but there was no record of who called him. He looked through the visitor's book and it was apparent that McDonald was expected but there was nothing to indicate who put his name in the book. Deacon then retrieved the CCTV footage from the cell area and took it to the tech lab to be viewed.

While Deacon was at the front desk Lewis called the custody Sergeant from the morning shift and told him what had happened and ordered him to come in immediately.

When Deacon returned to Lewis's office Lewis had calmed down considerably, he apologised to Deacon for his earlier outburst but Deacon diplomatically told him to forget it, HE then related to Lewis what he was told at the front desk and Lewis said: 'I reckon McDonald is connected to this Thomas character and that is why Pierce was adamant he had his own solicitor and why the details of his visit are so vague.'

While they were talking a knock came on the door, Lewis called: "come in". A Woman Detective Constable entered, she told Lewis that the Pathologist had arrived at the cells and he was inspecting the body. Lewis thanked her then with Deacon he went down to the cell.

When they reached the cell the Pathologist was still inspecting Pierce's body, he was wearing a white overall with shoe covers, skull cap and latex gloves. He told Lewis and Deacon that death had occurred two to three hours ago but cause of death was not known at present but, he wouldn't rule out poison because there was a needle mark just below the muscle on his left arm and there was a small blood spot, it appeared that the body had been deliberately placed in such a position that he was laying on it so it wouldn't have been seen immediately, he said he would have to wait until he had him on the slab and ran more tests before he could give any definite cause.

The Pathologist arranged for the body to be taken to his lab and Lewis called in SOCCO and forensics to go over the cell.

When Lewis and Deacon left the Pathologist Lewis returned to his office, there was a note on his desk informing him that the Sergeant had arrived and was waiting in reception Lewis called reception and had him sent to his office. When the Sergeant knocked on Lewis's door Lewis said: "Come" and Mike Darling entered. Without looking up he told Darling to sit down, Lewis was writing and kept Mike waiting a few minutes, eventually Lewis put his pen down and looked up, he spoke saying: 'Ok Mike you know why you are here, this is a very serious matter and there is going to be an internal enquiry, I have to interview you on tape I'm afraid.' Lewis started the tape, he then said: 'Now Sergeant, when was the last time you saw Pierce alive?'

'Well the last time I was positive he was alive was when I took the solicitor into his cell.'

'Does that mean you didn't check him when you let McDonald out, why not for God's sake?'

'I did look at him from the door but the brief said he had been falling asleep while they were talking, he said he didn't even eat his meal, I had no reason to disbelieve him.'

'Didn't that sound just a little strange to you, what about when you first opened the door, did he seem sleepy to you?'

'Well no but he was sitting on his bunk when I opened the door and I told him to stay where he was until I had relocked the door, I can't be sure but I think he was ok.'

'You think—YOU THINK! God man, it's your job to ensure the safety of prisoners on your watch.' . . . . Lewis paused disgusted at what he was hearing, then said: 'Ok, now, once more for the record, did you physically check

Pierce yourself at any time during McDonald's visit or afterwards?'

'No I didn't, I assumed he was asleep and didn't wish to disturb him.'

'Ok, I'm sorry Mike but the buck stops with you, he was in your custody and you should have made sure he was alright. I'll do what I can but the rules are clear. I will have to wait until I hear from the Chief Constable but I'm pretty sure you will be suspended on full pay pending an enquiry. Now don't do anything daft and resign, just keep your head down and I will let you know when I hear something.'

Meanwhile the body had been taken to the lab and the Pathologist was performing the post mortem while forensics and SOCCO were going over the cell, many fingerprints were found which was no surprise considering how many prisoners and Police staff had passed through the cell, they would have to be eliminated one by one before they could begin processing any from that day, however they did find a cap from a syringe under the bunk which was bagged for testing, otherwise nothing else was found so Lewis urged forensics to process the print and cap immediately.

"Some time ago while in prison for trying to throttle an Ex girlfriend, Darren Thomas heard about an expedition to the Mexican jungle to find a newly discovered "lost city." "There was supposed to be ruins and a crumbling Temple in which it was said stood a giant effigy of the "SUN FIRE GOD." "It was alleged that in the forehead of the effigy was an enormous jewel which from the description the locals offered, sounded like a large ruby".

"Thomas was told a recent exploration team discovered the city and had found gold and other treasures while excavating the site. However before they were able to remove any of the treasures they were either struck blind or had died at the scene. Apparently local people had warned them that the "SUN GOD" was protected by spirits of the original inhabitants of the city. Thomas had just laughed when he heard the story".

"The four survivors two of whom were blinded, were in a bad way when they were found and could only remember parts of their experiences, but they eventually revealed that the temple doors were only just about standing and they had been easy to pull open with minimal effort. They discovered a very large statue at the back of the temple and there did appear to be a "large ruby," in the statues forehead. It was then the team became ill, two were struck blind and the others had just died almost instantly. The couple that stayed outside of the temple—a woman and a man were unaffected so they collected as much of the gold and jewels as they could carry then helping the blind couple they made their way back into the jungle, they were on their own because their native bearers had seen what was happening and ran off into the jungle".

"After trudging their way through the tangle of undergrowth and trees, negotiating a large waterfall and river, plus losing their way several times they were eventually found at the edge of the jungle all but dead. They had no treasure with them and they were never able to explain properly what had happened to them or the others as they were too traumatised".

"They all died mysteriously within two months of being found. Many medical experts in tropical diseases examined them and ran numerous tests while they were alive and even after they died but could find nothing to explain their symptoms or why they died".

"Thomas hit on the idea of forcing Sam to come up with the money so he could finance an expedition of his own to find the city because he considered the curse as rubbish. Two of Thomas's men—John Palmer and Richard Bird—never knew the details of Thomas's plan, all he told them was that they would be richer beyond their wildest dreams, being greedy and not too bright they were happy to agree to anything Thomas said".

"After Clifford failed to come up with the money for Sam, Thomas changed his plans and convinced a Director of a million pound IT company to stake the expedition, Thomas had a hold over him because when he was in jail he discovered that the businessman was a fraud and was also a tax evader".

"Thomas's plan was to Kidnap Elaine in an effort to persuade her company to process and market his ill gotten gains when he returned from Mexico. He also had a backup plan, he was going to demand a half a million pound ransom for Elaine in case the expedition went pear shaped.

The businessman had a made a helicopter available to Thomas to fly him and his team out to Mexico where he had a team of professional guides to help them find the city".

"He was taking Simpson and two new recruits with him, Bird and Palmer were unaware of the new recruits because Thomas planned to dispose of them later. The solicitor—McDonald became another member of Thomas's team after he was disbarred for gross misconduct, Thomas used him to get his top men out of jail with the odd bribe or two, McDonald was also unaware of Thomas's actual plan but, was happy to go along with what he was told as in the past Thomas had always paid him well to follow his orders, the most recent was to dispose of Pierce".

Clifford waited up all night sitting in an armchair drinking numerous coffees waiting for some news; however in the early hours he eventually drifted off to sleep until he suddenly awoke with a jolt, he looked at his watch, it was five twenty am and he was still in his work clothes from the previous day so he decided to shower and have a shave. After putting on clean clothes he thought he should eat something as he would need his strength to keep him going. He made some toast and marmalade and a cup of coffee but could only managed to eat one slice as he felt guilty, not knowing if his Elaine was being fed or even if she was still alive. He was also thinking but dreading the thought that she could be lying at the bottom of a ditch or in a field somewhere and hadn't been seen in the dark, he decided he would take another look along her route home in case he had missed her the night before.

He looked out of the window and it was beginning to get light, he took the lift to the foyer and spoke to the security man who happened to be Jim the security officer who he and Elaine often chatted to, he told Jim he was going out to see if he could see Elaine and asked him to continue monitoring the cameras in case someone or something suspicious should happen. Jim assured him that the night guard had been doing that and he himself had continued the operation from the start of his shift. Clifford said he appreciated their help and said goodbye.

He took the lift to the car park and went to his car; he drove out of the side street and set off slowly looking in all the places he thought Elaine could be laying. He reached her work building and was turning around to go in the opposite direction when a security guard approached his car and held his hand out to stop him. Clifford stopped and opened his window and said: 'Good morning is there a problem?' The guard replied: 'I was just going to ask you the same thing sir, can I help you?'

'Well yes actually, my name is Mr Jessop, my wife is Elaine Jessop the MD's PA . . . . The guard cut in: 'Ah yes of course, I am sorry Mr Jessop it's a terrible business. Have you heard any news? We did a search of all the buildings and the surrounding area last night but there was no sign.'

'Well, thank you anyway; no there hasn't been any sighting of her as yet but I am retracing her route home again just in case she is lying hurt somewhere.' Do me a favour would you, if she should turn up here please call me?'

'You have my assurance Sir and I will pass on the message, good luck now and I hope you find her soon.'

Clifford left the guard and started his drive home, he drove down all the lanes and alleys as well as the rear of shops and businesses, he also attempted to go into the rear car park of the store Elaine was taken from but it was sealed off with police incident tape and two constables stood guard, as he approached they held their hands up gesturing to him to stop, he pulled up and one officer came to his window, he told Clifford: 'I'm sorry sir the car park is closed, we have a major ongoing incident . . . . Clifford interrupted: 'Yes I know officer, it is my wife that is missing. Are there any senior officer's on site?' The officer apologised and said there were no other officers at present but he was sure there would be later. Clifford went on to tell the officer his reason for being there and said he would continue with his search. The officer bid him goodbye and good luck. Clifford reversed the car and continued on. Eventually he had to admit defeat, he didn't know what to do so he decided to go to the Police station and see DCS Lewis.

He arrived at the front desk and asked to speak to Lewis. The desk Sergeant told him that Lewis and Deacon were in their offices and had left strict instructions not to disturb them unless it was an emergency. Clifford informed the Sergeant that not only was it his wife that was missing but he was a close acquaintance of the Chief Constable, this did the trick and the Sergeant called Lewis, Clifford could hear him getting an ear bashing and although he felt sorry for him he also considered his actions justified. The Sergeant hung up the phone and told Clifford that Lewis had said to go straight up.

He reached Lewis's office and knocked the door, Lewis shouted: 'Come in.' Clifford entered and Lewis said: 'I don't know why you are here Mr Jessop, DI Barnes did tell you we would contact you as soon as we heard anything. We are very busy at present as you are probably aware, anyway as you are here now how can I help you?'

'I don't really know Superintendant, I am sorry but I felt so guilty and useless sitting around at the flat, I felt I had to do something, I know Elaine is out there somewhere and I don't know if she is alive or not.' Lewis lightened up and said: 'I'm sorry Clifford—can I call you Clifford?'

'Yes of course, please do?'

'Look Clifford I know we have had our differences and I do admit that we did have you down as a suspect in

Sam's murder, nearly all murders are usually committed by family members or a close friends but, be assured you are well and truly off the suspect list now.'

'Well that is something to be grateful for I suppose.'

'Actually as you are here I do have some news . . . . Clifford cut in: 'is it about Elaine, is she alright?'

No! 'No that was stupid of me, I'm sorry, no it is about Pierce the man we arrested on Monday, he was found dead in his cell yesterday, it is unofficial but it is looking like murder.'

What! 'How on earth can that happen? He was our only lead.'

'Unbelievable as it may sound it appears that his solicitor injected a lethal substance into his arm while he was supposed to be talking to him in his cell, we have found out since that the Solicitor hasn't been officially working for two years since he was disbarred for intimidating a witness in a murder case. We now have to find out how he got involved in this case. My theory is he is working for this Thomas guy and he has tied up a loose end for him. We have to wait for test results from The Pathologist, SOCCO and Forensics but, there is not much doubt it is murder. Actually Clifford our two tech boys are about to leave for your apartment to monitor your calls, perhaps you would meet them down in the car park and show them the way. Now when and if you do get a call don't forget keep them on the line as long as you can so we can put a trace on the call.'

Clifford said he would try but Elaine's safety was his prime concern. Lewis said he understood and would also keep two plain clothed men in an unmarked car outside the apartment building to shadow Clifford for his own safety. Clifford acknowledged Lewis's remarks then said goodbye and made his way down to the car park, he climbed into his car and waited a few minutes for the men to appear. Eventually they arrived, one of the men waved to Clifford as a signal they were ready, and they set off.

They reached the apartment car park and Clifford took the men up to the Lobby and he told them they would have to book in at security, on the way up the men told Clifford their names, one was called "Keith Boyce" and the other "Brian Saunders".

They exited the lift and approached the security desk, Jim greeted Clifford and he told Jim who the men were and Jim booked them in, Clifford also alerted Jim to the fact that there would be plain clothed officers outside the building at all times.

When they then went up to the apartment Clifford asked whether the two men would like some tea or coffee, they both opted for strong black coffees, Clifford left them and went to the kitchen, a few moments later he returned with the drinks.

Once the phone equipment had been installed and ready to go,Keith reflected what DCS Lewis had mentioned regarding a possible ransom demand and keeping whoever called on the line so they could be traced, stressing the added importance if it came on his mobile because it took longer to trace those calls. Clifford said he would do his best depending on Elaine's situation, he then told the men that if they wished they were welcome to watch the television, he also told them that there was plenty of tea and coffee plus food in the fridge so help themselves because he was going to lay on his bed and rest assuring them he would take his mobile with him.

Clifford made his excuses and retired to the bedroom. He noticed that his mobile battery was low so he removed the charger from a bedside locker drawer and placed the phone on charge.

Thomas waited until twelve thirty five before making the call to Clifford's mobile. The call alert brought Clifford out of a deep sleep and he took a few seconds to become aware of what the noise was, once it occurred to him it was his mobile he sharply sat up and grabbed it and went quickly into the lounge. Brian and Keith had already started the tracing procedure, Keith then said: 'Right on the count of five press the call button and speak, Keith counted down from five he nodded and Clifford pressed the call button and said: 'Hello Clifford Jessop.' Thomas answered: 'Hello Mr Jessop we are honoured to have your charming Missus staying with us .... Clifford interrupted: 'Where is she? What have you done to her? How is she?' Thomas came back: 'Well she is fine at present and she will stay that way as long as you conform to my demands. I want five hundred thousand pounds in used unmarked notes by six o'clock tonight and no later. Put it all in a black bin bag and bring it yourself to the sports centre in upper lane and put it in the rubbish bin directly outside of the tennis courts entrance. Once you have done that turn around and walk back to your car and keep looking straight ahead, do not turn around. Drive straight off and don't look back "AND NO POLICE" or your Missus will suffer .... Clifford cut in: 'What about my wife? I'm not giving you a penny until I know she is alive.' Thomas let out a loud lengthy sigh and Clifford heard him say: 'Com here girly on your feet, your hubby wants a chat.'

Elaine came on the line and said weakly: 'Clifford is that you, Oh darling, do as he says, I beg you .... Before she could say anymore Thomas snatched the phone from her and said to Clifford: 'Right, now remember, six o'clock, I must go now or your boys there will trace my call, by the way be sure to use heavy duty bags.' He laughed to himself then hung up.

Clifford looked at Keith but he shook his head saying: 'Sorry no good, he was obviously timing the call, he knew just how long to stay on the line.'

Clifford was very quiet so Keith asked if he was ok, Clifford remained quiet for another second or two then said: Yes! 'Well no, it's just that when I went out this morning to try and find my wife I went right up to the sports centre .... Keith cut in: 'Look I know what you're thinking but this guy seems too switched on to have the money dropped anywhere near the place they are actually holding her, rest easy sir you missed nothing.'

While Keith was speaking he received a call from DCS Lewis, he put it on speaker phone, Lewis said: 'Hello Clifford we heard the call, it's a shame we couldn't trace it but, that's how it goes sometimes. However we are doing everything in our power to find Elaine, we have been doing a search of all empty buildings as well as garages, sheds outbuildings etcetera within a ten mile radius of the convenience store. By the way we have received the SOCCO and Forensic reports back from the cell, as expected there's not much to go on, the syringe had no DNA on it or a usable print, the only print's in the cell were of Pierce and past residents and staff, however the Pathologist report was more useful, there was a significant amount of Heroin in Pierce's system which was the actual cause of death.

Now I don't know your opinion Clifford but it is normally our policy where possible not to negotiate with kidnappers but following the death of Sam and Pierce it is clear we are not dealing with your average kidnappers. I will contact the Chief Constable and request they release the ransom money and I will call as soon as he gets back to me, don't worry you are in good hands I assure you. I will go and make that call then I am coming over there to oversee proceedings.'

After Lewis ended the call Clifford decided to give Elaine's boss a call and let him know she was alive. Ford was ecstatic at the news, he asked Clifford: 'Are you paying the ransom? What are the Police advising?'

'They feel that this man is desperate enough to go through with the threat so they are in favour of paying.'

'Right then Clifford don't worry about the money, the company will front it, all our staff are insured against these kinds of circumstances. I will get right onto it and the money will be with you in good time.'

'Thank you John but, that puts me in a bit of a predicament, DCS Lewis is speaking with the Chief Constable at this moment to try and get the money released, I don't quite know what to do now.'

'Not a problem Clifford you are assured the money from the company, I will call Charles Price and put him in the loop. I'll speak to you soon.'

'Ok John, thank you, it's a big weight off my shoulders.'

An hour later Lewis arrived and spoke with his officers, he then approached Clifford and asked to speak to him in private. He told him that the CC had advised him of John Ford's offer and had decided that would be the best way to go as it would take a while for a decision to be made by the Commissioner. He told Clifford the money would have to be checked in front of the carriers as it was a considerable amount. Clifford said he would go along with whatever Lewis decided because he would need his professional guidance.

Thirty minutes later John Ford called and Lewis told Keith to clear the line so Clifford could speak in privacy. John told Clifford that the money was on the way in an unmarked car with two plain clothed private security men, Clifford told John that he and Lewis would meet them in the foyer and escort them up to the apartment.

Ten minutes passed then Jim called Clifford to say that two visitors were in the foyer requesting to see him. Clifford and Lewis went down and met up with the two men, one had a large black case chained to his wrist. Lewis showed his Id and he told Jim they would not be signing in.

They went up to the apartment and Clifford led them into the bedroom and closed the door, the guard with the case laid it on the bed and unclipped a key from a chain on his belt, the other guard did the same and they each unlocked one of the catches. The case was opened and Clifford gasped seeing so much money. Lewis said: 'Daunting sight eh Clifford, Let's just hope it does the trick and we get Elaine home where she belongs?' Clifford nodded slightly.

The money was in five thousand pound bundles each made up of twenty and fifty pound notes. Clifford and

Lewis checked that it was all there and once they had the case was relocked. The guard unchained the case from his wrist and handed it to Lewis; he chained it to his wrist and locked the bracelet. The guards asked for Lewis's signature and said the money was now his responsibility.

Clifford went escorted the guards back down to the foyer and to the front door. He returned to the apartment and called John Ford to inform him that the money had arrived and had been checked, he assured John that Lewis was now in control of the case until it was time for the drop off. He then added his thanks and hung up.

CHAPTER FOURTEEN

The night of Elaine's kidnapping went very slowly, she didn't sleep at all as there was no way she was going to lie on the disgusting filthy mattress, the chair was also too hard and filthy and the damp atmosphere was making her choke. She knew that if she stayed there much longer she would soon be ill.

It was about eight thirty am when Richard Bird—one of her guards—arrived wearing a white hood. He unbolted the door and ordered Elaine to stand against the wall. He then opened the door just wide enough to slide a tray of food in on the floor. He began closing the door when she shouted: 'Hey stop, I need to get out of here, it's damp and I am feeling ill, I'll die if you leave me in here. I need to use the bathroom as well. Please I beg you?' Bird paused and thought for a minute he then opened the door a little wider and peered inside, he looked around then said: 'It doesn't look too bad to me now shut up or I will tie and gag you again. There's a bucket there if you need to use it.'

'You can't see properly from there come in and look.' I can't exactly do anything can I you're bigger and stronger than me after all?' He paused again then edged a little further into the small dimly lit room. Elaine said: 'Smell it, look there is mould all over the walls and they're dripping with moisture, it's dangerous and inhuman to keep me in here, and I want to use a proper bathroom. 'Bird smirked and said 'Yeah, yeah ok but I can't do anything until the boss gets back and don't ask me when that will be.'

'Please, tie me up but take me somewhere else, please?'

'Look I can't, I told you, I have to wait until he gets back, now eat your breakfast and shut up and I'll see what I can do.' Elaine babbled she couldn't eat anything, she picked up the tray and hurled it against the wall then she slumped onto the chair and burst into tears.

A long time passed before the door was opened again, she had no idea of the time because her watch was wrenched from her wrist when they manhandled her into the vehicle. This time Bird and another man came in—his name was Palmer—he was also wearing a white hood. He roughly put a hood over her head with no holes cut out and grabbed her by her arms and between them they dragged her out, and she was sure they led her over the same patch of gravely ground that they had the night before.

She was bundled back into a vehicle and one man held her arm tightly while the vehicle was driven off. After about ten minute the vehicle came to an abrupt halt sending Elaine sliding to the floor. Soon after the doors were pulled open and someone dragged her for what seemed about three minutes. She then heard a door being unlocked and with the hood still on she was pushed inside, the man said sarcastically: 'Here you are me lady your new five star accommodation.'

The man was Darren Thomas, she recognised the voice from when he had called Clifford and heard him demand the ransom money, she was petrified when she heard him ask for so much because she knew Clifford couldn't raise anywhere near that amount. Although frightened she was glad to have had the chance to speak to Clifford even though Thomas told her what to say, at least she knew he would be relieved to know she was still alive although she would have loved to have heard his voice as well but Thomas had snatched the phone away from her too soon.

Elaine cringed when she was forced onto the chair, she bravely asked how long he intended keeping her, He replied: 'Don't worry you're pretty little head about that, all in good time my dear, now turn around and I will take your hood off but don't look back until I have closed the door there's a good girl.' He smacked her bottom quite hard and went out laughing shutting the door behind him.

When Clifford finished talking to Ford Lewis had returned to the lounge and was sitting on the couch, the officers were sitting in the armchairs watching television. Clifford joined Lewis who said: 'Right Clifford when you take the money tonight there will be plain clothed officers spread out around the area . . . . Clifford butted in: 'He said no Police or Elaine would be hurt.' Lewis continued: 'That's what they always say but they know we will be somewhere observing, after all we are dealing with a shrewd and dangerous man but don't worry nothing will be left to chance.' Clifford was worried though but Lewis was obviously experienced in such matters so he felt he had to trust him.

The rest of the afternoon went slow, it seemed ages until at last Lewis advised Clifford he should get some bin bags ready so they could transfer the money from the case.

Clifford went to the kitchen and Lewis followed him, Clifford opened a cupboard taking out a roll of black bags, Lewis suggested taking the case and bags into the bedroom, Clifford agreed.

They laid the case on the bed and Lewis unlocked it and they commenced filling the bag's but, they were unable to get all the money in one bag because it was so heavy the bag couldn't be carried without the bag splitting.

Clifford surprised himself by quipping: 'Maybe we should have followed Thomas's suggestion and bought heavy duty bags.' Lewis looked at Clifford not knowing whether to react with a laugh or say nothing, he decided on the latter. Clifford appreciated the gesture then said: 'Perhaps we should use three bags one inside each other.' Lewis just replied: 'Yes perhaps we should.'

Once they had bagged and tied up all the money they had two full bags and one half full. It was fast approaching six o'clock so Lewis took his radio from his jacket pocket and using the prearranged call sign "Jackdaw" he rallied his plain clothed officers to their allotted places. Clifford glanced at his watch, It was fifteen minutes to six, He estimated that it took just over ten minutes to reach the sports centre. Before he set off Clifford had notified Jim the security officer that he was off to the drop off point, and told him the tech boys were still in his apartment, he said that it was possible they may drop Elaine off outside the building once they had hold of the money and asked that he keep vigilant. Jim assured him he would.

Lewis helped Clifford to his car with the bags and they placed them into the boot. Lewis was in a different car to his usual one and said he would follow at a distance and that he was meeting Deacon at their prearranged site. Clifford was still apprehensive at the Police being around but tried to concentrate on getting the money there on time.

He reached the sports centre at four minutes to six. The tennis courts were at the end of a narrow road that ran alongside the main sports hall, he reversed his car down the short road so he would be facing the way Thomas told him to after he had dropped the money off. Reaching the car park to the tennis courts he stopped the car leaving the engine running, there was a small car parked in the car park Clifford paused and looked at it, he didn't look too hard though in case Thomas had eyes on him so he went to the boot. He took one bag out and placed it in the waste bin, the bag half filled the bin so he knew that that he would only get the other bag in the bin and he would have to place the half full bag on the ground alongside it. This worried Clifford, he was thinking they may not take the half bag because it wasn't in the bin and would harm Elaine because they didn't get all the money. However he couldn't hang around he had to leave right away.

He returned to his car and drove off, by then Lewis had joined Deacon in his car and they were watching with night vision binoculars. Unfortunately the tennis courts were partly hidden from all watch points so there was a large blind spot. Lewis radioed all units and enquired if anyone had eyeballs on any suspects but the answer was negative from all units. They continue watching when all of a sudden there was an explosion from the rear of the sports hall lighting the sky up above the roof of the building and a blanket of smoke blotted out the area. Oh my God! Lewis exclaimed. 'What the hell was that?' He immediately put a call out to all units asking what they could see they all reported that they could not see anything because of the smoke and flames. Lewis took a chance and ordered all units in he also put out the call and alerted the fire brigade.

The heat from the burning car was so intense that the first Police officers on the scene could not approach it, when Deacon and Lewis arrived Deacon ran to the boot and took out an extinguisher he got as close to the car as the heat would allow and began to spray the car, other officers followed suit but they were not making much impact on the fire, meanwhile Lewis braved the heat to check the bin but all the bags were gone.

As soon as the car exploded Bird and Palmer who had taken cover behind the sports hall in the blind spot leapt out and gathered up the bags, they slipped back up past the tennis courts between a row of bushes and a high wooden fence, using the confusion of the fire as cover. The path they took brought them out at the rear of a large house, as they approached the house they heard voices. There were people in the rear garden watching the smoke and glare from the fire, so they took cover at the end of the path behind a large tree and waited for the people to go back inside. When they had Bird and Palmer crept out and along the garden fence until they reached the front of the house, there they had to be careful as there was no cover until they reached their car, once they reached their car and placed the bags in the boot they climbed in and gave each other a "high five".

Clifford had only gotten a little distance away from the sports centre when his attention was drawn to the glare of the fire in his rear view mirror, he stole a glance then looked back to the front, as he did so he was blinded by a cars full headlights shining directly at him he stamped on his brakes and skidded to a halt. The minute the car stopped the driver's door was yanked open by Thomas who was shining a torch in his eyes and a hood was pulled over Clifford's head. Thomas told Clifford he had a gun on him and to get out slowly. Clifford complied and he tried to ask what they wanted but Thomas told him to shut up.

As soon as Clifford was on his feet the ex-Detective—Simpson—came up behind him throwing his arm around his neck before marching him to a car. Thomas leant in the back seat of the car and pulled out some white cable ties, he pulled Clifford's arms behind him and put one around his wrists, he then eased him backwards until the backs of his legs were up against the car telling Clifford to sit on the seat.

Thomas kept the gun on Clifford while Simpson put a tie around his ankles then between them they lifted Clifford's legs and swung him into the car, Thomas told him to stretch out across the seat so he could not be seen from the road he then asked Clifford where his mobile was, Clifford told him it was in his left hand jacket pocket, Thomas found it and threw it across the road into some bushes, he then slammed the rear door and climbed into the driver's seat while Simpson climbed into Clifford's car. Thomas reversed his car and turned around then he drove off at top speed, Simpson followed close behind.

Clifford was convinced it was connected to Elaine's kidnapping, what he couldn't comprehend was why, he tried once more to find out, he asked: 'you're Thomas aren't you? Why are you doing this? 'I've done everything you asked.'

'Yes you have, you also brought the old bill and I told you no cop's although I expected nothing else. Fortunately I had a contingency plan in place while they were dealing with that we lifted the package right from under their noses. Did you see my little display?'

'If you mean the glow in the sky back there then yes I did but, I never saw any Police, I told them not to interfere as you ordered. What about my wife you haven't harmed her have you?' Thomas just laughed then said: 'You needn't worry about your little missus you will be seeing her soon enough, in fact you will be keeping her company for a little while.' Clifford asked what he meant but Thomas just said: 'Wait and see now shut up and keep your head down.'

CHAPTER FIFTEEN

Clifford estimated the journey took about twenty minutes, Thomas stopped the car and got out, he opened Clifford's door and told him that he still had the gun pointed at him. Thomas told Clifford to sit up while he and Simpson lifted his legs and swung them out of the ca He then cut the tie from Clifford's legs and told him to stand up, Simpson helped by linking his arm through Clifford's steadying him while he stood up. Clifford was then guided for a few yards, he heard a door being unbolted and he was turned around, the tie on his hands was cut off and he was turned back around and was pushed forward sharply in through a door, Thomas began closing the door and said with a sneer: 'Here you are little lady, hubby's come to rescue you.' He then slammed the door shut and bolted it.

There was silence for a while then he heard Elaine's voice: 'Clifford; is that you?' Clifford lifted the hood but his eyes were bleary for a while, Elaine however as soon as the hood came off squealed excitedly: 'Clifford; oh my God I am so glad you are here.' She ran over to him and they wrapped their hands around each other, it was then though it sunk in that he was now a prisoner as well and realised what she had said. Elaine asked: 'What's going on? Why have they taken you? Couldn't you raise the money? I know it was a lot, oh darling what are we going to do?'

'Calm down darling, panicking won't do any good. I did raise the money, John Ford paid it . . . . She stopped him saying: 'John Ford, how will we pay him back?'

'I don't think he is worried about that right now Elaine, in any case the company's insurance paid it, What I don't understand is, I left the money where I was told to and they collected it but for some reason they have taken me too. It was that Thomas Character who nabbed me but I can't fathom it, what good can it do him? He has something else up his sleeve that's clear, but what? Anyway how about you? Have you been here all the time? It's disgusting, how can he expect to keep us here? We have to get out.'

'I know but I was in a different place at first, if you think this is disgusting you should have seen that. I pleaded and pleaded with them to move me and at last they did this morning to here.'

'Poor darling, right let's get this sorted—come on.' Clifford took her hand and led her to the door. He said to her: 'Do as I do we'll make them move us.'

Clifford started banging on the door and shouting: 'Hey you out there, you can't keep us in here, let us out, come on get us out of this disgusting place. Elaine joined in and this went on for a few minutes until a voice shouted back: 'Look shut that noise up in there, you are staying where you are this is not a holiday camp. However they carried on banging and shouting then they heard Thomas's voice shout: 'Alright alright enough already.'

The bolt was pulled back and Thomas wearing a hood put his head around the door and told them they were being moved the next day and they would only be there for the night. Clifford shouted back demanding they have some blankets and some heat, Thomas growled angrily: 'you haven't been here five minutes and you are stirring it up already, you two are a good match. I'll get you a heater, now shut up or I'll separate you.'

'You can bet we're a good match, you may have run rough shod over my wife but not me, now when are we getting blankets and a heater?' Thomas just replied in his usual sarcastic manner: 'Ooh let me see, it's two months to Christmas, that's two months then.' Thomas slammed the door shutting and bolted it. Clifford turned to Elaine and said: 'Sorry darling, I think I have made matters worse for us, let's hope he still gets us a heater and blankets then we will have to see what tomorrow brings.'

Later Thomas sent Bird in with two blankets and a portable heater and they spent the night huddled around the heater, at daylight Palmer unbolted the door wearing a hood, he pushed a tray of toast and coffee in and Clifford seized the opportunity, before Palmer could shut the door he dashed over and jammed it with his foot. Palmer put all his might against the door but couldn't make Clifford move his foot so he took a gun from his pocket and shouted: 'You are heading for trouble pal, now move your dammed foot.'

'Not until we know where you are taking us and when, you have the money so there's nothing to be gained by this.'

'I have no idea what the boss has planned, I know he has something up his sleeve and you are part of it somehow, keep this up though and he will keep you here indefinitely.'

'Well he won't get away with it whatever it is, the Police are all over the sports centre they will find something, the smallest particle can tell them a lot these days and you lot aren't clever enough not to have left some evidence. You have already committed two murders and one of those was in Police custody, you won't go unpunished.'

'Don't try intimidating me because I know nothing about any murders now take your foot away and eat your food or I will shoot your damned foot.' Clifford relented and moved his foot and Palmer slammed the door bolting it from outside.

Clifford and Elaine ate their breakfast in silence each wondering what was in store for them, by now though the toast was cold and soft and the coffee lukewarm, nevertheless they forced it down because they didn't know when or if they would eat again.

Mid morning Thomas unbolted the door and Palmer and Bird were with him and they were all wearing hoods, Thomas told Elaine and Clifford to turn around and put their hands behind their backs. Palmer and Bird tied cable ties around their wrists and Thomas put hoods over their heads, they were then led to the same van Elaine was taken in first, they were bundled inside and driven off.

Palmer sat in the back with them and the other two sat in the front. As Elaine had done, Clifford tried to detect where they were going by listening for sounds but like Elaine he was foiled by the racket the van made, however he estimated they were only on the road for ten minute before the van stopped and the doors were pulled open and they were hauled out and led to another building, once inside they were manhandled upstairs and into a room, Palmer and Bird cut the ties from their wrists and Thomas told them once the door was closed and locked they could remove their hoods.

They listened to hear them close and lock the door then quickly yanked the hoods from their heads and looked around. The room was bigger than the last one with a table and two chairs in the centre, on one wall there was a boarded up fireplace and two windows, the windows were also boarded but up from the outside and the handles and catches were sawn off. There was another room off to the left hand side so they inspected that and they were pleased to see it was an en suite bathroom, that window was very small but was also boarded up.

Back in the other room there was a kitchenette and two tatty arm chairs plus small a couch. It was dim because of the boarded windows and just one light bulb shone down from the ceiling.

When they had all gone down stairs, Thomas told his men that he was leaving the next evening but he should be back in about two weeks then they would all be very rich. He told them: 'Keep our "guests" safe here and don't let them escape they are crucial to my plans, I will not be a happy man if I come back and find out you have lost them.' He gave Palmer a wad of notes and told him to get plenty of food in as he didn't want attention drawn to them coming and going because the locals would know the house was empty and someone would be bound to get nosey.

CHAPTER SIXTEEN

DCS Lewis and DCI Deacon were returning from the chaotic scene at sports centre when he received a radio message from DI Barnes, he told Lewis: 'A man's body has been found on waste ground at the rear of the trading estate in lower lane. Uniform are there and the Pathologist is on his way, SOCCO have also been dispatched.'

'Do we know who it is?' Asked Lewis

'No Sir.'

'Ok I'm on my way.' Deacon remarked: 'Some night this is turning out to be. Should I put the claxons on?'

'No if he's dead he's not going anywhere.'

When they arrived at the scene, a white tent had been erected over the body; they approached the tent and collected forensic overalls and over shoes, they slipped the overalls on and put a mask over their mouths. They entered the tent and the Pathologist called them over, he was kneeling down inspecting the body which was naked. Lewis asked if they had found any ID with the body, Ben stood up saying: 'No and the face is too badly beaten, we will have to wait for DNA, dental records or prints. He wasn't killed here though there isn't enough blood. The body was on its side when it was discovered but it had been lying on its back, you can tell by these purple marks on his back, I am afraid you will have to wait for cause of death until I do the PM but I can tell you he has been dead for about eight to ten hours.'

Lewis thanked Ben and said: 'I don't have to remind you I need you report "yesterday", do I?' Ben replied: 'No Andrew I'm on it.' Lewis then asked one of the attending Constables who had found the body, he told Lewis: 'A couple walking their dog, apparently their dog sniffed it out; they are in their car over there.'

Lewis and Deacon went over to the car and Lewis tapped on the driver's window, the husband was in the driver's seat and the dog was on the woman's lap in the front passenger seat, it jumped up and started yapping when the man wound down the window, Lewis showed him his ID as did Deacon, they enquired whether they could ask some questions the man said: 'Sure.' and he and his wife got out of the car leaving the dog behind. Lewis asked their names, the man said: 'I'm Ronald Carter and this is my wife Margret.' 'Was it you who found the body?'

'Yes—well no, "Teddy" did really.' He pointed to the dog in the car.

'Ok then which one of you saw the body first, apart from Teddy I mean?'

'Oh yes, of course sorry, we both did, you see Teddy was making such a racket we thought he was hurt so we both ran over.' His wife added: 'It was awful I have never seen a dead body before.'

'I dare say Madam, did either of you see anyone or notice anything odd—apart from the body of course?'

'No we were the only ones here we bring Teddy up here because it's always so quiet.'

'Ok thank you, if you remember anything else please call the station. We will need you to come in just to make a statement though.' The couple said they would call in the next day. Lewis thanked them and bid them goodnight. SOCCO had arrived by then so Lewis and Deacon left to let them do their jobs.

When Lewis returned to his office, he checked his E-mails, there was one, the full report on Pierce's death from the Pathologist, it read: "DNA tests of saliva traces on syringe cap confirms it to be from James McDonald, probably from him taking the cap off with his teeth. Pierce was killed by a massive dose of Heroine injected directly into the blood stream." "There is bruising on the left wrist indicating it was gripped tightly and pressure marks on the chest which indicates that it was knelt on, probably to subdue him while he was injected."

Lewis glanced at his watch and saw how late it was, he was about to curl up in his chair and grab some sleep when a knock came on the door, it was Di Barnes he said: 'Excuse me sir but Clifford Jessop has gone missing, he hasn't been seen since he made the drop, we've called his apartment building security but they haven't seen him since you and he left with the money.' Lewis was speechless for a second but responded by saying: 'Are the tech boys still at the apartment?'

'Yes sir it was them that called it in, they said they would hang on there.'

'Right get them some relief and tell them to look around the apartment for a recent photo of Clifford Jessop, get it copied and get a house to house of the whole area of the sports centre organised, I know it's very late but someone may have seen something and time is not on our side, If anyone gives any grief then refer them to me, also find out if there are any traffic cameras in the area and get the tapes, I'll put out an APB on his car . . . . God dam it, they must have taken him right from under our noses, question is why.'

The DI left and Lewis called Forensics to find out if they found anything at the sports centre. The technician said: 'No not much, we did find a freshly used cigarette stub, we got DNA from that but the results are not in yet.' Lewis said: 'Ok, but I want that report ASAP because the husband has disappeared now, right after dropping the money off it seems. Is there anything back from Ben on the latest body yet?'

'No not yet, wheels of industry and all that.'

'Well speed the wheels up we have a running disaster on our hands, as soon as you get anything call me.'

Although it was the early hours Lewis thought he should still notify the Chief Constable of Clifford's disappearance, and the new body discovery. The CC said that under the circumstances there would be limitless recourses for the solving of the case, he then asked whether there was any information regarding the latest body, Lewis confirmed that there wasn't at that point, he was waiting on test results. However he did give CC the results of Pierces Post Mortem the CC said in the circumstances he would instruct all departments to make Lewis's case a priority.

After Lewis had finished talking to the CC, DC carter called from the house to house saying that a man living at the rear of the Tennis courts was out jogging at just after six pm, he said he was passing the road that led up to the sports centre and witnessed what he thought was a road rage incident. His attention had been drawn by shouting and car headlights. He said that two cars were involved but the glare from the cars lights had made it difficult to see properly. They were on his side of the road but some distance away. He said one was facing towards him with headlights full on, he thought the other one was facing the other way but both were very close together. Lewis told Deacon to send SOCCO along to that part of the road and take a look.

Eight thirty Thursday morning Ben the Pathologist came to Lewis's office with the preliminary report of the latest body, He said he had a hit with the DNA and prints, he also told Lewis: 'It's your Solicitor McDonald; he had been dead for at least eight hours but no longer than ten. As I first thought he died elsewhere and had been lying on his back for a long time before being dumped. He died from several blows to the face and head with a large brick or stone and there were sand and dirt particles in the wound and on his body and he had eaten a burger meal shortly before he died but I am carrying out further tests on the body.' Lewis thanked him and then called Deacon and to him a rundown of the report, Deacon remarked to Lewis: 'He is certainly cleaning up isn't he? I fear for that couple, try as I might I am at a loss as to why they have taken Clifford Jessop instead of letting his wife go, after all he has the money, so obviously he has another agenda.' Lewis replied: 'I must admit I have my doubts about their safety now considering how quick he has dealt with Pierce and McDonald, he seems to be well informed. look

I know SOCCO has been all over Pierces pad but take a uniform with you and have another look around, you never know they may have missed something.'

As Deacon left, Lewis's phone rang it was Forensics with the cigarette butt results.They said they had extracted DNA from the butt but there was no match in the data base.

CHAPTER SEVENTEEN

Clifford and Elaine were awake' most of the night worrying over what was to become of them. After they had settled into their new "jail" Clifford told Elaine what Lewis had said about Pierce dying in his cell. Elaine didn't react very well to the news, she said that not only had they lost a key witness and a lead, it scared her into thinking that Thomas would not let them stay alive once he'd finished what he had planned for them.

Prior to going to bed the previous evening Clifford had checked the rooms out to see if there was any way to escape, it was clear though Thomas had taken every precaution to ensure there wasn't. Clifford however was not one to give up, he told Elaine: 'I think we will have to work on the guards, I reckon the short one is approachable because when I jammed my foot in the door he looked panicky, I am sure we could wear him down.' Elaine warned him: 'Be careful Cliff these men are hardened criminals, they've already killed three men and I thought I would never see you again, I can't bear the thought of anything happening to you now.'

'I know darling but I'm going nowhere, not without you anyway . . . . He hugged her and continued: I'll work something out we'll just watch them for a day or so.'

At lunchtime Bird unlocked the door and shouted for them to go in the bedroom and close the door. Once they had Clifford listened intently hoping to note something that may aid an escape attempt. He heard the door open and something being placed on the table the door was then closed again. Clifford waited a couple of minutes then peered out, Bird had gone so they came back out of the bedroom. Bird had left a tray on the table with sandwiches and a pot of coffee. They sat and ate the food both thinking of how they could escape.

The following evening at Eleven o'clock Thomas and Simpson met up with the two new recruits. They met at a private airfield ten miles outside of Chelsea. Thomas had told them to take rucksacks and tropical gear he also told them to take good walking boots. Simpson had asked why they needed that sort of gear but Thomas just told him to wait and see.

The other two men arrived separately and met up with Thomas and Simpson, not long after they all heard the sound of a powerful engine, Thomas announced: 'Right lads, our ride's here.' The sound eventually became louder and they saw it was a helicopter and soon it was hovering above them. Thomas held a powerful torch and flashed it three times at the helicopter, immediately it began descending.

When the helicopter landed the door was slid open and Thomas told them to get aboard quickly, they were all confused but knew not to question Thomas so they all obeyed his command. They boarded one by one with Thomas getting on last, the second he was aboard the pilot told him to close the door and he took off.

Once in the air Simpson took the initiative and asked Thomas: 'Come on boss what is this all about?' Thomas just answered: 'That is all on a need to know basis, I need to know, and you need to do what I say.'

'Look you whisk us away in a chopper to God knows where, I say "us" but I don't even know who "us" is, you owe me an explanation after all I have done some serious stuff for you, it's about time you were straight with me.'

'Ok enough with the grief, firstly "us," are you, me and our new friends here. Simpson; meet John and Nick, secondly we are all going on a fruitful little holiday.'

Holiday! 'You said we had a job on. What are we going to be doing exactly?'

'I did say a fruitful holiday did I not? However as you asked, firstly we are going to Frankfurt airport then we take a chartered flight to Mexico and that's when it gets interesting because, there we are meeting up with some expert guides who will lead us into the jungle to find a lost city and that's where we get rich, very rich indeed.'

'Are you mad? Why didn't you tell us? I sure as hell wouldn't have come nor I'm sure would these two.' Nick and John nodded in agreement. Thomas paused before he answered, he then said: 'That's exactly why I didn't say anything, come on lads it will be a bit of an adventure, I have planned this down to the finest detail but if you don't want to come, there's the door.' Thomas said as he opened the door lightly. Simpson got the message but then Nick piped up asking: 'Where's the money coming from for all this, it must be costing a fortune to fund, how much are you expecting to get from this "holiday"?

'Well, all I will say is that I have a benefactor that has made all this possible admitted he will get the lion's share but there will be plenty left over, then we will all live like kings, admitted it will be hard going but the rewards are worth it.' The three men looked at each other but said nothing they just sat contemplating what Thomas had just told them.

Eventually the helicopter landed on a private landing strip close to Frankfurt airport, advanced check in had been arranged and they travelled business class so they arrived reasonably fresh at Mexico main airport. It was just past four forty am local time when Thomas's party was collected from the airport by a tatty old pickup truck with a Mexican driver, didn't speak very good English so he said precious little once it was confirmed that they were the party he had been sent to collect. He loaded all their gear into the open back of the truck and then opened the passenger doors. Thomas told his men to get in and He sat next to the driver.

The truck moved off and Thomas asked: 'Ok Pedro how long have we got to sit in this tin can?' With a grin the driver continued to look directly ahead, then said: 'Oh yes I understand Senor "tin can" yes, very good Senor.' He chuckled to himself then continued: 'We drive twenty minutes maybe more Senor.' Thomas looked behind at Nick and John; they had grim faces and both raised their eyes to the sky.

Finally the truck stopped next to a wooden building, alongside were two more off road vehicles. They were met by a man who Thomas assumed correctly was another Mexican, and the head man. Thomas was also glad he spoke better English than the driver. The second man led them to the two vehicles, four other men appeared from nowhere and they followed carrying the men's gear. The second man told Thomas: 'Ok Senor Thomas, my men and I will travel in this first truck, you and your men follow in this one.' Thomas asked for how long, the man said: 'We will drive for three days and nights then you meet your expert guides, you then go on foot through the jungle for four days.'

Simpson turned on Thomas Saying: 'You said nothing about sitting in a steaming hot truck for three days and then trekking through the jungle for four more, there is no way I am putting myself through that.' He looked at Nick and John and asked: 'What about you two?' The two men glanced at Thomas who gave them a look that said: "Go on then answer him" at the same time he placed his hand on his gun holster that was strapped to his belt. Not wishing to cross Thomas they looked the other way, so Simpson replied: 'Ok I'm on my own then am I? Fine, I'll go along but it had better be worth it.' Thomas ignored Simpson and told them to get in the truck so they could get going.

At the end of their first day into their long hot arduous journey, they were at their wits end with the heat and the horrendous roads. The vehicles were tossed around, constantly sending them from one side of the road to the other. Thomas and his men squabbled endlessly and more than once he considered calling the trip off, it was only his greed that kept him going and the fact he wouldn't live long if he went home empty handed, his backer would see to that so he kept going.

Camp was set up for the night fairly close to a stream and just off the road, they were each given some cold meat and hot sweet potatoes which was cooked over the campfire, they were also given a billycan of hot strong bitter coffee.

They ate in silence then the head man pointed to some sleeping bags saying: 'Ok Senor's sleep well we leave at first light.'

The next morning after they had breakfast Thomas called his men to one side out of earshot and took his gun from the holster, he threatened them with it saying: 'If there's a repeat performance of yesterday then I will shoot the first one to start.' Simpson grabbed a small tree branch from the ground and heaved it at Thomas but it missed. Thomas rushed over and rammed Simpson against a tree and said: 'Look none of you lot are indispensible so don't push it, now grab your gear and get on that damned truck.'

The second day the roads were worse than the one before due to them driving over rough tracks with deep pot holes and raised tree roots.

The following day fared no better, early in the afternoon the journey came to a sudden and disastrous halt when the lead truck hit a deep hole and shattered the rear suspension and they were about Seventy miles from their destination. Thomas's truck screeched to a halt, He got out and went to survey the situation and he was unfairly furious with the driver saying he should have taken more care but, the head man defended him saying that truck had hit a deep hole that had been hidden by leaves and debris, Thomas walked away but turned back and asked: 'What's going to happen now?' The head man replied: 'We will have to continue on foot, the driver and one other man will take your truck with the gear and meet up with your guides, He will explain why you have been delayed and they will have to wait for you.' Thomas kicked off arguing he had paid to be taken to meet his guides by road and not walking, he couldn't understand why they couldn't all go in the other truck, the man explained: 'There would be seven people Senor and there are only five seats in the truck.'

'That's ok two can go in the back.' Thomas replied. The man said all the equipment from their truck would have to go in the back and with their gear there would not be room.

Thomas reluctantly backed down and after notifying his men of the situation which brought about the same response as Thomas's, he said: 'Ok Pedro, you know best now get the gear on the truck and get us out of this "hell hole". The man replied: 'Marco, Senor, my name is Marco.' Thomas replied sarcastically: 'Ok Pedro, oops, sorry, Marco, can we get on with it now?' Marco ignored Thomas and taking three rifles from the back of his truck he kept one, giving the others to his two men. Thomas asked why he and his men had no rifle's Marco explained that there were only three the others had gone in the truck.

CHAPTER EIGHTEEN

DCI Deacon and a constable arrived at Pierce's flat on Thursday morning at around eleven twenty. The flat was on the second floor of a multi story building which was run down with graffiti on the walls and some of the flats had their windows smashed. The lift was out of action so they had to walk up two flights of stairs to the floor Pierce's flat was on which smelt of cooking and stale cigarette smoke. As they approached Pierce's flat they passed a young dark haired woman walking in the opposite direction, as they reached the door to the flat the woman turned and walked up to them and said: 'Excuse me, are you going to number sixteen?' Deacon said: 'Yes miss, why do you ask?'

'It's my brother Stuart's flat but he's not in, who are you, what do you want with him?'

'I'm sorry miss I am DCI Deacon from Chelsea CID.' He showed her his ID card and said to her: 'Look Miss shall we go inside? I will explain everything to you.' Deacon opened the door and stepped back allowing the woman in first. Inside she looked around and saw the flat was in disarray. she asked: 'What's going on? Where is Stuart? Look at this mess, has he been burgled?' Deacon advised her to sit down; she sat on the edge of sofa looking at all the mess. Once she was seated and Deacon had her attention he continued: 'I'm very sorry Miss but I must tell you, your brother was killed on Tuesday afternoon.' She gasped and asked: 'Killed how? I only spoke to him on Monday, what happened?'

'Actually Miss I'm afraid he was murdered.'

'Murdered, I can't believe this. Who would want to murder Stuart? Have you got the person responsible for killing him? Did he suffer?'

'No Miss, by the way, is it Miss?'

'Yes it is, but please call me June.'

'Ok June, no he didn't suffer, as for the murderer well that is a little more complicated, you see the murderer has since been murdered. He took a deep breath and continued: 'Let me start from the beginning, Stuart was arrested for stalking and intimidation as well as car theft, he had been following and photographing a married couple in a stolen car. He was working for a vicious criminal and the couple were later kidnapped and they are still missing . . . . June cut in: 'Do you mean the couple that were on the news?'

'Yes that's correct, Look I'll try and explain, the Solicitor that your brother chose to represent him actually was responsible for killing him while he was in his cell, he too seems to have worked for the same man. It appears he injected a lethal dose of Heroine into your brother's arm, the Pathologist says he would have died almost immediately.' June looked horrified, Deacon told the officer to make some tea and continued: 'Unfortunately June it doesn't end there, last night the Solicitor's body was discovered, he has been murdered as well. I know this is very shocking Miss—sorry—June but if you are up to it I'd like to ask you some questions about Stuart, would you mind?'

'No I don't mind but I can't tell you much, I had no idea he was mixed up in anything, he had a steady job.'

'Yes he told us but he also owned up to previous car thefts. When we interviewed him he told us he had no family, do you have any idea why he would say that?'

No! 'Admitted we didn't see each other very often just birthdays and Christmas normally, in fact we were supposed to go out today for a meal, it's my birthday and that's why I'm here. We have no family in England just an aunt in Canada and she is very old, we haven't seen her for years although I have written to her occasionally but she never replies.'

'Well June I would like to wish you happy birthday but under the circumstances . . . . Deacon paused then continued: 'I'm sure Stuart was a decent guy deep down, he probably just wanted to keep you out of all this. Did he ever mention the names Thomas, Simpson or Sam to you?—With that the officer came in with a tray with a tea pot and cups etc. Deacon poured June and himself a cup of tea telling the officer to help himself, she took a sip of her tea then answered: 'He did mention the name Sam once, a couple of weeks or so ago actually, he said he had just died but he didn't elaborate further.'

'Ok June. What about you, do you work?'

'Yes I do, I work at Somers dry cleaners in the high Street.'

'Did Stuart know any of your friends or work mates?'

'Not as far as I know, he didn't go out much at all, he hasn't . . . . or I should say hadn't a lot of money, we were only going for a drink and a burger today.'

Deacon explained as much about the case as he was able and afterwards he asked if she wanted a lift home, June declined saying she had her own vehicle outside.

Deacon then told her that he and the constable had to do another search of Stuart's flat and if she wished to she could remain. She said she would rather not so he asked the officer to take down her details saying that he may wish to speak to her again.

She enquired if she would be able to see Stuart and when she could bury him, Deacon told her she would have to identify him first and he would let her know about burying Stuart as soon as possible, he then offered his condolences to June and said goodbye.

After June had left, Deacon and the officer commenced the search of Stuarts flat, Deacon took the lounge the constable went to examine the bedroom. Deacon carefully checked the drawers in the wall unit and down the side of the chairs and the sofa. After feeling the cushions and seats for hidden object's he moved to the television checking behind and inside the TV cabinet as well as checking the video unit. Finding nothing relative to the case he headed to the bathroom, he checked the wall cabinet above the wash basin and in the vanity unit under the sink. He had no luck there so he lifted the lid on the toilet system, still he found nothing. The bath panel had already been removed by SOCCO although he did check under it again but it was clear there was nothing there either.

He had just decided to join the constable when he heard him call out: "Sir I think you want to see this." Deacon stepped inside the bedroom and found the officer was on his knees with his head inside an old dark wooden wardrobe. Deacon asked: 'What have you found Davies?'

'Here sir, take a look.' Davies moved aside and Deacon peered inside the wardrobe, he saw that Davies had discovered a loose panel in the base, he had lifted it and hidden there was a brown paper parcel tied with string. Following procedure they had taken a camera along with them so Deacon told the officer to retrieve it from the lounge where he had left it, Davies soon returned with the camera and Deacon instructed him to Photograph the find.

Deacon lifted the parcel and stood up, taking the parcel over to the bed he took a penknife from his pocket and cut the string and opened the parcel which contained five wads of twenty pound notes.

The constable photographed the contents then he and Deacon counted the money. There was four thousand, four hundred and twenty pounds in total. A lot of money for someone who was supposed not to have any! Deacon exclaimed. He then said: 'Ok if there's nothing else let's get this back to the station.'

On their return Deacon sent Davies straight to evidence to book the money in and he went to DCS Lewis's office. After hearing Deacon's report Lewis said: 'Interesting, I think we should speak to the sister again. Bring her in under caution and we'll tape the interview, it may well unsettle her and persuade her to change her story, at least we will have it on record. While you were out we received the report on the dirt and sand found in McDonald's wounds, the sand is common builder's sand but the dirt isn't so common, it's organic and the only organic soil within a ten mile radius of the trading estate is at Parker's organic farm just three miles west of town. SOCCO and Forensics are out there now and DC Peters and two uniforms are questioning everybody on the farm.'

Two hours later DC peters reported back from the farm, he told Lewis: 'We haven't got much accept for one worker who has not been seen for three days, his name is John Holland. I have his address he lives just a mile away from the farm but here's the best bit—he is a part time builder and—DRIVES A RED PICKUP.'

'Good work Peters, has SOCCO or Forensics turned up anything?'

'No, accept for a sample of soil, they are bringing that back right now to have it tested.'

'Ok you take the other Officer to Holland's house and find out what you can, let me know immediately if anything turns up.'

When Peters and the PC arrived at Holland's house; there was no sign of his red pickup so Peters sent the officer around the back, while he knocked on the front door. There was no reply so he knocked harder, just then a woman's voice called out: "He's not there". Peters looked around and saw a large woman standing on the doorstep of the house next door. He walked over to her and showed his ID card, she continued: 'He's not been there for three or four days,' Peter's asked: 'Is his name Holland, John Holland?'

'Yes it is, he's normally quite chatty but a week or so ago he became very quiet walking around as if he had a heavy load on his mind, then as I say he disappeared with his truck and I haven't seen him since.' Peters asked if Holland was married, quite clearly enjoying being the centre of attention, and only too happy to give the information Peters wanted, the woman said: 'Yes but she left him over a year ago, she took their little boy with her, he must be about two and a half years old now. I don't know why she left him, although they had started arguing a lot a few months before she went.'

Peters thanked the woman telling her she had been most helpful and gave her his card asking her to call if Holland came back or if she remembered anything else. Peter's also asked her name, to which she replied Mrs Jane Talbot.

PC Peters left the woman and headed round the back of Holland's house to join the uniformed officer and met him coming back around the side of the house, Peters asked: 'Is there any way in at the back?'

'Yes there is a broken window in the back door' the officer told Peters. He said that would do and they both headed around to the back. The rear door consisted of small square panes of glass with wooden panels underneath. The broken pane was on the bottom row nearest the door handle, Peters using his elbow gently but firmly hit the window breaking the rest of the glass. He and the PC put on latex gloves then reaching in through the window turned the key in the lock and opened the door.

Cautiously they entered the property, Peter's called out: "POLICE OFFICER'S WE ARE COMING IN". There was no response so they ventured further into the kitchen and then into the lounge. On the wall there was a silver framed photo of a small child about eighteen months old, a man and a woman stood either side of him holding his hands. On the mantelpiece was a pair of candle sticks and two more frames with photos, one was of the boy and the other of the couple with their arms around each other, Peters told the officer to bag them. In a drawer of the wall unit there were bills for credit cards and utility services which were also bagged, however there was nothing else of interest downstairs, and it was the same story in the rest of the house so Peters decided to turn their attention to the back garden. They poked around in the grass and flower beds then the officer looked inside a wooden shed which stood at the end of garden, he suddenly called Peters saying: 'I've found something.' Peter's walked down to the shed and went inside and saw the officer holding a pair of green bloodstained overalls, Peters told him to bag them for evidence then poked about himself, he moved a pile of sand bags and beneath them was a pair of safety boots with blood splatters on the toes and sand and earth buried in the tread. Peters bagged the find up and after another look around he said that they were finished there and should head back to the station.

Once outside Peters locked the house up and put the keys in an evidence bag, he and PC Davies then went to Mrs Talbot's house and Peters knocked the door. Mrs Talbot opened the door and Peter apologised for disturbing her again and showed her the pictures from the house, he asked: 'Is this Holland?' She confirmed it was and said the boy was his son and the woman his wife—"Margret." Thanking her once again Peters bid her goodbye and the two men returned to the station.

On their return the constable booked the items found at Holland's house into evidence while Peters went and reported to the DCS Lewis. Lewis listened intently to Peters' report, when he had finished talking Lewis clapped his hands and said: Yes! He cleared his throat then said: 'When SOCCO and Forensics have finished at the farm

I'll get them to Holland's house and they can take the place apart—oh and by the way Peters—well done.'

After Lewis had notified Deacon of the find he decided to get a cup of tea and some lunch so he told Deacon to meet him in the canteen. They sat down with their drinks and meals and they both ate in silence for a few minutes, then Lewis finally spoke: 'I have told the lab that the CC has deemed our tests take priority over all the other departments, they said we should have a result on the soil and the items Peters brought in within a couple of hours.' Deacon replied: 'Strange isn't it they can get tests done very fast when the powers to be clap their hands, pity they can't always be so efficient.'

Too right! 'We could wrap up cases a lot faster if they were, still I may forgive them if they give us some answers.'

They were on their way back down to their offices when Lewis's mobile rang, it was SOCCO reporting from the farm saying they had found the red pickup concealed under a pile of hay inside a barn, they had discovered sand, blood and soil in the back of the truck, a half of a wall brick covered in blood was also found in the barn.

Later that afternoon Forensics reported that the blood from the back of the pickup was definitely McDonald's, also the sand and soil was a definite match with that found in McDonald's wounds. When SOCCO and forensics had finished processing Holland's house they reported that they had collected hair from the waste trap in the bathroom sink, as well as finger prints from all over the house. Lewis reminded them of the CC's orders and he was promised the results ASAP.

CHAPTER NINETEEN

Being locked up for three nights—the fifth for Elaine—was getting to the Jessop's. Their guards were very cautious each time they opened the door and they were only provided with plastic plates, cups and cutlery which they had to wash to use again after every meal. Coffee also came in a plastic jug as did the milk plus the food and coffee was never more than lukewarm.

They were told to wash what clothes they were wearing and hang them to dry in front of the electric fire. Clifford had tried to say that it was all unacceptable but Palmer just replied sarcastically: "Complain to the management".

Clifford became more and more determined to attempt an escape, at the outset they considered Palmer to be the easiest target but as time went on it became clear Bird would be a better choice.

After their evening meal of baked beans on toast and lukewarm coffee Clifford said to Elaine: 'I have been thinking and I have a plan to get us out of here.'

'What have you in mind? Whatever it is it won't be easy, they are on their guard all the time.'

'I know but I don't think they would actually dare harm us though, Thomas seems to want us alive for whatever reason and that could work in our favour. Look, I reckon if we could get them off guard we could make our move, we would need a weapon of some sort though.'

'Oh hang on I happen to have a machine gun in my bag, where on earth are we going to get our hands on a weapon?'

'Ok clever clogs don't panic, I will think of something.' promised Clifford not feeling as confident as he appeared. She kissed him and told him: 'I love you, Clifford Jessop.' Clifford said he loved her and she said she was going to have a bath and have a think.

While Elaine was having her bath, Clifford sat on the sofa and fell fell into a deep sleep; he was suddenly woken though by Elaine poking him in the chest announcing: "Wake up, wake up Darling, I have it". He responded quickly saying: 'Well whatever it is you keep it to yourself, it might be contagious and I don't want to catch it'. He had no sooner said it though when he immediately apologised for joking, then asked: 'Ok what have you got.' She told him: 'Well remember you said that Thomas wouldn't want us harmed, well we could use that, why don't we start arguing loudly and violently and throw things around the room? We can use the cramped space to pretend we are getting on each other's nerves being so confined together they are bound to come in to shut us up. We could break off a couple of chair legs and when they come in we can have them behind our backs, then we could surprise them and hit them then make our escape.'

'Wow when did you think that up?' Elaine said it was when she was in the bath, she then told him: 'I thought tomorrow morning would be as good a time as any.' Clifford admitted it was a good plan so they agreed to give it a try, he suggested they try and get some rest as they would have to be razor sharp in the morning.

Morning came and they were awake early after spending most of the night mulling over their escape plan. Bird and Palmer were usually quite punctual bringing their food in so when it was almost time for breakfast to arrive they prepared scene for their performance, Clifford had already broken off two chair legs and they listened at the door waiting to hear footsteps. Elaine heard the footsteps first, they waited until they were sure their voices could be heard then started arguing. Elaine began yelling: "YOU PIG, YOU NEVER COULD STAND BEING ALONE WITH ME FOR LONG, NOT EVEN HERE WHEN I NEED YOUR SUPPORT. YOU DON'T LOVE ME; I'M JUST YOUR SLAVE". Clifford shouted back at her: "SLAVE? I DON'T THINK SO, SLAVES DO AS THEY'RE TOLD . . . AND THEY DON'T ANSWER BACK."

Elaine was just about to reply but she only just managed to say: "WHY YOU . . . . When the door was opened sharply and Palmer yelled while waving a gun at them: 'What the hell is going on in here? 'I thought you two were inseparable.' Clifford barked back: "INSEPERABLE YOU MUST BE JOKING". With that he brought his chair leg from behind his back and hit Palmer over the head knocking him to the ground. Elaine then swung her chair leg at Bird catching him on the side of his head, Clifford hit him a second time knocking him out and grabbing the gun.

Clifford told Elaine to get out and run for her life. She didn't need telling twice and she took to her heels but, as she drew level with Palmer he reached out his leg and she tripped over banging her head on the wall close to Bird who was coming round, he seized the opportunity and reaching out he grabbed her arm pulling her roughly in front of him using her as a shield and forced Clifford to drop the gun. Palmer had recovered and reached out for the gun, Clifford reacting quickly for a second time stamped on Palmers hand and grabbed the gun instantly pointing it at Bird, He said: 'Shoot and you will hit her.' Clifford's adrenaline was rushing by then though and he told Bird: 'That's fine by me the sooner she's out of the way the better.'

Elaine forgetting the plan for a second became worried he would shoot her and she gave him a look of shock and disbelief. Bird replied: 'Give it up, you don't know how to handle a gun, put it down and we will forget this ever happened.' Clifford laughed and said: 'I handle guns much bigger than this pea shooter every day at work, now let her go.' He continued pointing the gun at Bird who was quick to let Elaine go as he believed Clifford would really kill him and he thought that at least with Palmer and him alive there was a slim chance they could reverse the situation.

As soon as Bird released Elaine Clifford told her to run once more, this time she made it and once outside she looked around, just ahead of her she saw a path running to the right and the other way was a dead end closed in by shrubs and trees. She made her way towards the path and ran as fast as she could, when she thought she was a safe distance away she took shelter behind some bushes, after ten minutes she became worried because she thought

Clifford should have been with her by then so she decided to head back and get a little nearer to the house and watch for him. She was almost there when a shot rang out from the house, she unwittingly screamed but then she realised her mistake and stopped.

Inside the house Clifford had forced Bird to pull a curtain from the window and tear it into shreds to tie Palmers hands and legs together, he then told him to tie his own legs. After Bird had done that Clifford placed the gun on the sofa and turned to pick up a strip of curtain to tie Bird's hands, however as he turned Bird lunged forward taking Clifford by surprise and was pushed back against the wall as Bird threw himself at the sofa, going for the gun; however Clifford was quicker grabbing the table and hurling it at Bird hitting him on the back, even then Bird managed to get a hand on the gun but Clifford lunged at him again and they both slid along the vinyl floor. They hit the wall and Clifford grabbed Bird by the right arm wrenching the gun from him but Bird's finger was on the trigger and the gun went off—Which is what Elaine had heard—and the bullet nicked Bird's left ear. This only succeeded in riling Bird further and he fought even harder for the gun, Clifford however managed to maintain his grip on the gun and wrenched it from Birds hand pointing it at his head, stopping him in his tracks. Bird raised his hands up and muttered: 'Ok buddy you win, for now.' Clifford told him to turn over on his stomach and he successfully secured Bird's hands.

Panting heavily Clifford walked outside breathing in the fresh air, he had locked and bolted the door to the room and the building and had thrown the keys as far as he could into some hedges. Elaine by then had all but reached the house. She saw Clifford and rushed over crying with relief. Clifford though half in anger and half in relief scolded her for coming back then lightened up and assured her he was fine.

That afternoon back at Police headquarters Forensic scientist Giles Taylor called Lewis with the official test reports on Holland's house and truck, he told Lewis: "The blood on the clothes and boots found in Holland's shed was a positive match to McDonald, also the blood and hair found in the back of the truck also matched McDonald's, as did the blood and skin tissue on the brick." "The sand in McDonald's wound and hair was also linked to that in the truck and the tread of Holland's boots, also the soil found in the wound and on his body definitely came from the farm." Taylor went on to tell Lewis that the hair from Holland's bathroom sink was tested for DNA and some of that was definitely Holland's, there was other hair found but that with the DNA and fingerprints from the house, was not in the data base.

Lewis thanked Giles and immediately called Deacon who responded saying: 'Well all we have to do now is find Holland.' Lewis replied: 'We have no proof yet it was actually Holland who killed Mc Donald but, I think it is a fair assumption. I think we'll call a news conference for seven o'clock tonight and get Holland's face posted all over the country, also I think I'll fax it off to Interpol.' Lewis hung up but almost immediately his phone rang and it was DI Barnes, he told Lewis: "A burnt out car has been found on waste ground at the edge of a small forest near an airfield. It's virtually a wreck and the number plates have been removed, however SOCCO opened the boot and discovered a minute spot of paint that had remained intact where the rubber seal would have been a scraping has been lifted and is on its way to Forensics, hopefully they will be able to trace the manufacturers and check the paint code, they should then be able trace the dealer who sold it and give us the name of the buyer. We also have reports from about a mile away from the airfield of a glow that was seen in the sky from the area three nights ago so it could be Jessop's car.' Lewis thanked Barnes and hung up.

CHAPTER TWENTY

The first day of Thomas and his crew's unplanned hike wasn't exactly hard but they did get their first taste of what was to come. Late afternoon one of Marco's men had a narrow escape as a highly poisonous snake suddenly appeared above him hanging from a branch. Marco managed to hack it down with his hatchet but it sent an air of panic for a few seconds.When the light began fading Marco suggested setting up camp for the night which suited Thomas and co as they were exhausted, they soon dropped their rucksacks and plonked themselves down on the ground.

Earlier Marco had gone into the undergrowth and shot a large snake and was busy skinning and gutting it,Thomas was curious so he wandered over and asked why he was doing it. Marco informed him that it was their supper and Thomas immediately barked he wasn't eating that. Marco calmly reminded him that they had to send everything away with the truck as they could only carry their gear and essential items so, they would be eating whatever was available and that snake tasted just the same as chicken.

Thomas continued protesting but slumped off back to his perch as he was too tired to argue further.

Marco continued preparing the snake chopping it into small pieces and adding other natural ingredients he had gathered earlier he then placed it all into a tin pot and added water. He hung it over the fire and stirred the mixture regularly for about twenty minutes then announced that dinner was served. Nick, John and Simpson didn't hold back, they were first in the queue holding their billycans out as they were so hungry from their days hike. Marco using a wooden ladle filled their containers with what looked like a thick soup. Marco's men were next licking their lips in anticipation of food, Thomas however held back although he was ravenous he wasn't sure whether to attempt the mixture. He watched his men as they shovelled their portions down, Simpson noticed this and told Thomas that it was good and he should have some before it all goes. Thomas still held back but when Nick also said it was good he got up and went to Marco holding his can out. Marco couldn't resist a wry smile as he scooped up some of the soup and poured it into his billycan. Thomas eagerly spooned some into his mouth; he thought about it for a second then began shoving the rest down his throat almost without taking a breath.

Thomas being Thomas finished HIS portion and immediately went and poured another large one into his dish. Marco reminded him to leave enough for the others. Thomas though just grunted and took an even larger portion.

After supper Marco advised everyone to get some sleep as the next day was going to tough and long. As usual Thomas moaned that he wouldn't be able to sleep on the ground, Marco shrugged his shoulders and said that couldn't be helped. Eventually everyone went to sleep, even Thomas but in the early hours when everyone was asleep in their beds, suddenly they were all awakened by a loud piercing scream. Thomas and his men arose quickly on hearing the commotion and saw Marco standing by the fire with one of his men talking in their own tongue, and they sounded distressed. Marco was holding a thick tree branch and he smacked it against a rock breaking a piece off the end.

Thomas asked what the hell was going on and Marco told him: 'My man on guard let out a scream and now he has disappeared.' He told Thomas that he and his remaining man were going to look for him and Thomas asked what he and his men were supposed to do and reluctantly Marco gave Thomas his rifle and told him to keep his men together until He got back.

Marco then plunged the tree branch into the fire embers and managed to get it to light then he and his man made their way to where his other man had stood guard. They searched for signs of where he could have gone and discovered blood and drag marks leading into the deep thick grass. Using the light from the flaming branch they followed the marks and soon they came across the man's gun lying on the ground and close to it was a pool of blood which trailed off into the undergrowth. Marco retrieved the gun then they followed the trail but the further they went the thicker the blood became and it was becoming obvious that it was unlikely he was still alive, however they continued on. Eventually the trail led to a patch of bloodied grass where they found blood soaked shreds of his jacket and trousers, plus one shoe. The blood trail then disappeared into the dense undergrowth and Marco knew it was hopeless so he and his man made their way back to camp.

When they returned Thomas was standing with the rifle pointed at them and he told Marco and his man to drop their guns. Marco complied with Thomas's wishes but asked what he hoped to achieve with such actions, Thomas ignored him and asked: 'Where's the other guy? Call him to come here and tell him no tricks.'

'I cannot do that Senor, he is gone.'

Gone! 'Gone where?'

'It appears Senor Thomas he has been taken by someone or something, he was dragged into the trees bleeding badly and regrettably it is highly unlikely he still lives. Why don't you give me the gun Senor? There are dangerous creatures and bad men all around us and you are only playing into their hands with this behaviour, we all have to stick together now.' Thomas ignored Marco and ordered his men to collect the three guns and keep one each, Marco told Thomas the gun Simpson had was the lost man's gun and it was bad luck to take dead men's possessions. Thomas said: 'Yeah and it is bad luck if you get killed because there aren't enough weapons.'

Simpson asked Thomas what he was planning because they needed Marco to get them through the jungle, Thomas though told him he was running the show from now on and he ordered Simpson and Nick to get all the gear together so they could get going.

The next morning when it was light enough for them to set off Thomas told Marco to lead and he would follow. Simpson and the other man walked behind Thomas with John and Nick at the rear. Thomas told everyone to keep their eyes and ears open, Marco was about to say something but Thomas prodded him with rifle and told him to keep quiet and walk.

"Marco was going to inform Thomas that the most important thing of all—the water containers—had been left behind". Marco had second thoughts and decided to remain silent knowing that as experienced trekker's he and his man knew how to survive without water and it would give them a hold on Thomas when thirst kicked in."

At Chelsea Police headquarters, DCS Lewis had managed to get home for a while and had snatched a few hours sleep while he waited for the rest of the test results to come in.

He had just showered and was sitting watching television with Karen after eating a nice meal and was so comfortable slumped in his deep plush armchair he dropped off to sleep. However he was soon brought back to reality when the phone rang, Karen reached over and lifted the receiver and handed it to him. She had no doubts what the phone call meant so she went into the kitchen and prepared some sandwiches for her husband to take to work.

The caller was DCI Deacon informing Lewis that the tests of the paint sample taken from the burnt out car did match the paint used on the same make and model of Clifford's car, the dealer was traced and they confirmed Clifford did buy the car from them. Deacon also told Lewis that there were no scheduled flights in or out of the airfield the night Clifford had disappeared, however a house to house enquiry of properties in the surrounding area revealed that several people heard an engine and some saw a light in the sky, on or around the outskirts of the airfield late the following night. Lewis replied: 'Ok, so are we to assume the Jessop's were taken out of the country, if so why? Martin; prepare a team meeting in the incident room for eleven o'clock tomorrow morning, I want everybody's input on the case so far, also contact Interpol and put them on the alert, tell them this enquiry has all the makings of a major incident and send them Clifford and Elaine's pictures. Meanwhile I will call the CC and bring him up to date.' Lewis ended the call and immediately called the CC, he told Lewis that he would meet with the joint chiefs first thing in the morning to discuss their actions if, in the event the Jessop's may have been taken abroad.

After Lewis had ended the call he looked at his watch and saw it was almost ten thirty, he told Karen he should go back to work, handing him the sandwiches she said: 'I anticipated that, the only calls we get these days are from the station.' He kissed her on the cheek and went upstairs to get dressed.

On his return to the station Deacon met him in the corridor outside his office; he informed him that when they spoke earlier he had forgotten to say that he had arranged for Pierce's sister to go in for further questioning at nine thirty the next morning, and to identify the body. Lewis thanked him and went to his office.

The next morning when June Pierce arrived at the station she was shown into an interview room. She saw the recording machine on the table and the CCTV camera on the wall.

Deacon entered the room and took his seat, he switched the tape on and announced the commencement of the interview, then said: 'Hello again Miss Pierce, I guess you're wondering why you have been called in so quickly?'

'Yes that's right, why am I here? I told you all I knew the other day.'

'Well June when we searched Stuart's flat after you had left that day we found a large bundle of money concealed beneath the bottom of Stuart's wardrobe. Do you know anything about it?'

'No I don't .... when you say a "large bundle" exactly how much are you talking about?' Deacon told her it was over four thousand pounds and asked why she said her brother never had any money. June replied: 'As far as I know he didn't, it can't be his because he wouldn't be able to resist bragging about it and splashing it around and he definitely wouldn't have been taking me for just a burger today.' Deacon then asked her: 'Now you have had time to think about it, are you positive you don't remember Stuart mentioning any other names apart from the dead guy Sam?'

'No I told you I hardly saw him, now if there's nothing else I'd like to go now and see Stuart then I need to get to work'.

'No that's it for now, we know where to find you if we need to talk again. I must impress on you though if you do know something and don't tell us, that could make you an accomplice. June swore she knew nothing so Deacon told her not to leave the area without notifying them first. June understood and said goodbye. Lewis had been watching the interview on a monitor from the room next door, they met outside and Lewis said: 'I'm still not convinced she is telling all she knows, put a tail on her, lets rule her in or out once and for all.'

CHAPTER TWENTY ONE

It took Elaine and Clifford a few minutes to gather their thoughts; once they had Clifford glanced around to get their bearings. Elaine told him as far as she could tell the lane seemed the only way out. Clifford looked at the sky and the sun was going down, he paused for a second thinking, then said: 'Chelsea is in the south and the sun goes down in the west so if the lane goes right up to the road, which I think it does from what I can remember, we turn right at the bottom. The lane is too narrow for a vehicle to drive up so it can't be very far from the road as it only took us a few minutes to walk to the house.' He took her hand and said: 'Come on.' And they ran quickly down the lane.

They reached the end of the lane in a few minutes, to their amazement a tatty old black van was parked just off the road. Clifford tried the doors but they were all locked. His hopes dashed he said they should begin walking, Elaine on the other hand was more forthright, she put her hand under the offside wing and found a key in a small metal box attached by a magnet. She yelled "eureka" and Clifford hugged her saying: 'Where would I be without you?'

'About five hundred yards down the road.' She replied. They had a chuckle then climbed in the van and set off. Clifford then said: 'I never imagined you as a car thief; I'm beginning to see you in a different light.'

Meanwhile Bird and Palmer were struggling to get out of their ties, eventually succeeding. Bird was cursing Palmer saying he was responsible for the escape, Palmer told him to shut it and help him get up from the floor. His head wound was bleeding profusely and his hand was swollen and painful from Clifford stamping on it, Bird was also in pain from hitting the wall with his arm while struggling with Clifford.

Bird attempted to haul Palmer up but he was not a light man and he could only use his left arm, he tried a few times but had to give up. He thought for a minute then said t: 'Try to get up on your knees and shuffle over to the sofa and I will help you climb onto it. The plan worked and once Palmer was on the sofa Bird mumbled: 'Thomas will kill us for this the only thing to do is run before he gets back.' Palmer replied angrily: 'We are not running those two are not getting away from me.'

The door to the room opened outwards, they approached it and began hurling themselves at it but with no success due to the pain they were in, they rested for a while then bird went to the sofa and threw all the cushions and seats on the floor, he called Palmer over and told him: 'If we drag the sofa over to the door we can stand it on its side and topple it over against the door, there should be enough weight to smash the door down. Palmer shrugged his shoulders and said: 'We could try I suppose, it could work.' After Palmer agreed to give it a go, they dragged the sofa to the door, standing it on its edge they heaved it at the door as hard as they could and as they hoped it shifted from the hinges, Bird said they should give it another go and that would probably be enough. The plan worked and the door shifted further away from the frame, it then took just a couple of kicks to force it off the hinges. Bird was cock 'a' hoot his plan had worked, he taunted Palmer but he could only reply: 'Yeah so you were lucky, and by the way I'm not your pal.'

Once they had clambered over the broken door and made their way along the passage into the front room, Palmer opened a drawer in the wall unit and pulled out another gun which he had hidden in case of an emergency, he turned to Bird and said: 'Come on if we're quick we are bound to catch up with them, after all they're on foot and we have the van, where did you put the keys?'

'I never had them Thomas drove the van didn't he?'

'Oh hell, look around he must have left them here somewhere.'

They looked for ages but the keys weren't there, Palmer eventually said: 'Come on this is a waste of time they're getting further away.'

They went to the front door and found it locked, Bird said sarcastically: 'You have a gun, if you know how to use it, shoot the lock off.' Palmer replied: 'I'll shoot you if you don't start treating all this seriously.' He lifted the gun and Bird ducked down, Palmer aimed the gun at the wood above the bottom hinge and fired two shots, the frame shattered and they both gave the door a sharp kick and the door came away from the frame and they were out.

As soon as they were outside Palmer urged Bird to get going as they had a lot of ground to make up. It was nearly dark so Palmer went back in and brought out a torch and they set off as fast as they could with their aches and pains. Palmer was way ahead of Bird who was struggling with pain in his leg which he hadn't noticed he had until he started walking his left leg also began to stiffen up and become painful with each step he took.

He was just a few yards from the end of the lane when he heard Palmer shout out: 'I don't believe this, the damned vans gone; they have taken the damned van.' Bird caught up and said: 'WE don't know it was them, it could have been anyone, Thomas could have taken it after all we couldn't find the keys could we?" All I know is that it has stuffed up any chance of catching up with that pair.'

'Well I'm in agony, we should go back and rest then we can get away in the morning.'

"YOU JUST DON'T GET IT DO YER? WE AINT RUNNING."

'We have to run, even if we get them back Thomas will never forgive us for letting them escape. We're dead.'

'Yeah and you'll be dead if you don't man up.'

CHAPTER TWENTY TWO

Thomas's party had hacked and tramped their way through the undergrowth which was now becoming denser. Marco was still in the front hacking a path for them to follow. Earlier Thomas had questioned why they had to go that way and not take an easier route; Marco explained that if they go the easy way they were more likely to be attacked by bandits, however Thomas continued to question Marco asking: 'How do you even know we can get through this way?'

'I don't Senor but we have a better chance than going the other way.' Marco replied trying to stay calm with Thomas while answering his questions. Thomas accepted the situation but he was still not happy, however they continued on.

By late morning the sun was unbearably hot and the humidity was getting to them all. They were lucky enough to find shade under some thick leafy trees to rest it was then that Thomas was made aware that he had left all the water behind. He blamed Marco saying he was the expert and he should have realised and said something, Marco just shrugged his shoulders and replied casually: 'WHAT can I say Senor?' Thomas went to hit him with the rifle but Simpson stopped him saying: 'You blame everyone but yourself; you said you were in charge so it's your fault.' It was clear that Thomas was about to strike Simpson but John shouted: 'I don't think so Thomas.' He had his rifle trained on Thomas so he paused and backed off. Simpson asked Marco: 'Is there any chance we can get water?'

'I'm not sure Senor, we must rest now though.' Nick told Thomas that Marco should be back in charge as Thomas had no idea what he was doing. John and Simpson agreed and handed Marco their rifles but not before they forced Thomas to hand his over, Thomas insisted he was keeping his pistol though.

After resting Marco said they should get going because they had to reach their next set of guides or they would pull out, as the area around where they were waiting was renowned for bandit attacks.

They got going again but Thomas still continued moaning he was thirsty, Marco ensured him he would get a drink when they camped that evening. Forging their way through the thick undergrowth they managed to get a fair distance through the jungle until suddenly a loud throaty cry came from the rear of the line, which stopped everyone in their tracks. Thomas and Marco rushed back to see what was happening and found Nick and Simpson straining to see into the thick undergrowth and trees, and they were clearly disturbed about something. Marco asked what had happened and Simpson muttered nervously: "John has gone." Thomas asked what he meant by "gone"

Simpson replied: 'Gone, Just like the other guy, he just disappeared somewhere in there.' He pointed into the dense bushes and trees and continued: 'One second he was here and the next he was gone. He gave out the most horrible scream.' Thomas said: 'Yes we heard it, now get out of the way.' Thomas pulled Simpson away and peered into the bushes himself but there was no sign of John and it was impossible to see through the dense vegetation, just then another ear piercing scream rang out, Thomas pushed Simpson and NIck out of his way yelling at the top of his voice: "THAT'S IT I'M OUT OF HERE." He grabbed his kit and ran back the way they had come, this panicked everyone else and they all followed suit.

They regrouped further down the path and Marco suggested remaining there to regain their composure and talk options. After thinking a while he addressed everyone: 'Senor's I am sorry for the loss of your friend but I think we should make haste. Senor Thomas I will need my man up front with me, I need his expertise, he has helped lead many people through this part of the jungle, he also has a good sense of danger.'

'Well he didn't sense the demise of John, or your man, did he?' Thomas remarked. Then continued: 'Anyway before we go I need water.'

'That is where my man is needed once more, he is an expert at extracting moisture from certain plants essential for our survival, he has been doing this for many years and saved many lives. I myself have had to rely on his methods and I am happy to say that is why I am here to tell the tale.' Thomas had no answer to this so Marco spoke to his man and He sauntered off into the undergrowth, minutes later he re-emerged his pack overflowing with shoots and plants, Marco handed some around and told them to suck on the stems to obtain the moisture from inside, he then called everyone together and they set off.

They hiked on for the rest of the day until Thomas and his men said they couldn't walk another yard. They had reached a partial clearing and Marco agreed they should stop for the night as the light was fading. Marco asked his man to prepare something to drink so Nick and Simpson volunteered to help while Marco went to gather wood for a fire, but Thomas just sat and waited.

Marco soon returned with wood and food, mainly consisting of grubs, fungi and a small snake. Thomas voiced his disgust but Marco told Thomas there was nothing else edible in these parts because of the jungle, it is so dense that the sun doesn't penetrate the trees so nothing can exist other than insects snakes and grubs like these.' Thomas tried fighting off being violently sick but eventually he rushed to a bush and vomited profusely three times. When he rejoined Marco he was as white as a sheet, Marco remarked: 'Better out than in Senor.' "For what Marco surmised was probably one of a very few times in his life, Thomas was speechless."

Marco started preparing dinner, Simpson asked: 'what's on the menu?' Thomas said nothing he just wanted to get as far away as he could from the smell and the sight of grubs.

Marco smiled then he and his man took some of the roots and other jungle produce from his bag, he held small bundles of the shoots and laid them in the bottom of a large metal dish. Then using a large stone he slowly crushed them until they emitted a clear liquid. Nick was fascinated by this and watched avidly. Once all the shoots had been crushed he did the same with all the other roots this produced a milky looking liquid.

Marco's man then cut the stems into pieces about a half inch long and placed them in the can with the milky liquid and stirred the mixture. He then placed the can of clear liquid onto the fire and slowly heated the mix up then did the same with the shoots and milky liquid stirring constantly.

Meanwhile Simpson had followed Marco to see what he was preparing, he watched as Marco laid his hat on the ground, when he saw the grubs he—like Thomas—had to go and vomit although not so violently. Nick saw what was occurring and came over, and when he spotted the wriggling creatures he kicked the hat spilling most of the grubs out onto the ground, Marco immediately fell to his knees and gathered the grubs up again then said loudly: 'As you are all so disgusted I assume nobody wishes to eat supper this evening.' Thomas called out: "Too damned right". Nick and Simpson said nothing but they didn't seem too keen either. Marco said: 'That's fine Senor's there will be more for Miguel and I.

Meanwhile Miguel was lifting the can of hot steaming liquid from the fire using his neckerchief to hold the handle. Nick went to his bag and took his billycan out and returned to Miguel and held it out for some. Miguel responded saying: 'No sorry Senor you cannot have any yet, it has to be filtered, it is too toxic as it is at present, you must have patience.' Nick was really thirsty as were all of the party but he acknowledged Miguel and tentatively went back to see what Marco was doing. Marco had began preparing the grubs, he gathered a heap of large leaves and intermingled them to form a flat sheet then tipped all the grubs onto it and folded the leaves enveloping them forming a hollow pocket in the centre. He approached the fire and placed the bundle onto it. Nick blurted out that he had put them on the fire alive, Marco responded saying: 'That's the way to cook them Senor if they are dead the fluids dry up too quick and they become too hard to eat.'

When the grubs had been on the fire long enough Marco raked the glowing parcel from the fire with a stick, holding it down with the stick he used his knife and cut the leaves open, although disgusted Thomas and Simpson slowly crept over to inspect the end result. The sight amazed them, instead of slimy wriggling creatures they looked more like a large kidney bean but lighter in colour.

Miguel was the first to take one, licking his lips he took it and placed it in his mouth, it was obviously hot but eventually they heard a loud crunch. Thomas cringed and turned away, Nick and Simpson however remained motionless. Marco then took one, placing it in his mouth he too crunched his and looked at Miguel who just nodded with a satisfied smile on his face. Marco then offered one to Nick as he was the only one who hadn't vomited. He tentatively took it and looked at it, Marco said: 'Go on Senor it will not kill you, in fact it will keep you alive.' Nick put out his tongue and tested it. Simpson and Thomas looked on with interest and disgust at the same time. Nick however eventually bucked up courage and placed it in his mouth, he left it for a second or so but there was no actual taste so eventually he bit into it screwing his face up but then his expression changed to a look of surprise, he happily chewed away and swallowed it holding out his hand for another, immediately popping it into his mouth. The three men chewed and crunched away on several grubs then Simpson relented and came over saying: 'leave some for me.'

He took one and thought about it then he closed his eyes and took the plunge, like Nick he didn't bite it straight away but, when he did he soon discovered the taste was pleasant and joined the feast. Thomas wasn't going to be the odd man out for long he gathered up his courage and joined the others.

When they had eaten all of the grubs Marco said to Miguel that the drink should be ready so Miguel went and fetched it, the juices had been filtered through special leaves into a container made from goat's skin. Miguel offered the first drink to Thomas but as normal he was not going to try it before anyone else so Marco drank first followed by Nick, he only took a small sip but surprised at how nice that was he took a larger drink. Miguel had some then Simpson took a swig and handed it to Thomas, he hesitated then his thirst got the better of him and gulped some down. Marco suggested he should leave some for the next day so Thomas took another swig and handed the container to Marco.

After they had all had filled their bellies they all turned in and went to sleep hoping for no more rude awakenings.

CHAPTER TWENTY THREE

In his haste to get Elaine and himself away from the house, Clifford hadn't realised how fast he was driving. It was getting dark and they were about two miles from town when flashing blue lights lit up the rear view mirror. Clifford looked at Elaine and he could see relief on her face, he too was feeling good assuming that it was the Police and they had been found, however they were not prepared for what was to follow.

Clifford slowed up and pulled over and a Police car pulled up behind them, Clifford released his seat belt and opened his door but, a uniformed officer wearing a peaked cap appeared and told Clifford to remain in the van and close the door. Elaine was looking in her door mirror and noticed that another officer was at the back of the van, he was looking at the tail end and talking into his lapel radio transmitter, she guessed he was relaying the registration number to their control.

Clifford wound down the window and tried to tell the officer who they were, however the officer stopped him saying: 'YOU will have your say in a moment sir but for now I need to see your licence, insurance and MOT please.' Clifford replied: 'I don't have them this is not our vehicle.'

'Who does the vehicle belong to then sir and why are you driving it?' Elaine attempted to lean over and tell the officer about their situation but he told her that he was talking to Clifford and he would talk to her later. Clifford then answered the officer saying: 'I don't know who it belongs to, as I was trying to explain before . . . . He was interrupted by the other officer who had come to whisper in his partners ear: "The van was stolen ten days ago".

The first officer stepped back and ordered Clifford out of the van, grabbing him by his arm he turned Clifford and told him to face the van and announced: "I am arresting you on suspicion of vehicle theft". He then read Clifford his rights and handcuffed him and led him to the Patrol car.

Clifford was so shocked he couldn't think for a moment, he regained his senses though as the officer opened the car door, he dug his heels in and once again tried to identify himself by saying: 'Look officer you are making a mistake, I am Clifford Jessop and that is my wife Elaine in the van.' The officer ignored Clifford and guided him roughly into the car followed by Elaine, who had also been led to the car in handcuffs and the rear doors were slammed shut. The first officer opened the driver's door, lifting the car radio mike he reported the incident, Elaine was crying because she had really believed their troubles were over, Clifford reassured her saying: 'It's alright Darling don't fret they are only doing their jobs, it's obvious they don't recognise our names, we will sort it all out at the station.'

Meanwhile the second officer had returned to the van to check the inside, finding nothing he locked the van and returned to the police vehicle. As he climbed into the front passenger seat and drove off towards the police station, Clifford made another attempt to say who they were and they were missing the chance to catch their kidnapper's. They travelled a little further then suddenly the driver stamped on the brakes and the car screeched to a halt, he looked at his partner and excitedly said to him: 'Kidnapper's—yes of course the Jessop's we had the report a few days ago over the radio, Oh my God it's them.' He turned around saying:'I am so sorry Mr Jessop—Mrs Jessop but we had no idea.'The officers climbed out and opening both back doors to the car, they helped the couple out and instantly removed the handcuffs. The driver asked if they minded answering a couple of questions then they would get them back home. The word "home" brought a spark of joy back to Elaine, she linked Clifford's arm with hers and gave him a little smile. Clifford said he didn't mind some questions so the officer asked: 'How far away from here were you held, are the kidnappers still there?' Clifford answered: 'Not far and they were.' in that order.

Clifford went on to give them a description of where they had escaped from. The other officer then asked: 'Can you describe any of the kidnappers?'

'Yes we can and they could be armed.' Elaine chipped in.

'Right thank you, Ok I will call control and get someone on to this immediately.'

The officer called in and reported that they had found the Jessop's saying they were alive and well, he also reported that they were currently not far from the place they were held, and the kidnappers could still be there and may be armed.

DCS Lewis received the message almost immediately, he was in his office going over the case files with Deacon, leaping from his chair he yelled: 'We got them, the Jessop's, they've been found. Lewis composed himself and gave a little cough, he then told the officer on the phone to get directions and relay them to armed response, adding: Deacon and I will be there right away.' Lewis hung up then said to Deacon: 'The Jessop's their safe.'

'Yes, I got that Gov, I'll get by coat.'

Back at the car the officer told The Jessop's what was happening, Clifford said they didn't know the address but, he was sure they could take them to the house. Elaine nodded and added: 'Yes I'm sure we can but as we told you they could be armed and they are vicious.' The officer reassured her that Armed Response were on their way and would not put her or her husband in any danger.

Armed Response was the first to arrive followed quickly by Lewis and Deacon. Elaine and Clifford greeted the DCS and Clifford remarked 'I never thought I would be pleased to see your face again.' He held out his hand smiling to the DCS and they shook hands. Lewis never responded to the remark, he just said: 'How are you both? I see you have hurt your head Clifford. Do you require hospital treatment?'

'No I'm fine, thank you,' replied Clifford.

'Well it's nice to see you in such fine spirits considering what you two have been through, now if you are ready shall we go? I must point out, for your own safety we will only let you take us so close leaving you a safe distance from the house, then you will be taken back to the station. There will be some fresh clothes for you both and you can shower and freshen up.' Elaine was quick to quip: 'Why do we smell that bad?' Lewis laughed and assured her that they didn't. He then turned to speak to the Sergeant in charge of the ART then turned back to Clifford and asked how far the house was. Clifford said it was about fifteen minutes away, Lewis then asked: 'Are you sure you will be able to find your way back in the dark?' Clifford assured him that they could because the road was fairly straight apart from a couple of bends, Elaine added she thought she would be able to recognise a couple of land marks on the way, so Lewis clapped his hands and announced: 'Ok all units board your vehicles and follow the patrol car, keep your radios on I will warn you when we are close.

They set off back to the house driven by the officer who had earlier arrested them, Clifford sat on the left and Elaine on the right in the back seat with Lewis as the meat in the sandwich, Deacon and the ART followed close behind. The officer drove at a sedate pace giving the Jessop's every chance to pick up something memorable. Elaine had said she remembered seeing a very old rickety house which would now be on her side, she noticed it because it seemed to be leaning like the kind of house seen in old horror stories, and it was close to where the road straightened up from the second bend. She said that just up from that there should be a rail crossing and the lane that leads to the kidnap house was not far from there on the left.

Five minutes went by then Elaine yelled out: 'Look that house, that's it.' The driver slowed down, Clifford looked then told Lewis Elaine was right. They drove on and as Elaine had told them they went around a left hand bend, then they drove over the railway crossing. Clifford said: 'We're not far away now there's just one more bend to the right. Soon after they reached the bend and Clifford told the driver: 'Right keep a look out there is a staggered crossroad with a pub on one corner to our right then a few yards past that on the left is the lane. Lewis called the other units and told them they were almost at the lane. He also warned them to be on the lookout for the kidnappers.

Soon the lights of the pub came into view and then the lane, Lewis told the driver to pull up just past the lane to allow Deacon and the ART to pull in behind them, Lewis then asked the Jessop's the location of the house, Clifford gave him the directions Lewis then asked what they could tell him about the house. Elaine and Clifford gave Lewis as much detail as they could, Clifford added that he had locked and bolted the front door and threw the key away, Lewis commended him on his actions and thanked them both and said he and his officers would take it from there, he then told the two officers to take the Jessop's to the station.

After the car had whisked the Jessop's away Lewis gathered the Sergeant and Deacon together and gave them the layout of the house, he opened the boot of his car and took out a loudhailer he also took out two bullet proof vests and hand guns handing one of each to Deacon. They both put on the flak jackets and helmets and once all of them were ready Lewis gave the word and they proceeded cautiously up the lane.

When they reached the top and the house came into view, everyone crouched down using the bushes as cover.

Lewis estimated they were approximately twenty yards from the house.

The ART carried night vision binoculars with inferred vision, Lewis asked the Sergeant to give a pair for himself, the Sergeant handed them to Lewis and he scanned the house and the surrounding area. He announced quietly via the radio that he could not see any form of life in the house or the surrounding area but, for everyone to remain alert and vigilant, he continued to say that when he deemed it was safe to approach the house he would give two clicks on the radio, Lewis advised the Sergeant to take his men and circle the house when he gave the signal but do nothing else.

They watched the house for a while until Lewis considered it safe, he then gave the signal. The ART moved slowly towards the house spreading out so that the house was completely encircled, Lewis and Deacon then moved in and approached the front door. They could see the door had been smashed down, although Lewis was sure the house was clear he put the loud haler to his mouth and announced: "ARMED POLICE PUT YOUR WEAPONS DOWN AND COME OUT WITH YOUR HANDS ABOVE YOUR HEAD. YOU HAVE THIRTY SECONDS TO RESPOND."

Thirty seconds passed and with no response Lewis ordered the Art in, the Sergeant and three men took the downstairs, the rest went upstairs. The downstairs group swooped through the house screaming out: 'ARMED POLICE STAY WHERE YOU ARE.' Once the whole ground floor was declared clear Lewis and Deacon entered the building, the sound all clear was soon heard from upstairs as well so Lewis sent the ART officers back outside to keep watch, he then said to Deacon: 'Give SOCCO and Forensics the nod and get them down here I want this house torn apart.' Deacon carried out Lewis's request then they looked around without disturbing too much evidence but finding nothing useful they left the house. They replaced the door as best they could and Lewis asked the Sergeant to leave two armed officers there until SOCCO and Forensics arrived.

CHAPTER TWENTY FOUR

It was hot and humid when the expedition stopped for the night. The exertions of day three—the hardest so far, was taking its toll with thirst, hunger and the heat, plus the loss of two men was still on everybody's mind. There was a high point however when they stumbled across a small water hole that had been sheltered by a group of trees, however their spirits were soon dashed when they discovered it was virtually dried up but, there was a small clearing to the side of the pool which provided an ideal camp site so they set up camp. Marco and Miguel built a large fire while Thomas and his men collected as much water as they could in small billycans and goatskin pouches. The water was very cloudy in fact it was virtually liquid mud but Marco said Miguel would filter it and it would be fine to drink.

On their return from collecting the water they found Miguel preparing more grubs he had collected, Thomas complained that they had them the night before and although they tasted ok it wasn't something he wanted every night, Marco said he understood but that was all there was at the moment, Miguel added he had found different grubs which he would cut up and mix with special shoots and it would make a thick nourishing soup.

Simpson and Nick were watching Miguel crush the shoots between two rocks, he then went into the undergrowth but Thomas stopped him and asked: 'Hold it Pedro, where do you think you're going? Get your butt back here.' Marco pulling Thomas to one side told him: 'It is ok, he is only collecting leaves, go with him and see.' Thomas thought about it then said: 'Ok come on then Pedro.' Marco told Thomas to stop calling them "Pedro" Thomas just gave a shrug and headed off with Miguel.

After they had gone a little way into the undergrowth Thomas watched Miguel as he hacked down several tall bendy stalks that had large green leaves at the top. He chopped off about thirty of the largest leaves gathering as many as he could carry, he then looked at Thomas and said in broken English: 'You carry Senor?' Nodding with his head at the remaining leaves, Thomas grunted but bent down and grabbed an armful of the leaves thinking they were connected with his supper.

When they returned to camp, Thomas dropped the leaves in a pile and promptly sat himself down under a tree. Everyone except Thomas gathered around Miguel and watched as he laid the leaves out intertwining them in such a way they formed a dish like shape. He then cut long vines and attached them to the stalks of some of the leaves. Finally he tied the other end of the vines to a tripod over the fire. He had constructed the tripod out of three thick tree branches bound by thin vines at the top.

Meanwhile Marco began throwing grubs into the large dish adding water which he had filtered and then chopped up more leaves. He stirred them into the mix adding the remainder of the juice left over from the night before and then stirred it all together. Thomas's crew were amazed that no water leaked out of the makeshift dish, Marco said the meal would be ready in about half an hour so everyone sat down in whatever shade they could find and rested.

Periodically Miguel stirred the mixture, once it was beginning to boil he threw something else into the dish, Thomas wanted to know what it was, Marco told him that it was just seeds that would add flavour to the meal, Marco then asked who wanted some first; Nick volunteered and Marco poured some "soup" into his billycan and he took a sip, nodding he said: 'Yes very nice.' Simpson was next up, quickly followed by Thomas. Nick waited until Thomas had taken a couple of mouthfuls then suddenly dropped to his knees moaning out loud gripping his stomach. Thomas immediately dropped his dish and ran to the water container and drank a mouthful rinsing his mouth out. When he turned back he saw Nick holding his stomach not in pain though but in uncontrollable laughter, Simpson and the two Mexican's were also in tears laughing. Thomas caught on and had a look of thunder on his face and went for Nick but Simpson stopped him and said: 'Come on boss, where's your sense of humour?' Everyone was still laughing, Thomas just gave a smirk and walked over to the fire and refilled his billycan.

After they had all eaten Miguel went and fetched more water that had been filtering and made everyone a drink.

Once he had finished his supper Thomas headed for his sleeping bag, but found it hard to sleep with all the others talking round the camp fire, he yelled at them to shut up and with no one wishing to antagonise Thomas they all headed for their beds, except Marco who took first watch.

They set out the next day ultra early with the thought in their minds that it was the last day before they reached their destination. Marco was hoping to reach the other guides by mid afternoon and although the jungle was the worst they had encountered everything was going well. They had eaten the last of the soup for their breakfast washed down with the last dregs of the water, and they had all slept reasonably well so were in good spirits.

It was just past eleven o'clock when they stopped for a rest, there were fallen trees for them to sit on and they were only too glad to take their back packs off and rest their feet for a while. Marco suggested that he and Miguel venture out and find some food and he reluctantly gave Thomas a rifle saying they would be no more than half an hour.

Marco and Miguel set off and disappeared into the bushes, they hadn't gone far when they heard rustling in the undergrowth, Marco signalled with his hand saying Miguel should make his way around the back quietly to flush whatever it was out towards him.

Miguel moved around the bushes trying not to step on twigs or dry leaves that would spook their prey while Marco waited patiently, suddenly a loud wailing cry came from within the bushes, Marco stood up from his crouching position and called out to Miguel but his call was greeted with a loud cry which rang out through the jungle followed by a gunshot. Marco called out again but there was just silence so he turned and made his way quickly back to the others. Thomas and his crew had heard the cry and shot and they were stood on their feet. 'What was that noise Marco?' Simpson asked as soon as he appeared through the thicket. Marco told them what had happened and said he wanted a volunteer to go back with him to look for Miguel and Simpson said he would go. Marco told Thomas and Nick to be alert with their rifles ready to fire then he and Simpson headed to the spot Miguel disappeared from. They reached the area and Marco started hacking his way through it. They come out the other side and found a large pool of blood close to a large gap in some other bushes, they investigated further and saw that the blood continued on through the gap but then suddenly stopped. Marco knew there was no hope of getting his friend back, he told Simpson they should head back to the others.

As they were turning to go back Simpson spotted Miguel's rifle lying under an overhanging canopy of some trees, he stooped to pick up the rifle but stopped dead staring at a gap between two bushes. Marco looked and saw the top half of Miguel's body lying in pools of blood and there was a look of fear etched on the face. Marco was stunned into silence for a while then recovered slightly and told Simpson: 'I have never seen anything like this in my life, usually wild animals tear pieces off of their kill but Miguel has been torn clean in half.' Simpson nodded and said they needed to get back to the others, FAST!!

They ran back with the news and Thomas was the first to react, saying. Hell! 'Who's going to be next? I can't believe this is happening, we were meant to be getting rich not slaughtered.' Marco said: 'You were warned at the outset Senor that this is a dangerous place with ferocious animals and bandits, I am scared also Senor, I have never known this to happen before and I have been in the jungle many times. If you want my advice we should move on, it appears whatever is out there it is following us, the largest animal in this jungle is the panther but that wouldn't bite a man clean in half so I have no idea what is out there.'

Nick could see Marco was upset and offered his condolences for the loss of his man, Marco thanked Nick and said: 'You are very kind Senor, yes it is sad especially as Miguel was my friend WE grew up together.' He then fell silent so Nick ushered the others away and left Marco alone for a few minutes while they discussed the situation amongst themselves, then when Marco rejoined them they decided to carry on.

CHAPTER TWENTY FIVE

When they arrived at Chelsea Police headquarter, Clifford and Elaine were taken by a WPC Forbes to a large room with armchairs and a table. On a cabinet against the wall was a microwave and a kettle plus a coffee making machine. The WPC asked if they would like some coffee or tea, they both asked for tea but they were surprised when she left the room. Shortly she returned with a tray on which was a teapot with two cups and saucers plus milk, sugar and biscuits, she told them she made them fresh tea as this was just a rest room and there were only cheap teabags in the cabinet. She told them to enjoy their tea and said she would wait outside, she added that when they were ready she would take them to the officer's washrooms where they could have a nice refreshing shower and put on clean clothes.

This was music to their ears and they thanked her. They soon finished their tea and Clifford stood up and opened the door telling the WPC they were ready. She led them to the washrooms where she asked Elaine if she could speak to her quietly. Elaine nodded and The WPC diplomatically asked her if the kidnappers had harmed her in any way, because if they had it would be wise for Elaine not to shower just yet. Elaine looked at the WPC and assured her she had not been harmed, the WPC smiled and said she would be back in half an hour.

In their respective changing rooms were clean towels and white robes. They stayed under the soothing and hot refreshing water for sometime washing the last few days down the drain. Finished they each dried themselves off and donned their robes. WPC Forbes had left them a selection of clothes to choose from, Elaine chose a pair of black slacks and a red tee shirt and Clifford chose a white sweatshirt and black joggers, they also had trainer style shoes to wear.

Once they were dressed they sat on a padded bench in the passageway outside the washroom until the WPC returned, she led them back to the rest room and said: 'I imagine you are both hungry.' Clifford and Elaine said they were starving. The WPC said that there was Shepherd's pie followed by apple crumble they both said eagerly that sounded wonderful so the WPC went to fetch the meals.

Just after thirty minutes she returned with their food on a tray, a male Police officer followed with two dishes of apple crumble and a jug of cream. They placed the food on the table and the WPC wished them both bon-apatite and left. Elaine looked at her meal and glanced at Clifford, he looked at her and they both gave a little grin.

They demolished their meals in double quick time then sat back in their chairs not speaking for a while. After a few moments Clifford who was looking straight ahead of him said: 'Do you know Elainc you stuffed that down your gullet as if you haven't eaten for days.' She took the cushion from behind her and threw it at him.

About fifteen minutes later the door opened and DCI Deacon walked in, Deacon said hello to Clifford then turned towards Elaine and said: 'I assume you are Mrs Jessop, I haven't had the pleasure.' Elaine shook hands with Deacon and said: 'Please you must call me Elaine.' She then asked: 'Have you got them, the kidnappers?' Deacon replied: 'No I'm sorry we haven't they were gone I'm afraid, we found the front door smashed down and the place was empty, SOCCO are there now tearing the place apart. I've just come to tell you DCS Lewis will be down shortly, he thought you would prefer to talk here rather than in his office, they said they would prefer that. Deacon acknowledged them and said he would see them later and left the room.

Five minutes later Lewis knocked the door and entered the room, smiling he said: 'Hello again you two, I take it the DCI has brought you up to speed. He sat down then said: 'I have to tell you it was such a relief when I heard you were both free and unharmed but, I do think you should get that head seen to Clifford.' Elaine couldn't resist quipping: 'I have been telling him for some time now he should get his head seen to.' Lewis laughed and remarked again how good it was that they still had some spirit left. Elaine said it was their spirit that got them through it all. Lewis added: 'I'm sure it was. Now if you are up to answering a few questions for me we can then get you both back home?' They both nodded with a large grin, so he asked: 'Ok, firstly then Mrs Jessop, can you run me through your abduction? Before you say anything though would you mind if I record this?' Elaine said she didn't mind then answered Lewis's question running through Tuesdays events from the time she left work, Clifford squeezed her hand reassuring her each time she faltered at the memory of what happened.

Lewis waited till Elaine had finished, he told her she had been very brave and wise not to have antagonise her kidnappers too much. He then asked Clifford: 'Ok Clifford can you give me an account of your kidnapping?' It was now Elaine's turn to squeeze her husband's hand as Clifford began his account: "Well as soon as I dropped the ransom money off, I returned to my car and immediately drove back down the road, I was almost at the end when I saw a bright glow from the area of the sports centre in my mirror but, when I turned back to the front again I was blinded by a car's headlights coming right at me. I stamped on my brakes and as soon as the car had screeched to a halt, the driver's door was yanked open and I was dragged out by a guy wearing a hood, he was pointing a gun at me and told me not to try anything and I recognised the voice, it was Thomas. Seconds later my legs were tied with cable ties by another man then I was physically forced onto the rear seat face down and my hands were tied behind be, again using cable ties and I was ordered to keep quiet.

Clifford went on telling his story Lewis just sat nodding his head occasionally but saying nothing. At the end Lewis paused then said: 'Well that is some story, you two certainly don't do things by half do you? Ok, now if you don't mind we'd like to get our sketch artist in here and ask you both to help with a sketch of the two men at the house? Afterwards we will take you to your apartment and you can grab some things, then we will take you to a safe house until we apprehend these two men.' They agreed and Lewis using his mobile called the sketch artist and asked him to go to the restroom.

The sketch artist arrived after ten minutes and they commenced describing Palmer and Bird to him. After they had finished Clifford and Elaine were in agreement that they would rather go back to their own apartment, they said their own security would be on full alert so they were sure they would be safe. Lewis replied: 'Well that is your prerogative of course although I don't recommend it, but If we go along with it I insist we put a couple of plain clothes boys in the foyer, and station some men in cars around the clock outside the apartment building. I would also like the tech boys to come back in, as the kidnappers may get in touch.' They agreed to Lewis's terms and he wished them luck then he rang the car pool to have an unmarked car take them back to their apartment.

CHAPTER TWENTY SIX

Bird and Palmer were on their way back to the house when Palmer suddenly stopped and said: No! 'We're not going back to the house, I've just thought, if that pair gets to the cops they are coming straight here aren't they?. Bird agreed so they turned around and walked back to the road, at the bottom Palmer turned left, Bird followed but after going a few yards he asked Palmer: 'Why are we going this way, town is in the other direction.' Palmer told him that if they went that way the Police would probably see them when they come to the house, he said it would be best to go that way and try and thumb a lift. Bird asked how he intended doing that as no one would stop in the dark to pick them up. Palmer waved the gun in Bird's face and said: 'Maybe but this is a good persuader don't you think? I am sure we will get lucky.'

They walked for over ten minutes but not a single car came along from either direction. They walked a little further and came to a left hand bend and just up the road on the left they could see a light coming from an upstairs window of a house. Palmer pulled Birds arm to stop him and whispered: 'Come on and keep low.' Palmer told Bird they were going to the house, Bird asked why but Palmer just said: 'You'll see, now shut up and follow me.'

As they drew closer they crouched down behind a tall hedge at the side of the house, Palmer peeped around the hedge and saw there was a white early model Audi car parked in the drive. He told Bird to "stay put" and crept up to the car to see if the keys were in the ignition, they weren't so he tried the door but it was locked, he then peered through the letter box of the house and spied some keys on the hall table, plus a phone.

He went back to Bird and said: 'Right our ride is waiting for us all we have to do is collect it.' Bird asked what they were going to do. Palmer replied: 'We'll just knock the door saying we have broken down and need to use the phone, then while I keep them busy pretending to make a call you grab the keys, we will then leave and wait a few minutes before we snatch the car."

Bird agreed it was a good plan but was very apprehensive, Palmer told him to stop acting like a fairy and follow his lead.

When they knocked the door a well dressed lady answered. Palmer spilled out his story about their car breaking down and asked to use the phone. At first the woman was unsure but pretending her husband was in the lounge watching TV she let them in. She pointed to the phone on the hall table and Bird lifted the receiver and pretended to dial a number while Palmer kept the woman busy talking to her.

Bird pretended to talk to someone on the phone while sneaking the keys into his pocket but, he wasn't quick enough, the woman spotted him and Palmer realised and grabbed her arm pulling her to him before she had time to react. He had taken his gun out and warned her to stay quiet or he would shoot her and then her husband, she obeyed and he told her well done and to slowly and quietly make her way to the front door and the car.

As they made their way out Palmer told Bird to get in the driving seat. Bird however informed Palmer he couldn't drive, Palmer sighed loudly and told the woman she was driving and pushed her into the driver's seat, without waiting for Bird to shut his door Palmer told the woman to drive off and hit the gas. He told her to drive slowly back to town keeping to the back roads where they were less likely to be spotted, on the way they were forced to pull into a petrol station to top the Audi up as it was running low on fuel, they also took the opportunity to buy a few provisions using what little money they had left from what Thomas had left them. Palmer was very cautious though and gave the woman the money and made her go in so he or Bird wouldn't be caught on the CCTC cameras warning her not to do anything stupid or he would hurt her.

The woman returned with a plastic bag, she got into the car and Palmer told her to give him the bag he then told her to start the car and get out of the garage as soon as she could in case someone came in and recognised them.

As soon as they were on their way Palmer ordered the woman to head for town and to keep to the speed limit so not to draw attention to them.

Once in town they made their way to the rear of the police car park entrance stopping just short of it. Palmer told the woman to go there because he was sure the Jessop's would be taken there eventually.

'What exactly is your plan, apart from getting us thrown in jail that is?' Bird asked Palmer.

'Oh you of little faith, we my friend we will wait here until that couple are brought back, which they will because they'll want to question them before they take them home.' Bird didn't respond to Palmer's sarcasm, instead he said: 'Well if we are to wait here for God knows how long then we may as well have some food and drink.'

'Ok, I'll go for that.' Palmer said and opened the bag; he took out the water bottle and removed the cap and began waving the bottle about, he then asked: 'Ok who wants a little "drink" then?' Bird put his hand out to take the bottle but Palmer ignored him and put the bottle to his mouth and took a large swig himself. Bird unclipped his seatbelt and leant over the seats, he angrily tried to snatch the bottle from Palmer's hand but it was sparkling water so it fizzed up and spouted out of the bottle into Palmer's face and lap.

The woman was scared but managed to tell bird that there were some tissues in the glove compartment, Palmer ordered Bird to give him some tissues and Bird threw the box at him, Palmer wiped his lap and face then drank some of the remaining water, again Bird held out his hand for the bottle but Palmer threw the tissue box instead. Bird responded: 'Very funny, the bottle man, give me the damned bottle.' Palmer looking at him and with a sly grin placed the open bottle on the floor between his feet, he then said to Bird: 'Did your mother not teach you to say please and thank you?'

'Give me the damned bottle.' Bird demanded once more, Palmer grinned then threw the bottle at him spilling the rest of the water over his lap and on to the floor.

Bird resisted reacting and sat staring straight ahead, fuming. Palmer then took a mobile from his pocket and gave it to the woman, he told her to call her husband and tell him she had been kidnapped by the Jessop's kidnappers and to inform the Chief Constable. She did what Palmer ordered and he snatched the mobile back.

Over an hour later, as Palmer had predicted the Jessop's car arrived and they were ushered through the rear door, Bird enquired: 'Ok clever dick, what now?' Palmer didn't answer he just kept watching.

About three hours later they saw a movement in the shadows at the rear entrance. They watched as a man in plain clothes came out and walked to the car park, a minute later an unmarked car drove up to the station door then three people emerge from inside, two men and a woman. Palmer kept watching as one of the men walked to the car and opened the rear door and the man and woman climbed in, then the man then went around to the near side passenger door and got in. Palmer was gloating saying: 'I told yer Birdie that has to be them, start the engine woman but keep your head down I think we're in business.'

The woman complied then Palmer and Bird ducked down below the dashboard until the car had pulled out, Palmer though kept his head just high enough to watch the car.

Palmer had heard the woman say her name was Joanne when she made the call to her husband, he said: 'Right

Joanne follow the car but keep your distance and don't be stupid and try something to attract their attention.'

When the unmarked car arrived at the apartment building the driver drove down into the underground car park. The officers escorted Clifford and Elaine to the car park lift, Clifford said he would have to collect the apartment keys from security in the foyer. When they reached the foyer Clifford said hello to the security guy and asked for the keys. The guard said he was pleased to see them and that they were alright and handed Clifford the keys. Clifford informed him that the two plain clothes officers with them would be posted in the foyer and asked the guard to look after them, which he said he would be happy to do. Clifford also informed him there would be other officers in two unmarked cars watching outside. Clifford thanked the guard and the two officers said they would escort Clifford and Elaine to their apartment and check it out to make sure it was safe before they went in.

They reached the penthouse floor and one of the officers took the keys from Clifford and opened the door, they looked all around the apartment and said that it was clear. The officer handed Clifford the keys and said: 'Welcome home.' Elaine and Clifford thanked the officers and bid them good night, the officers said they would be in the foyer if they needed them.

Clifford closed the door and Elaine plonked herself down on their sofa and gave out a gigantic sigh. Clifford joined her and they sat in silence looking around. Clifford broke the silence by reaching out to hug Elaine and saying: 'I love you Elaine. I couldn't live without you.' And taking her by the hand led her to the bedroom.

After Lewis had de-briefed the Jessop's he and Deacon returned to their respective offices, Lewis slumped in his chair and called a constable and asked him to fetch a hot strong coffee. He commenced reading his E-Mails, one was from SOCCO saying they found several DNA samples and finger prints from the kidnapper's house but there was only one DNA match and two finger print matches on the data base. The DNA and one set of prints were from Palmer and the other prints were from Thomas.

Palmer's prints were from his past criminal records when he had been arrested for robbery with menaces and actual bodily harm, he and Thomas had done time together and that was how they met.

Lewis was reading the rest of his mail when his phone rang; it was Chief Constable Price he said: 'Hello Andrew, I'm sorry for the lateness of the call but we have a problem, we need to get the Jessop's to a safe house immediately. We have some reliable information that suggests the kidnappers may attempt to retake them. A woman—Joanne Woods—has been abducted from her house less than a quarter of a mile from the house they were held. She was taken just prior to your arrival at the kidnap house and her car—a white Audi—is also missing. Later she called her husband from an unregistered mobile phone, saying she had been taken by the Jessop's kidnappers, they sent the message for me, taunting us that they had her. I advise you to use safe house "Number Four" it's the lesser known and nicely tucked away.

CHAPTER TWENTY SEVEN

In the jungle, it was half past two when the diminished party finally set off on what should have been their last day before reaching their meeting place. Marco had said it would be best if they carried on until it was too dark to continue, so they could get as many miles under their belt as possible. Thomas and crew agreed but with reservations, they were concerned that the dark would make it easier for whatever it was out there to attack them. Marco reassured them that most jungle animals didn't hunt at night and they could make torches out of dry branches which should keep all the animals away.

This appeased the men so they plodded on through the dense under growth sticking as close together as possible. Unfortunately after an hour the sky clouded over and rain threatened so Marco was forced to call an end to the day.

They set up camp and Marco said he would go to find something for supper and collect some fire wood, surprisingly he asked Thomas to accompany him. Thomas eagerly grabbed a rifle and followed Marco.The cautiously and quietly edged their way through the undergrowth, it wasn't long however before they heard rustling in some bushes;Thomas stopped and held back aiming his rifle, but Marco reassured him saying that the bush was too small to conceal whatever had attacked their men. Thomas was relieved and Marco suggested he quietly make his way around the back of the bush and flush whatever it was out. Once Thomas had reached the other side he started bashing the bush with his rifle butt. Marco watched holding his rifle in readiness, it didn't take long though to flash the creature out which happened to be a large fat wild bird similar to a turkey.

Marco downed it with one shot, he called out to Thomas to come back and He was pleased to see it was not a snake and said: 'Nice one Marco, one drumstick is mine.'

On their way back to camp they collected enough firewood to keep the fire going all night, back at camp they discovered that Simpson and Nick had collected water from a small stream that ran close to their camp; they had also collected wood and already started a fire. Marco remarked: 'We will make jungle experts out of you all yet Senor's.'Thomas replied: 'Not me Marco, I won't be going anywhere near a jungle again, I can promise you.' His men nodded in agreement then Marco held up his prize and said: 'Good tasty meat tonight Senor's.'

Marco commenced preparing the bird he plucked and cleaned it then pushed a stick though the carcass, next he placed each end of the stick in the "V" of two sticks he had pushed into the ground on each side of the fire.

In the meantime Nick had poured water into four billycans after it had finished filtering and handed them around.

While the bird was cooking they all sat around the fire drinking while contemplating recent events, during which Thomas amazed everyone by saying: 'Marco; I'm sorry for Miguel dying like that, I know he was your friend. Do you think we are safe now?' Nick and Simpson gave each other a shocked look but said nothing. Marco though thanked Thomas for his kind words and added: 'I wish I could say yes Senor, but if I am honest I can't, I have no idea what could be out there but it does seem to have been following us. Tomorrow though is our last day so fingers crossed we will have no more trouble.' Thomas tapped Marco on his shoulder and said: 'I hope you're right pal I really do.'

Everyone was silent for a few minutes then Marco suggested they should prepare their beds, making them from dry spongy grass and large leaves.

Once the bird was cooked Marco broke it up into portions, he gave Thomas his leg as promised then ripped the other leg off and held it above his head and asked who wanted it. Simpson and Nick rushed over but Simpson won the race and took the leg from Marco then went back and sat next to Thomas, Marco gave Nick a large portion of breast meat as compensation and they all chomped happily through their supper until they had picked the bones clean.

That night they all slept soundly and fortunately the rain stayed away but it made the humidity more intense.

When morning came Marco raised everyone early, they had some coffee but there was nothing left to eat, Marco said he would try to find something on the trail, so as soon as they were packed up and had put the fire out, they set off.

The sun was almost up and it was clear that it was going to be a hot day. Two hours into their walk Thomas began complaining about the heat and that he was hungry. Marco asked if Nick and Simpson felt the same, they told him they were ok but if he was going to find some food then they would not turn it down. Marco assured them that as soon as they find a suitable spot they would rest for a while.

It wasn't long after the trail took them to a large clearing, Marco stopped and threw off his kit and Thomas and co followed suit. Marco again asked Thomas to accompany him while he looked for something to eat, warning the others to remain alert.

The two men set off and ventured into the thinning undergrowth while Nick and Simpson prepared a fire. Thomas was alongside Marco when they heard noises coming from behind a bunch of small trees at the bottom of which grew thick spiky bushes. Marco whispered to Thomas: 'You stay here and keep watch; I will go and flush out whatever it is towards you.' Thomas looked concerned but agreed.

Marco crept through the bushes making his way around the thicket. All was quiet for a while but then Thomas heard shouting and gunshots and he froze on the spot, more shots rang out then just as suddenly all went quiet. Nick and Simpson heard the shots and Nick remarked: 'That was too many shots just to kill an animal, come on.' Nick pulled Simpson by the arm and grabbed a rifle, they rushed towards the direction of the shots and saw Thomas glued to the spot visibly shaking. 'What the hell is going on?' Nick asked. Thomas mouthed the words: 'I don't know.' Suddenly Marco appeared half walking and half falling before collapsing to the ground in front of them. There were several bullet wounds in his chest and stomach with blood pouring from them and his rifle was missing. Nick dropped to his knees and cradled Marco's head and asked what happened and Marco could only burble to Nick to put his ear closer to his mouth then whispered: 'Bandits Senor, I shot one and wound . . . . His voice then faded away and they knew he had gone. "Bandits he said bandits." Simpson blurted out. This brought Thomas back down to earth, he turned and ran the other two decided that he was right and quickly followed.

They returned to the clearing and Thomas grabbed his kit then turned to the others and said: 'Let's get out of here fast.' Nick said to Simpson: 'It's not often I agree with him but he's right, grab your gear and let's get out of here.' They hurriedly threw their kit bags on their backs, grabbed what rifles were left and set off then Thomas stopped and said: 'Hang on which way do we go.' Nick said: 'Shit that's right, which way?' Simpson remembered Marco had a compass in his kit and said: 'I know, he told me he was heading west all the time, we have to get that compass from his bag.'

Obviously there were no immediate volunteers so Thomas said they should all go, the other two agreed and they headed back to the gruesome scene. Nick said he would get the bag but they had to cover him, with this agreed he dashed over and grabbed the straps of the bag and ran back quickly to the others, they all turned quickly heading back the way they had come trying not to make too much noise.

When they were far enough away they stopped to rest, Thomas retrieved the compass from Marco's bag, there was also a map with the route marked out plus other odds and ends such as gloves, a small phial of snake antivenin and a sharp knife, and much to Thomas's joy a hand gun. The other items he showed to Nick and Simpson but the gun he kept to himself craftily sneaking it into his pocket. He took the antivenin and gloves and put them in his bag, the map and route he put into his coat pocket. Afterwards he stood up and announced: 'Ok as we have lost all our guides I am taking control, if either of you have a problem with that then tough, now grab your gear and let's go.'

Thomas looked at the compass and started walking, after nearly seven hours of walking, tripping, falling and being bitten by insects they finally broke free of the jungle and emerged into a vast green valley. There was a fast river roaring below the valley, it flowed off to the right and ahead of them were trees and several pools of water at the foot of a hill. Thomas threw his kitbag to the ground and dashed to one of the pools, Simpson and Nick quickly joined him diving into the water. They wallowed for ten or so minutes then one by one they climbed out. After they sat for awhile they went to one of the other pools and drunk some of the cool clear water before filling their containers.

Unbeknown to them just over the brow of the hill was their meeting place. The name of their next head guide was Hector and he was watching them through his binoculars; he was mystified as to why the party was so small. Nick asked Thomas: 'Which way do we go now?' Thomas took the map and route from his pocket, he laid them out on the grass and studied them, he looked up the hill and finally he said: "Up there."

Hector watched for a while then decided he was going down to meet them he got to his feet and called for three men to go with him. Taking guns with them as a precaution they went to the corral to saddle their horses. Hector rode off down the hill, his men close behind. Thomas was just about to put his arms through the straps of his kitbag when he spotted the riders coming down the hill, he yelled: "Shit bandits." The others looked up, seeing the men on horseback they made a run for it but the riders raced after them encircling them with rifles drawn. Simpson was trembling with fear, thinking he was going to meet the same fate as Marco, he said with a tremor in his voice: 'LOOK WE HAVE NO MONEY, WE ARE BRITISH .... Hector stopped him saying: 'It is ok Senor we are not bandits, you are the Englishmen who wish to find the lost city, yes?' Thomas replied: 'Yes—yes we are—thank God we thought we were finished you sure are a sight for sore eyes, isn't he lads?' The other two just nodded. Thomas put his hand on his chest and said: 'I'm Thomas so you can put those guns away now.' The men ignored Thomas, Hector dismounted and handed the reins of his horse to one of the riders then asked: 'Where are my compatriots Senor's, I don't see them with you.' Thomas knew by the man's tone he wasn't happy and the explanation referring to the animal and the bandits would sound lame, however he tried to explain and Nick and Simpson chipped in every now and again. They told

Hector what had occurred throughout their horrendous journey, after listening to the men's accounts of the deaths he spoke in Mexican to his men, he then remounted his horse and he set off up the hill telling his men to follow with the Englishmen.

CHAPTER TWENTY EIGHT

By the time they had reached the top of the hill, the three men were near collapse through sheer exhaustion, the riders guided them to the front of a large wooden hut. Hector dismounted and told the three men to sit on the ground and not to move, the other two men had dismounted and stood facing them still pointing their guns. Hector went into the hut then emerged with two other men. They went over to Thomas and lifted him by his arms, they turned him around and Hector tied his hands behind him with a thin leather strap. Thomas was protesting and struggling throughout all this, he shouted angrily: 'WHAT the hell are you doing, I'm paying you lot, what's this all about?' Hector just turned around and walked back into the hut and his men followed virtually dragging Thomas with them. Nick and Simpson were each treated in much the same manner but were taken to separate areas.

Thomas was roughly sat on a long wooden bench, Hector sat opposite at a long wooden table which separated them. Hector removed his cowboy style hat and placed it on the table, Thomas continued to protest swearing and cursing but he was ignored. After a minute of silence Hector asked calmly: 'Now once more Senor, where are my friends?' Thomas once again gave his account of how Hector's friends and John lost their lives to what appeared to be a ferocious mysterious animal and how Marco had died. Hector was still not convinced, he said to Thomas: 'Now Senor this puts me in a very difficult dilemma. If I believe you and consent to take you on to the lost city, how do I know the same fate will not befall me and my men? The driver that brought the truck back with your equipment has told us how you behaved towards my compatriots, you must see the position I am in.' Thomas appealed to Hector saying: 'I promise you I am telling the truth.' Hector then informed Thomas that while they had been talking his men had also been answering questions, and depending on their answers he would consider continue with the expedition to the lost city or call the authorities and have them all arrested.

Thomas made a last ditch attempt to profess his and his men's innocence but Hector just raised his hand to silence him and walked out of the hut.

Outside Hector gathered his men who had been talking to Nick and Simpson and compared their story's, he then told one of his men to bring Thomas out. Thomas was brought from the hut over to where Nick and Simpson were sitting on the ground, seeing his men still tied up he began to struggle but he was forcibly pushed to the ground to join them. Hector stood looking at them and then crouched down and said: 'Ok Senor's I have made my decision, based on what you men have said and reluctantly

I am inclined to believe your stories, two of my own men say there has been a tale of a large creature that has taken sheep and goats whole leaving only fragments of their bodies behind, they say goat herders have also been taken and a half of a human body was discovered in a state as you described so, I have decided to take you on to the lost city but I must warn you Senor's, I am in control of my men and I will not tolerate any interference, also we will only take you as far as the outskirts of the city, my men will not venture any nearer because they believe in the curse, Is this understood.' Thomas and his men nodded and Hector walked away telling his men to remove the men's bonds.

Hector had not walked far when he turned back and said: 'You will find food and drink in the other hut Senor's, eat well and then get some sleep, we leave early in the morning.'

After they had eaten Thomas and his men were shown into a bunkhouse. Some men were already in bed asleep. They were shown to the far end of the room where there were empty bunks. Nick jumped on the bottom of the nearest bunk, Simpson climbed onto one of the others on the other side of the room while Thomas took the bunk above Nick.

They soon fell asleep, at dawn Hector went into the bunkhouse and clapping his hands shouted for everyone to get up. Thomas growled at him saying it was still the middle of the night, Simpson too began giving Hector a mouthful of abuse for waking him. Hector just said: 'Ok Senor's I am happy to call the expedition off, go back to sleep gentlemen.' Hector turned to leave the bunkhouse but Thomas was off his bunk and stood in his underpants shouting after Hector, much to the amusement of Hectors men. Thomas quickly realised and pulled his trousers on he ran out of the hut after Hector, shouting at his own men to get dressed.

He finally caught up with Hector as he was about to enter the hut where breakfast was being served. Thomas apologised for his and his men's outburst, Hector didn't react he just told Thomas to go and fetch his men before all the food was gone, Thomas informed him that his men were on their way and followed him into the hut

Thomas returned to the bunkhouse after he had eaten his breakfast which consisted of bacon and eggs and strong bitter coffee. Nick and Simpson were only just coming out of the hut, Thomas told them to get a move on as he wanted to get moving telling them they had treasure to find. Nick was furious Thomas had not come back for them before he ate, Thomas just said: 'Well you should get up in the mornings.'

Once breakfast was over Hector gathered his men together and called Thomas to tell him that he and his men were ready to set off. The three men joined their guides. One guide gave them each a kitbag saying they contained light rainwear as the area they were heading for was very damp and humid, he also handed them insect repellent and told them to smother it thickly on their faces, necks and hands, he also advised them to wear their hats saying that the insects were large and their sting can be very toxic. Before they set off Thomas wanted to know where their weapons were. Hector advised him that his men would refuse to move if they had weapons. Thomas as usual protested saying there were animals and God knows what out there and they should be able to protect themselves. Hector apologised and said: 'The situation is out of my control Senor, so if you wish to continue then we should get under way as we are wasting time. Thomas seeing they had no option other than to agree reluctantly complied.

Hector took the lead with three guides with Thomas and crew following them. Six bearers carrying all the necessary equipment for sleeping, eating, cooking etcetera came next followed by four more guides who brought up the rear.

Apart from the usual complications of insects and rough ground the first day went well. The light was fading when they came upon an ideal place to set camp. The bearers and guides took care of everything including preparing everyone's sleeping arrangements and at last the three men had proper food. Their evening meal consisted of fish and potato's followed by freshly brewed coffee.

Tired and well fed Thomas, Nick and Simpson retired to beds. They were over the moon at having their own tents with sleeping bags and not having to sleep out in the elements. Next morning the three men were among the first up, Hector was stoking the fire and greeted the men with a good morning, Thomas just grunted but Nick and Simpson said hello and said they had slept well. After breakfasting on hot porridge and coffee they set off on what was to be another uneventful day. The camp was not as comfortable on the second night as the ground was more uneven but they were happy to be a day closer to the lost city.

The sun was already bearing down when everyone got up the next morning and it was apparent it was going to be the hardest day by far. Breakfast was quickly eaten and with the fire extinguished they made their way into the thick undergrowth to find the lost city.

They had a hard solid days trekking ahead of them, their guides hacked at the vegetation trying to make a path for them to walk through, they continually stumbled, spiders and snakes appeared hanging from the branches and leeches stuck to their necks and faces. They were all soon tired, their throats parched from lack of fluids and their arms ached from continually having to beat the mosquitoes away from their faces but, however they continued to battle their way through the jungle with the thought of being rich spurring them on.

The sun was unforgiving beating down tiring them out and they needed to keep stopping to catch their breath. Although they were wearing hats their heads still felt near to boiling point because of the intense heat and humidity. Hector could see they were struggling so when they reached a small shady area he stopped so they could rest and take on fluids. They each had canteens of water and after drinking some they poured a little over their heads to cool them, Hector warned them to conserve some of the water as they would need some later, he knew there would be plenty throughout the journey with running springs from the high mountains but, wanted to play safe just in case of any problems.

While they were all resting one of the bearers screamed making them all jump. Hector went and investigated, he discovered that while the man was drinking, a red, yellow and black striped snake fell out of the tree onto him, startled the man had jumped up and the snake had bitten him. Hector shot the snake then took some antivenin from his bag and administered it to the man as quickly as he could. Thomas and the other men stood watching while the man slowly recovered. Hector made his man comfortable then took Thomas's arm and led him to one side, explaining the bearer would be unable to continue on the trip and would have to go back to camp, he said he would be sending another man back with him. Thomas was visibly shaken by Hector's words and even more so when Hector explained they would have to share out the bearers load which would mean they would all have to carry extra items, Thomas looked at Nick and Simpson then looked at Hector in disgust and walked off.

After an hour the man was showing improvement so Hector instructed one of his men to take him back to camp and started to share out the man's load amongst his and Thomas's men. Once this was completed Hector apologised to the men for making them carry extra items and said they should make a move.

Much of the day had now been wasted so they continued hacking their way through the jungle until it was dusk, constantly getting bitten and attacked by insects. When the light became too dim to carry on safely Hector halted the party. They set up camp in a small clearing it was too small for tents so hammocks were erected between the trees. Supper consisted of dried beef and potatoes with special bread produced by the cooks back at the base.

Over breakfast an argument broke out between Thomas's and Simpson about who was going to carry the heavier load, Thomas reckoned that Simpson and nick should carry the most as he was the leader and should have the lighter pack, Hector interrupted saying they should save their strength for the hike ahead of them. Nick and Simpson gave Thomas a sly grin and walked away.

The rest of breakfast was eaten in silence until Hector gave the signal and they all got to their feet once more.

CHAPTER TWENTY NINE

Clifford and Elaine had just gone to their bedroom when their door bell rang. Elaine looked at Clifford and said: 'who can that be?' Without answering Clifford went to the door and peered through the spy hole, seeing Lewis and Deacon standing there he opened the door. Clifford asked Lewis what they were doing there, Lewis said: 'We are here to take you to a safe house, and this time we must insist. He explained the situation then said: 'If you would like to gather some items to take with you we will get going.' Lewis had arranged for plain clothed officers in unmarked cars to watch the area around the apartment building and for Armed Response to follow at a distance.

When the Jessop's were ready Lewis led them to the lift and they went down to the car park. Lewis looked cautiously around to see if the white Audi was present, satisfied there was no danger he called the Jessop's and Deacon out of the lift. They all got into a car and Lewis drove them out and onto the main road and headed for the safe house.

Earlier when the Jessop's were taken into their apartment Palmer told Joanne to continue on up the road and then take a right into a side road, then to go right again into a service alley behind a row of shops and businesses. He made her stop just inside the alley and pull right over to the left and switch the engine off. She thought they were about to kill her and started begging for her life, Palmer told her to shut up and stay in the car while he got out and walked off up the alley into the darkness. Joanne asked Bird to let her go before he came back, Bird said: 'No, I'm sorry Joanne but it would be useless because even if you get away tonight Palmer would find you and kill you for escaping.'

He had just finished talking when there was a sound of an engine, a moment later there was a knock on the window, Bird looked up and Palmer was standing alongside an old black mini bus. Bird opened the door and got out, Palmer said: 'Get everything out of the car and put it in the minibus, make sure you leave no evidence then lock the car and throw the keys away. Bird did as he was told and Palmer told the woman to get in the driver's seat of the minibus, she protested that she wouldn't be able to drive such a big vehicle but Palmer told her to stop winging and get on with it. Joanne saw that the window in driver's door was smashed and glass was all over the driver's seat so she knew he had stolen the vehicle. Joanne brushed away as much glass as she could and climbed in, Palmer climbed in behind her and Bird got in the front passenger seat. Palmer told Joanne to drive out into the main road and follow his instructions, telling her to turn right and to stop in the shadows of a low hanging tree.

Palmer knew that when the Police drove the Jessop's to the safe house they would have to pass the minibus, the lead car contained the Jessop's and they were followed by three unmarked cars, Palmer had suspected that would be the case and waited. When he was sure it was safe he told Joanne to pull out slowly and follow the last car, little did he know though, one car was a little further behind and saw them pull out. The officer instantly radioed the information to all the other units giving the vehicles details. Palmer didn't realised they had been spotted and continued to follow at a distance.

After about a mile Palmer told Joanne to take a right, the following car stopped and watched them disappear into the distance then radioed to confirm that the threat was gone.

When the car with the Jessop's aboard arrived outside the safe house Lewis told them to stay in the car and keep their heads down. He and Deacon approached the house on foot and Lewis unlocked the door. They went in and using their torches they looked around, the house was safe so Lewis sent Deacon back out to fetch the Jessop's. Lewis had put the lights on in the hallway and switched the heating on.

When Elaine and Clifford came in Lewis took them upstairs to one of the double rooms so they could unpack, he told them not to leave the house under any circumstances and there would be three officers downstairs at all times. He also said the fridge was stacked and there was plenty of coffee, tea and groceries in the cupboards. Advising them not to use any phones, he bid them goodnight.

Lewis and Deacon left the house and headed back to Chelsea but not before instructing all units to survey from a distance and to contact him the minute anything suspicious occurred.

The minibus had arrived in the area ten minutes before, Palmer knew where the safe house was because there was a number preset in his Mobile which Thomas had given him, Thomas told him only to use it in an emergency, he decided this to be an emergency so he had called the number and after giving a prearranged code he obtained the details of the safe house.

As they approached the house Palmer told Joanne to turn the lights off and go slowly into the drive, he then told her to turn around facing the road and leave the engine running. He got out and walked up to the front of the house and looked all around, seeing no lights on he went around the left hand side of the house to the back garden. There was a path at the side of the house to a wooden gate, he opened it and went into the garden. He saw just the one light on upstairs and one downstairs in the lounge. The lounge curtains were open so he peered through the window and saw the three officers watching TV but the Jessop's weren't to be seen convincing Palmer that the Jessop's were upstairs.

He went to the back door and found it consisted of half glass and half wood. Using his elbow he broke the window and waited in case someone heard and came to see. He then reached in and turned the key, muttering to himself "Stupid pigs, this is too easy."

He opened the door and ventured inside the kitchen ensuring he avoided walking on the broken glass. He had a small torch with him and shone it around making sure the beam was not shining too far ahead that it would attract attention. Satisfied it was clear he went out into the hall, taking his gun out he began climbing the stairs, half way up he stood on a squeaky stair, he stopped frozen to the spot expecting to be discovered.

Clifford had heard the noise, he put his finger to his lips to tell Elaine to be quiet and whispered in her ear: 'Did you he hear that, you stepped on that stair on the way up, quick get under the bed. He looked around quickly for something to use as a weapon, there was an ornamental lamp on the bedside table so he grabbed that, he then rolled the pillows up and stuffed them under the duvet to make it appear they were in bed

On the same wall as the door there was a walk in wardrobe with sliding doors, Clifford removed the light bulb from the ceiling light and climbed in the wardrobe leaving the door slightly open.

Palmer was relieved thinking nobody had heard the stair and continued on up to the landing. There were four rooms upstairs and Palmer tried to remember which room had the light on. Closing his eyes he retraced his steps and eventually located the correct room. Nervously he slowly turned the door handle, he pushed the door open and saw the light was off, he thought for a moment he had picked the wrong room but saw shapes in the bed where Clifford had put the pillows to fool him.

Cautiously he pushed the door open wider and stepped inside the room and crept towards the bed, on seeing Palmer; Clifford came out of the wardrobe as quietly as possible. Elaine was watching terrified from under the bed trying to breathe as quietly as she could so as not to give the game away.

When Clifford was within range he brought the lamp down hard onto the back of Palmer's head, he fell instantly to the floor seemingly unconscious. Elaine screamed and scrambled out from under the bed, Clifford told Elaine to put the bulb back in the main light, meanwhile he had picked up Palmer's gun and stood pointing it at him.

Elaine stood on the bed to replace the bulb, this distracted Clifford for a second and Palmer who wasn't actually knocked out leapt up and rushed him. They tussled for the gun and it went off and the bullet embedded itself into the pillow on which Elaine would have been sleeping.

They continued struggling but in the end Palmer managed to wrench the gun from Clifford, he pointed the gun at Clifford saying: 'I ought to shoot you where you stand but I need you both, now sit on the bed and you lady, do likewise.' Elaine who was unscathed pulled herself up and went to the bed and sat next to Clifford.

Palmer took the cords from their dressing gowns to tie the couple up, before he could though the three officers began running up the stairs shouting: "ARMED POLICE DROP YOUR WEAPONS." The door was open and Palmer greeted the officers holding Elaine in front of him pointing his gun at her, he told them to drop their guns then ushered them into the bathroom, he then backed out and locked the door from the outside.

He took Elaine back into the bedroom and told her to take a cord and tie Clifford's hands behind his back and to make sure they were tight, Clifford had been too afraid to move in case Palmer had kept his promise to shoot Elaine.

Palmer then told Elaine and Clifford to turn and face the bed then took the other cord and tied Elaine's hands tightly behind her back. After checking Clifford's bonds were tight he ordered them to turn around and walk towards the door telling Elaine to go in front of Clifford.

Outside, officers that were in earshot heard the shot and the alert was sent out, Lewis was alerted and he gave out full details of the safe house, and ordered all units who were parked up some distance from the house to move in on foot and get a vantage point out of sight, he also put the rest of the Armed Response team on standby. He radioed the officers in the house they reported the situation saying that Elaine and Clifford were unharmed at present.

Once close enough one officer got within about thirty feet of the minibus, creeping a little closer he saw that the engine was running and there were only two occupants. He crept back and spoke to his partner saying that the vehicle only had two occupants and that he thought they could surprise them, his partner said: 'Ok let's have a look.' They both crept towards the bus making sure they made no noise and staying out of sight. The second officer said that he agreed that he could only see two occupants, definitely one male in the front passenger seat but was unsure about the driver side.

They devised a plan and set it in motion, the first officer Detective Constable Chalmers crouched down low and crept around the back of the bus and up to the driver's door. His partner then sneaked up to the passenger door staying low to avoid detection in the mirrors. When they were in position both looked under the vehicle, Chalmers gave the signal and leapt up surprising the woman and yanked her door open, at the same time the other officer opened Bird's door overpowering him and pulled him out of his seat and onto the ground. Once Bird was handcuffed Chalmers put out the call that the van was secured. Joanne was shaking but happy, knowing that her ordeal was finally over.

When Lewis had received the call he and Deacon immediately headed back to the safe house. They were briefed on the events and Lewis told everyone to clear the area and stay out of sight; he then called for a WPC and asked her to take Joanne's place in the bus and Chalmers to replace Bird. He and Deacon then moved quietly up to the house, they discovered that at the far end of the drive was a small gap between the house and a wall that closed the drive off. They were able to squeeze into the gap and decided to wait there for Palmer to bring the Jessop's out either from the front or the back of the house.

Upstairs Palmer had placed himself behind Clifford and said: 'Ok down the stairs slowly and wait at the bottom.' Once downstairs Palmer pushed past them and cautiously opened the front door, he peered outside and satisfied it was clear he said: 'Ok you two come out quietly and slowly.' He made them walk towards the bus staying behind them with his gun pointing at Clifford's back. Lewis was peering around the wall and saw what was occurring, he whispered to Deacon that they would wait a few seconds then they would follow.'

When they reached the back of the van Palmer didn't notice that Bird and Joanne were gone, he opened the two doors and forced the Jessop's into the back, he then called for Bird to get out and give him a hand.

Chalmers climbed out slowly and approached the rear of the bus with his handcuffs at the ready. Palmer had his back to him so Chalmers immediately pounced on him, grabbed his left wrist and clamped the handcuffs on, immediately other officers pounced and Palmer was overpowered. The WPC then climbed out and helped the Jessop's out of the van.

Lewis in the meantime arrived at the scene but not before calling in all units and releasing the officers from the bathroom. He ordered that Palmer be marched to a car and was whisked off to the Police station, Bird had already been taken away. Lewis then called an ambulance to attend Joanne and the Jessop's and ordered all units to return to Chelsea while he and Deacon waited for the ambulance to arrive.

CHAPTER THIRTY

Clifford and Elaine were checked over at the hospital then a Police car returned them to their apartment, Joanne though was suffering from shock and was kept in but released later that day. The Police told both the Jessop's and the Joanne they would like them to go into the station at their convenience to make statements regarding the last forty eight hours.

After being processed by the custody officer Palmer and Bird were charged with kidnapping, possession of a deadly weapon assault on a Police Officer, they were then locked in separate holding cells to prevent another repeat occurrence of the Pierce catastrophe. Lewis had also ordered that no solicitor was to be permitted access to the cells area and fifteen minute safety checks by custody staff was instigated. Neither of the men had a preferred legal rep so two duty Solicitors were appointed, Lewis ensured both Solicitors were severely vetted and left orders that they had to be searched every time they arrived and left.

Not unexpectedly Lewis and Deacon were happy at the arrest but Lewis decided not to release details of recent events to the media in case it spooked Thomas and any of his associates.

The two men said nothing when they were charged other than to give their names, Lewis suggested to Deacon that they interview the two men simultaneously but, in separate rooms, he thought they could play one against the other by insinuating they were giving each other up.

Palmer had a record for serious assault and had served two years at the same time and at the same prison as Thomas. Bird had only minor offences against him for burglary and handling stolen goods, so Lewis reckoned Bird would be more likely to crack first.

Prior to interview the two men were seen by their Solicitor's in separate rooms while officers stood guard outside.

The interviews were set up for five thirty pm. Lewis suggested that he and DC Hines interviewed Palmer while Deacon and DI Barnes questioned Bird.

When everyone was settled at Palmer's interview Lewis switched on the recording machine and announced the start of Palmer's interview, he gave the date and time then named the people present.

He began by asking Palmer if he knew Sam, Simpson, Holland or Thomas, showing him their pictures. Palmer denied knowing them but Lewis informed him that Thomas had been identified as being at the house the Jessop's were held captive, but he still denied knowing any of them.

Lewis continued: 'Well we know Thomas recruited you and your friend Bird to aid in the kidnapping of Mrs Jessop and hold her against her will with the intention to extort a large sum of money from her husband. We also know Mr Jessop paid the ransom but then he was also taken by Thomas and one other man. He too was held against his will at the same house as Mrs Jessop, both have identified you and Bird as Thomas's men, what do you have to say to that?' Palmer answered: 'I have nothing to say and I know nothing about any kidnaps.'

'What do you mean you know nothing? You and your mate who by the way is in the next room spilling his guts, abducted an innocent woman last night in order to use her car to recapture the Jessop's which as you know we foiled. We also found you in procession of a fire arm which in itself is a serious offence.' Palmer looked at his brief who just nodded, Palmer then continued: 'OK you got me there, but I have nothing to do with any murder. All I know is a guy I met in prison called me out of the blue and asked if I wanted to earn some serious cash, I was skint so I agreed and ask Bird to help me.'

'It must of been very serious money for you to risk abducting an innocent woman at gunpoint and take her car, not to mention carrying and discharging a firearm in a public place, and on top of that assaulting a Police officer. I am afraid my friend you are in very serious trouble and unless you cooperate you will be going to prison for a very long time.' Palmer still maintained his innocence, Lewis then asked: 'Ok, let's move on, how were you able to find the safe house?' Palmer would not answer so Lewis said: 'As I said your pal has been singing like a Bird—if you'll excuse the pun—he reckons that you were one of the instigators of the kidnappings and he only went along with you because you threatened his life. He also says he had been promised a large sum of money from a "big job" you and Thomas have planned.' Palmer instantly sat bolt upright in his chair and blurted out: 'He's a lying git, he is as much involved as I am,' He suddenly realised he had said too much and clammed up. Lewis though responded quickly: 'So you admit to your involvement in the kidnappings and being party to Thomas's plans then?' Palmer remained silent so Lewis looked at his watch and said: 'Ok that will be all for now. Constable take him away please.'

Meanwhile Deacon was working on bird. He also denied knowing the four men in the pictures or anything about a "big job" but he was being a little more open about the kidnappings, he said though he didn't know how Palmer found out about the safe house. He said they were recruited to watch the Jessop's on the promise of a large pay out but didn't know why they were kidnapped or anything else. He sat back in the chair and said he had nothing more to say. Deacon ended the interview and had Bird was escorted back to his cell.

Deacon and Barnes left the interview room and went into a room next door, where Lewis and Deacon had watched the end of the interview on a TV monitor. Lewis told Deacon that he still thought Bird was the one to work on, he suggested waiting until he had dropped off to sleep then wake him up and drag him back up to be re-interviewed.

This agreed Lewis waited three hours then called for Bird to be brought back up. The custody officer opened Bird's cell banging the door hard against the wall and shouted for him get up. Bird awoke with a start and wondered where he was for a second; before he could recover the officer slapped handcuffs on his wrists and escorted him up to the interview room.

Bird protested all the way up, asking why he was being taken to be interviewed again so soon and demanded he saw his solicitor. The officer told him to pipe down and said he knew nothing he was just doing as he was told.

Bird was relieved to see his solicitor was already present in the room, Bird asked him why he was being questioned again so soon, his Solicitor told him they needed to ask some more questions and that was all he knew, he advised Bird not to forget what they had discussed regarding him being co-operative, saying it would go in his favour as he was already facing a long jail sentence.

When Lewis and Deacon entered the room they sat opposite Bird, they could see by looking at him that their idea worked and he was looking rattled. After a few minutes of shuffling through their paperwork Lewis announced for the tape: "Continuation of interview with Alan Bird" and gave the time once more. Lewis then asked Bird: 'Is there anything else you wish to tell us in connection with this enquiry?' Bird said nothing for a while then leaned over and conversed with his Solicitor, Bird then said: 'Ok, Palmer called me one day and said he had a job and he wanted me to help him. He said there was a big payout, we found out afterwards we were to help with the kidnapping, as far as we knew it was only going to be the woman; he sprung the husband on us the day of the ransom drop. He told us it was just about the ransom and the husband was just leverage. We learned later though that the money was to fund Thomas to go to Mexico but we don't know why . . . . Lewis interrupted him to ask: 'Why Mexico? What is he doing there?' Bird continued: 'Look you are going to think I am spinning you a line here but I swear it's true. He said he was given information about a "lost city" in the jungle, there is supposed to be a large fortune in gold and jewels. His main target though is a large stone that is said to be set in the forehead of a large effigy of some sun god or other, it is said to be worth millions alone. The woman was kidnapped to force her bosses to dispose of the treasure.'

'I see and how does he expect to find this "lost city". Lewis looked at Deacon and they both laughed and told Bird someone was pulling his leg and he must be very gullible to believe such a story. Even the solicitor had a smile on his face. Bird though insisted it was true and explained: 'Thomas had arranged an expedition to Mexico and it was to be led by local expert guides, he's probably at the "city" right now.

Deacon butted in: 'How did he get there and who has he taken with him?'

'I don't know who's with him but I do know he went by helicopter to Frankfurt then he was taking a plane to Mexico. Apparently this "lost city" is cursed; anyone who enters it is said to die or be struck down with blindness or worse. Thomas doesn't believe in the curse though and he said we would split the treasure evenly when he got back.'

Still grinning Lewis said: 'Ok Alan, we will break for a while, we'll send some coffee and sandwiches in and resume in twenty minutes.' Bird's nodded in agreement.

Lewis suspended the interview formally for the tape then he and Deacon left the room. Lewis told Deacon to get someone to notify Interpol and to fax them photos of Thomas, Holland and Simpson's and to make sure the passenger flight lists in and out of Frankfurt on or about the dates in question, were checked, plus all CCTV at the airport.

Lewis went to the canteen and had a coffee, he brought one back for Deacon and they restarted the interview. After three hours of questioning Lewis decided they had learnt all they were going to.

Bird was taken away and Lewis went to his office, he was filtering through the transcripts of the interviews when Deacon knocked the door. He informed Lewis Interpol had checked all flights out of Frankfurt and there were four men who had chartered a flight to Mexico, they had also checked the CCTV tapes and three of the men were definitely Thomas, Holland and Simpson, the other one they were not sure about as he was not in their data base, there has been no sightings as yet of them coming back into the country.

Lewis said: 'Well done things are starting to come together at last. I think perhaps we should have another chat with Palmer.'

Lewis called for Palmer to be taken back to interview room three, when he was brought in Lewis and Deacon was already there. Palmer was already sat down and a constable stood guard at the door. Palmer asked where his solicitor was and Lewis said he didn't need him because this was just an informal talk. When Palmer was ready Lewis said: 'Now earlier you said you didn't recognise the pictures we know now that was a lie, we also know you and Bird were ordered to guard the Jessop's until Thomas returned from Mexico where he is hoping to pull off this "big" job. The couple were insurance to force the woman's company to fence the treasure he is hoping to bring back, am I getting warm? Bird names you as Thomas's right hand man and said it was you who instigated the abduction of the woman last night, saying you wanted the car to take the Jessop's if you recaptured them, have you anything to say now?'

Palmer remained quiet before saying: 'Ok but I want protection because if Thomas finds me I'm a dead man and so is Bird.' Lewis told him as he had told Bird that he would have a word on his behalf but there were no assurances.' Palmer sat upright and coughed then said: 'Oh what the hell, Thomas is travelling with three other men but I don't know who they are. I admit helping Thomas in taking the Jessop woman and I concocted last night's abduction, it nearly worked as well.' Lewis said sarcastically: 'Yes well I have nearly won the lottery many times but nearly isn't good enough is it?' Now once again, apart from Thomas do you recognise any of the men in the photos I showed you?' Palmer nodded and explained: 'Yes but only that Sam bloke, I don't actually know him but I was with Thomas once in a pub where Thomas met him, Thomas was shouting at him: "Get it or else, I'm warning you Sam" he didn't look like he had two pennies to rub together though.'

'No he didn't, and he never will now because Thomas murdered him, he was badgering Sam to find half a million pounds but he couldn't so he executed him. Ok that's it for now, you are in court at eleven thirty this morning for your bail hearing, Bird is rejecting bail to keep out of Thomas's way, do you want to go down the same road?' Palmer said he would discuss it with his solicitor so Lewis said that was fine and bid him goodnight and the Constable took him back to his cell.

CHAPTER THIRTY ONE

After another two days of struggling against the harsh conditions Thomas's crew arose early in the morning, it was the day they were supposed to reach the "lost city." They rushed breakfast so they could get going and set off in good spirits. Early in the afternoon Hector halted his men and turned to Thomas and said: 'This is as far as we go Senor, you will have to go the rest of the way alone as my men will not go one more step in that direction, it took a lot of persuasion and the promise of more money to get them this far,' Thomas and his men saw that Hector's men had dropped to their knees and were praying. Hector said he and his men would stay there until they returned or until they are sure they were not returning. Thomas asked how far the city was and Hector said about one and a half hours away and it was easy going if they stayed on a straight course, then they should come to a valley lined with trees on each side, the city was about another two hundred metres ahead. Hector gave them each a canteen of water and some bread and cheese to sustain them until they returned.

The three men began walking in the direction Hector had said, all hoping they were soon going to be very rich. After about two hours they came to the valley, they stopped and rested for a few minutes and drank some water before setting off again. When they reached the end of the valley Simpson said he felt an eyrie sensation which had become stronger the closer he got to the city, Thomas said not to be so stupid and to act like a man. Simpson just looked at him expressionless.

A few minutes later they came across an arrow formed out of small rocks pointing straight ahead, they assumed it was pointing the way to the "city."

Walking on they at last came to the outskirts of the city ruins which were virtually engulfed by vegetation and the city walls were almost hidden by trees and overgrown bushes. Thomas said: 'Well this is it lads, are you ready?' The two men both nodded but at the same time seemed a little apprehensive. Nevertheless they ventured in through the entrance and slowly edged their way forward. After pushing their way through bushes and other vegetation they were suddenly overwhelmed by what stood before them. The most stunning structure they had ever encountered. The temple was still virtually intact, although the walls were a little crumbly but nevertheless they still looked strong.

Simpson stood staring but Thomas told him to move they were there to get rich and not to get sentimental over some old ruins. As they went closer they saw glints of something in the grass around the entrance. They suddenly realised it was the sun shining gold chalices and other items, they also spotted diamonds and jewels scattered around. Thomas rushed over grabbing handfuls of stones and stuffed them into his pockets then couldn't help dropping to his knees and chanting: "Were rich, were rich," then added: 'I told you lads, didn't I? Come on let's fill our boots.' Nick and Simpson just gazed in amazement until Nick recovered and blurted out: 'Well you can fill your boots but I am filling my bag.' He emptied his kitbag out and commenced scooping up the gems and gold pieces. Thomas spotted a larger jewel and put that in his bag, he then pointed to the Temple and said: 'Right let's go inside and get what we came for.'

Nick joined Simpson and Thomas at the entrance then froze, he looked at the other two and said: 'What if the curse is true we could all die.' Thomas just stood there and looked at him saying that he was not going to let some stupid custom stop him from getting rich, he hit Nick on the back of the head and told him to grow up and be a man. Simpson added that Thomas was right and they had come all this way and he was going home rich no matter what. Nick contemplated what they had said and reluctantly agreed.

Once they made the decision they gingerly made their way into the temple and stood just inside the crumbling doors, there wasn't much light but once their eyes became accustomed they stood opened mouthed staring but not quite believing what their eyes were seeing, six gold figures stood on stone slabs their eyes consisting of emeralds and diamonds. There were also carved wooden figures with precious jewels embedded into them. Other precious jewels were scattered over the floor.

Age was taking its toll on the inside of the Temple, tree roots and plants were forging their way between the cracks in the walls.The glassless windows allowed in some sunlight which shone on the effigy that towered above them. It was mounted on a concrete plinth which they estimated to be about fifteen feet high, the effigy stood about thirty feet above that. There was a large stone embedded into the forehead which Thomas had been informed was an opal.

They stood motionless for a while until Suddenly Simpson gasped, he grabbed Thomas's arm and pulled him towards him, he was trembling when he uttered: "Look". He was pointing at the floor around base of the effigy. Thomas followed his gaze and gasped. Strewn all around were human remains, bones, skulls and even whole skeletons, there were also decaying remains of animals, plus old boots, and bits of clothing. Nick took to his heels and disappeared outside and Thomas could hear him being sick. Eventually though Nick plucked up courage—although it was more like greed taking over.

Thomas had begun inspecting the remains, he looked at many of the more complete skeletons and skulls, after a while he called out: 'Come and have a look at this.' Simpson was still rooted to the spot. He called to Simpson again: 'Come here, look there's no curse, come here I'll show you.' Simpson slowly edged his way towards Thomas, when close enough Thomas pointed to several skeletons, bones and skulls showing him holes and chinks in them and said: 'They all died from bullets or knives maybe even swords look.' He showed Simpson that some of the bones still had bullets lodged in them, he continued: 'This has nothing to with any curse, these all died fighting trying to get up to that jewel. Where's that scared rat got to?' Simpson told him he was still outside. Thomas went out but Simpson stayed to grab some of the treasure. Thomas called to Nick to come back but he said he would make do with what he could find outside the temple. Thomas went up to him and said: No! 'Look I'll Show you, the curse had nothing to do with those bones, I've just shown Simpson, come and see.' Nick relented but eventually followed Thomas back into the temple. Simpson had a wide smile on his face as he told Nick everything was ok. Nick moved closer and Thomas pointed out the bones and explained his no curse theory. Nick looked gingerly around then relaxed a little. Thomas said: 'Right then lads I think we are ready to get rich.'

The men scrutinised the scene trying to decide how they were going to get the jewel down, Nick astonished the other two by telling them that he did a lot of climbing in his youth and if they had some rope he might be able scale the effigy. Thomas patted him on the back and said: 'I knew I picked the right crew.' Nick replied: 'We have no rope though.' Simpson spoke up saying that there were long vines all over the place outside and said he remembered Marco saying that they were strong enough to climb as he had climbed them looking for eggs and honey many times. Thomas said they should go and get some but Nick said they had nothing to cut them with. Thomas however said he had a knife he had taken from Marco's bag.

Simpson went with Nick to collect the vines selecting the longest ones. They came back with as many as they could carry Thomas asked how they should fix the vines to the effigy. Nick took a few minutes to think about the situation then said: 'The effigy has several good footholds but the plinth has none and it is very smooth. That isn't a great problem as such because I can use a vine to climb that by making a loop in the end then sling it up hooking it over the big toe of the right foot. Simpson said: 'Good plan.'

Nick tied two vines together making a large loop at the end of one. Swinging it up he tried to hook the loop on the big toe but failed; it took two more attempts before he had any success, he curled a spare vine around his neck then began his climb; although his boots were not the perfect climbing footwear. When he finally reached the top of the plinth he checked out each foothold carefully. Thomas shouted to him telling him to get on with it. Nick ignored him and began climbing slowly stopping every now and then to catch his breath, he continued climbing but parts of the effigy crumbled under his weight and crashed to the floor, Simpson, Nick and Thomas moved further back hardly daring to breathe in case Nick fell.

Finally he reached the shoulders and carefully swung the spare vine around the neck of the statue and securing it around his waist. Taking the knife Thomas had given him he carefully begun to chip away the stone around the eye socket. He used the knife like a chisel and began to edge the knife around the jewel.

Nick dug the knife in deeper scraping at the stone to reveal more of the jewel. Eventually where it had been stood for hundreds of years the effigy gave up the stone fairly easily, but it still took over an hour of chipping before the jewel was loose enough to lever it out of the eye socket. Sweat was pouring from Nick's forehead and he was absolutely shattered. He rested for a minute then he called down to the others that the jewel was almost free. They began dancing in pure joy and shouting they were rich.

Nick continued chipping away when all of a sudden the jewel popped out falling to the ground and smashing into little pieces.

It was soon obvious that the jewel was actually just glass. They stood staring in shock and disbelief. It took some time for them to recover, Nick who by then had climbed down remarked about all the things they were anticipating like the curse etcetera, and that the last thing on their minds was that the jewel could be just glass. He added: 'In a strange sort of way it's kind of funny.' Thomas bellowed: FUNNY! 'You call all the money, trouble and effort involved to get this thing, only for it to end up being glass. you think that's funny do you?' Thomas pushed Nick to the ground and shoving Simpson to one side he stormed outside.

Nick and Simpson looked at each other for ages worried as to what Thomas might do but eventually went outside to find him. Thomas was sitting on a rock staring into nothing, they approached him and he looked up at them with an angry look on his face, he then stood up as if to have another go but just walked back to his rucksack.

CHAPTER THIRTY TWO

In response to Deacon's enquiries Interpol faxed over the CCTV images from Frankfurt airport, they confirmed that the four men were Thomas, Simpson, Holland and one other but they travelled with false identities. The face of the fourth man was being run through their facial recognition system and that there was still no sign of them returning to the airport.

Interpol also reported that they were working in conjunction with Customs and Immigration and that they were staked out at Frankfurt airport, assuring that a mouse wouldn't get by them. Lewis faxed his thanks to Interpol and went to see Deacon, he showed him the picture of the fourth man and Lewis told him to go to the cells and ask Bird and Palmer if they knew him, before he did though Lewis told him he was beginning an investigation as to how Palmer found the safe house, he told him: 'Only the CC, the Assistant CC and I were privileged to that information. I deliberately omitted to reveal any details to you or any of the officers involved in the operation until it was absolutely necessary, by the time I did Palmer and Bird were already at the house. We need a thorough investigation into it. We'll have to get all of the phone records from the CC and ACC; I will need a warrant from the Commissioner for that. They will also have to be questioned. I'd better go and call the Commissioner and get the ball rolling, hopefully this will be taken out of our hands with an internal investigation.'

Deacon left Lewis and went to see the prisoners but both men said they didn't know the fourth man. Later that afternoon Lewis received Forensic and SOCCO reports from the house where Elaine and Clifford had been held. Deacon was in Lewis's office so he read it aloud: "DNA and fingerprints were found on cups, drinking glasses, as well as from a hair brush and toothbrushes in the bathroom. DNA was also collected from hair found in the waste trap under the bathroom wash basin. Most of the prints and DNA matched Thomas, Bird and palmer but the rest were unidentified. He then told Deacon that Bird and Palmer had their bail hearings that morning and both had been remanded in custody.

Later that day Lewis looked at the time and it was just past five thirty pm, he notified Deacon he was going home but wanted to be kept informed of any developments. He tidied up his desk and took some files with him to look over at home and left his office. As he walked past the front desk he was just about to say goodnight when the duty officer stopped him telling him that DCI Deacon wanted him to return to his office as something had turned up. He let out a noticeable "tut" turned around and went straight to Deacons office. Deacon was holding the telephone receiver with his hand over the mouthpiece, he whispered: "Secret Service" to Lewis and handed him the phone. Lewis took the receiver saying: 'Hello Detective Superintendant Lewis here.' A male voice replied: 'Hello Detective Superintendant, I am special agent Frank Pink from "The National Security Agency" we have some information regarding your current enquiries, we understand that Interpol recently sent you some images from Frankfurt airport of four men that interest you, Is that correct?'

Lewis replied: 'It is yes, but what have they to do with "NSA"? Ours is a murder and kidnap enquiry.'

The agent went on to say they were aware of what Superintendant Lewis and his officers were working on, he told Lewis: 'We monitor all investigations that involve Interpol so we put the unknown man in the party through our data base and we got a hit. His name is Nicholas James Tor, he was a person of interest to us a year or so back when he was flagged up for more than the average return trips to Germany, he would visit there about once sometimes twice a week over a period of three months. We picked him up a couple of times but he had nothing on him or in his luggage, we even searched his car and property but came up with nothing and his papers were always in order, so we had to let him go.'

Pink said he would fax the details to Lewis immediately. Lewis thanked the agent for the call and said goodbye and handed the receiver back to Deacon. He sat thinking then said: 'Well I didn't see that one coming.' He went on to relay what Agent Pink had just told him then said he would go to his office and wait for the fax.

When the fax arrived Lewis called Deacon and gave him Tor's details, he told him that he would request a search warrant for Tor's house and told Deacon to inform Interpol of the latest news.

The search warrant arrived an hour later. Lewis and Deacon took two uniformed officers with them to Tor's property. He lived just outside Surrey in a rented house. He was single but neighbours said he had a string of girls and women visiting regularly, they also said a rough looking man was also a regular visitor but never stayed for more than a few minutes each time. Lewis showed the four men's photos to the neighbours and they identified Thomas as the rough looking man. Afterwards they went into the house and commenced a thorough search.

Lewis and Deacon checked all around downstairs but there was nothing of interest in fact Lewis remarked to Deacon how bare the place was. They were just finishing up their search when a call from upstairs: 'inspector, I think you'll want to see this.' They both went upstairs and the two officers were standing next to a shabby single bed, Lewis asked what they had found. One of the officers said: 'Here sir in front of the bed.' A tatty rug had been pulled back and a floorboard had been lifted, the officer pointed to the space beneath the boards and continued: 'I stood on the rug and the floorboard was raised a little and seemed loose, I pulled the rug back and I was right, the board was just pushed into position and not fixed. When I lifted it I found that.' He kneeled down and shone his torch, there was a long white packet wrapped in polythene and sealed with brown parcel tape between the ceiling support timbers. Lewis told the officer to photograph the find then hand it to him. After the package had been photographed it was handed to Lewis. He placed it on the bed and asked the officer to take another photograph before he opened the parcel, Deacon remarked: 'It doesn't take much guessing what's in there.' Lewis nodded his agreement and took a small penknife from his pocket and carefully cut the tape and removed the polythene. Inside there was a clear plastic bag containing a white powder sealed with more tape, Lewis cut the tape and opened the bag and asked for more photos. He wet his finger and dipped it into the powder, he then tested the substance with the tip of his tongue, he nodded saying: "Heroine" 'Pure I would say, right I'll take it back with me, well done lads carry on.' He and Deacon went downstairs and Lewis remarked: 'That's one up for us, the NSA couldn't find anything. There's not much doubt that is what Tor was going to Germany for, I'd like to know though how he got it into the country. I think I just might give NSA a call, a little gloating is in order.'

While he was speaking the officers came down the stairs and handed Lewis an ordinance survey map, the route to the airfield Thomas had taken off from was marked out on it, he told Lewis: 'We found that in a bedside locker, apart from that though there was nothing else.' Ushering all the officers out Lewis locked the door and immediately ordered SOCCO and Forensics out to process the house.

Back at HQ Lewis and Deacon discussed the search; Deacon said it had been very fruitful and very helpful to the case especially the map. While he was talking Lewis was reading an E-Mail, it read "A relative of Tor has been located—his brother. He lives on a council estate in London, DI Barnes has contacted the MET to have him questioned." Lewis showed the E-Mail to Deacon, then said: 'Right on that note I'm going home—I hope.'

CHAPTER THIRTY THREE

Totally demoralised, Thomas, Nick and Simpson retrieved the backpacks and scooped up what treasure they could carry, including the smaller statue and wooded ornaments embedded with jewels and diamonds. Meanwhile Hector's men were getting increasingly restless waiting for them to appear, they constantly pressed Hector to abandon "The English Meddlers" believing that they were all dead or even worse coming back full of evil spirits. He managed to quail their fears each time but they were becoming visibly unsettled. Consequently when the men came into view Hector gave a huge sigh of relief. As they came nearer Hector's men edged away with fear clearly on their faces. Thomas saw this and called out: 'Ok, ok there's nothing to fear, there is no curse, and there was no large jewel either.' Hector enquired: 'What do you mean Senor, no large jewel? A lot of people have ventured into that place and many never returned. Those who did were inflicted with serious physical and mental problems.' Thomas replied: 'Sorry to disillusion you, but the only dead people in that place have been killed by each other fighting to get to the jewel, which actually turned out to be nothing else but glass, your people and everyone else have been taken for fools by a curse which doesn't exist. Hector swiftly took Thomas to one side and quietly said that he and his people had been living in fear of the curse for many years and he should not mock their beliefs because they were very sensitive. He added it was getting very late and that his men would not camp in the area.

Nick had heard the conversation and said maybe they should give Hector's men a few trinkets to allay their fears, Thomas wasn't sure about it but Nick told him that Simpson was right, and they should get it over with so they could get going.

They gathered up a few trinkets and approached Hector's men, Hector explained to them what was happening, they mumbled between themselves and finally one spoke to Hector in Mexican, Hector then told Thomas: 'They are very grateful Senor's and they assure you of their services on the return journey.'

As soon everyone was ready Hector rousted his men, the bearers attempted to pick up the Englishmen's bags, they reacted by stepping in front of the bags, Hector came over and told them that it was ok they were just offering to carry their bags for them. Nick and the others smiled at the bearers and allowed them to take their bags. The three men looked on in amazement as the bearers heaved the overflowing bags onto their backs as if they only contained cotton wool.

At long last they got going but the light faded fairy quickly as more rain clouds appeared. Hector watched the sky as they pressed on but after only a few hours he decided to halt the expedition. He chose a campsite encircled by tall thick leaved trees which offered a partial shelter. When camp was set up a fire was lit, Thomas asked if there was any food and Hector assured him that there was plenty, he told him: 'I shot some game while you were away, come I will show you.' Hector took Thomas to where one of his men was preparing supper, Hector said: 'There Senor, we eat well tonight.' His man was cutting up an animal similar to the one Marco had killed on the first leg of the expedition. They ate and drank very well and fortunately the rain stayed away.

After a good night's sleep and a good breakfast they set off at just after seven thirty am. The going was fairly easy with no undue problems. They rested occasionally but as the sky was overcast they never had so much heat to contend with as they had previously, unfortunately though the insects were just as bad and they were constantly bitten, mostly by Mosquitoes.

Simpson was bitten the most because he removed his hat at one of the rest stops not realising his mistake until it was too late. He was bitten continuingly on his face, neck, and head. His head got the worst of it because the mosquitoes had become trapped in his thick hair. Hector applied antiseptic cream and insect repellent to the bites and the rest of Simpson exposed skin.

They made camp early that evening and ate well again, Simpson had a bad night due to his insect bites but fell asleep eventually through sheer exhaustion. The next morning was greeted happily with them all knowing it was the last day of trekking as they had made such good progress.

When they finally reached the guide's encampment the huts were a welcome sight, as they approached the brow of the hill they saw a helicopter set down close to the camp. Hector stopped and crouched down, his men did the same. He told Thomas: 'Senor Get your men down there are strangers in the camp.' Thomas asked Hector: 'Are you talking about the Helicopter? Because if you are that is for us, it's our transport out of here.' Hector stood up and beckoned his men on. They entered the camp and Thomas saw the helicopter pilot sitting on a grass mound eating. He sat next to him and the pilot put his plate down and said: 'Mr Thomas I presume.' Thomas confirmed that he was and said: 'You are a welcome sight, the sooner we get out of this stinking country the better.' Hector had heard Thomas and said quite bluntly: 'This stinking country Senor has made you a very rich man.' Thomas picked up on his tone and diplomatically said: 'Sorry Hector, no offence meant.' Hector said no more on the subject instead he said: 'I was not aware you were leaving by helicopter, I was under the impression you wanted the trucks to take you back to the airport.' Thomas just said there had been a change of plan. Hector continued saying that he was intending to offer to handle the fencing of his treasure for him as he could get a good price. And that was why he deliberately didn't take any of the treasure they offered his men. Thomas apologised saying that would be taken care of back home. Hector shrugged his shoulders then went on to advise Thomas not to fly out that evening as the light was already fading. Thomas asked the pilot for his opinion and he agreed with Hector but added that he was paying so it was up to him. Thomas agreed with Hector's advice and they would leave early the next day.

In the morning the three men needed no wakeup call, they were up and washed and eager to go as soon as the sun came up, Simpson though was still not feeling that special, he assumed it was the reaction of the insect bites.

They were among the first in the queue for breakfast and feasted on bacon and eggs with bread and jam, followed by hot fresh coffee. Hector came over and wished them good luck on their journey home, he told Thomas that he had prepared a rucksack of food and water for the trip.

CHAPTER THIRTY FOUR

When Lewis finally left for home he called his wife to let her know he was on his way. When he arrived home and hung his coat up in the hallway. Karen called out to say she was in the dining room; she was sitting at the writing bureau finishing a letter to her sister Sophie who lived in Canada. Karen had received a letter from her two days earlier inviting her and Andrew to visit. They had moved to a large six bedroom house in Toronto six years before. Her husband was a successful business lawyer working mostly for large consortiums. Lewis didn't get on too well with him because he tended to brag about his success and their wealth too much.

Lewis leaned over and kissed Karen, he read part of Sophie's letter and remarked: 'I don't know when she wants us to go over but I am pretty sure I am extremely busy that day.' Karen playfully dug her elbow into his stomach which prompted Andrew to say: 'That's it home for two minutes and your beating me up already, if that's the only reception I get I am going for a shower.' Karen called him as he walked out of the room saying: 'Your dressing gown is wet, I washed it today and it rained so I couldn't get it dry.' He told her not to worry and continued on upstairs.

He shaved and showered, when he had towelled himself off he remembered about his wet dressing gown so he grabbed Karen's pink fluffy one and put it on, it was a little tight and only just met in the front but tied the cord together and went downstairs.

Karen was in the kitchen whisking eggs in a glass bowl for scrambled eggs, she didn't look up immediately but when she did and saw him in her dressing gown she almost dropped the bowl and virtually collapsed and shook with laughter, when at last she recovered Lewis remarked: 'Well at least you don't have to stir the eggs anymore.' She warned him he would wear the eggs if he wasn't careful.' He then said: 'I take it the "yoke's" on me then.' He put his arm around her shoulders and kissed her on the cheek, she said: 'Thank God you're home it's been a long time since I laughed so much.' He got the last word in quickly and replied: 'Why, is the mirror broken then?' She grabbed the first thing to hand which luckily for him was the tea towel and threw it at him. He threw the towel back at her and she told him to sit at the table and be quiet or he wouldn't get anything. Using his thumb and forefinger he imitated zipping his lips together and picked up the newspaper to read while he waited for his supper.

Next morning Lewis woke in his bed for the first time in days, he had a leisurely bath then slipped on his now dry dressing gown and went downstairs. Karen was in the kitchen, she had cooked breakfast and was about to take it up to him on a tray. He took the tray from her and placed it on the kitchen table, he wound his arms around her waist and gave her a lingering kiss and thanked her. The morning newspaper was on the tray he placed it on the table alongside his plate and began reading the headlines. Karen sat opposite him resting her chin on the palm of her hand just looking at him saying nothing.

He was eating his food while reading the paper but looked up wondering why she was so quiet, she was still staring at him so he looked at her and said: 'What?'

'Nothing I was just thinking that I don't see you for days, when you do come home you just insult me and go to bed, then in the morning you ignore me.'

'I'm sorry darling it was very rude of me.' He closed the paper and continued: 'Right I'm all yours.' She replied sarcastically: 'Good morning to you too darling, I take it you slept well, from the way you were snoring it seemed like you did.'

'Yes I did sleep well the office chair is no substitute for my cosy bed. Now what are your plans today?'

'I have no plans so maybe you can take me to town, and then we can have lunch somewhere nice.'

'Ah yes well, I was actually intending to go back in today, that Thomas guy is expected to get back anytime soon and plans have to be made, plus I am waiting for a call from the Commissioner.' Karen didn't reply instead she got up and started putting the dishes in the dishwasher, he soon knew how she felt though when she came and took his plate from him before he had finished eating his breakfast. She scraped the remaining food into the waste bin and angrily dropped the plate into the machine and stormed out of the kitchen.

He was at a loss what to do as Karen never usually behaved like that. He sipped his coffee for a while then got up and went to find her; she was in the lounge patting the cushions on the sofa a little more exuberant than usual.

He walked up behind her and gently took her arm and began to turn her around, she snatched her arm back and continued banging the cushions. Lewis turned to leave the room, as he reached the door she said: 'I am warning you now, when you have finished with this case you are taking some time off and "WE ARE" going to see Sophie in Canada.' She stopped bashing the cushions and slumped down onto the sofa, he went back and sat next to her and said: 'Ok darling, you have a deal, I'm so sorry I have been away so much but this is the most frustrating and difficult case we have ever had to deal with. No sooner we get a break then another hitch comes along. However we have caught the kidnappers and the couple are safe and well.' She replied: 'I know I heard that on the local news. Look when do you think it will be all over Andrew? We are nothing more than strangers at the moment.' Lewis nodded his head in agreement and said he understood how she felt; he said he would not go into work until after lunch so they could spend some time together.

Karen wiped her eyes and went upstairs to change, she reappeared and they put their coats on and went to the car.

As Andrew drove out of the drive his mobile rang, he reached in his pocket and gave it to Karen saying: 'Switch it off I don't care what it's about, I'm sure someone else can deal with it.' She ignored him though and took the call and it was Deacon, she told him Lewis was driving and asked him to hold on. Lewis pulled over and Karen handed him the mobile and whispered that it was Deacon. He took the phone and said: sharply 'Yes what is it?' Deacon sensed the coldness in Lewis's voice so he said cautiously: 'I'm sorry to disturb you sir, but we have a tip off from an anonymous caller that Thomas isn't coming back via Frankfurt, in fact he is coming all the way by helicopter, and he is on his way this very moment. The caller has even given Interpol the numbers on the chopper and apparently he has his men with him, apparently they are loaded down with priceless treasure from this "lost city". The only thing he didn't know was the actual destination.'

Lewis told Deacon he would be right in and ended the call. Karen just said: 'Well that's that, let's get back and I'll get some food up together for you and I'll pack you some clean clothes.' Lewis told her he was sorry but Thomas was on his way back into the country, and he had to go back in.

Back inside the house Lewis went and dressed more appropriately, when he went downstairs Karen had an overnight bag packed ready for him, he told her again he was sorry and kissed her then said he should be going, he said sorry again then added he would call her later.

"Hector was the mystery caller, he had decided to grass on Thomas because he turned down his offer to fence the treasure, plus the disrespect he constantly showed to him and his men".

On arrival back at HQ Lewis called Deacon to his office asking to be updated with events. Deacon told him that the owner of the helicopter had been traced and it was registered to a wealthy businessman and major shareholder of a very successful "IT" company called "It's the Solution".The company was situated in Duncan Street in West Chelsea but that was only one of five branches, one of which was in London and another in Germany. His name was Alex Templeton. The company built Computers and provided advice and/or assistance to major businesses, the government and the Military. Deacon went on to say: 'I think we have found Thomas's backer, although I can't see for the life of me see why someone with such a vast empire in his control would risk mixing it with the likes of him.'

'Well yes but then again this "jewel" is said to be worth million's so he may have thought having that much untaxed money in his hand was worth the risk.'

Deacon continued saying: 'Yeah I suppose, anyway we have questioned him but he says he is not the only person to use the helicopter, in fact he said he hasn't used it himself in ages. It's based at the airfield we are sure Thomas flew out from, I called the airfield myself, they checked and the chopper was booked out just over a week ago by Templeton himself over the phone, a normal practice apparently. He'd said it was for one of his employees—Marcus Thompson, he was supposed to be going to a convention in Switzerland. Templeton though denies any knowledge of the booking or of this "Thomson" but, the surname does imply it was for Thomas, don't you think? I have sent a couple of uniforms to the airfield to collect the CCTV tapes for the day the chopper was collected, I also asked Templeton if he had a regular pilot. He said he did but he is in hospital with appendicitis, we have checked and it's legit.'

Lewis sat and digested the news then looked up and asked Deacon to check with all airfields—Military, RAF and private to see if any pilots were missing or had left their place of work within the last year. If so then he was to get their details and check them out himself. Lewis asked him while he was waiting for news to set up a team meeting for two o'clock, he said he would contact air traffic control and get them to watch for the chopper in case he came in somewhere other than the airfield and carried on by road, adding that he would also put out an APB within a twenty mile radius and have all traffic cameras monitored.

As Deacon was leaving the room Lewis said: 'The Commissioner has ordered an internal enquiry into the safe house leak. I was dreading having to interview the Chief Constable and co, myself but luckily he has asked for an independent enquiry.'

Deacon arranged the "team talk" for two O'clock, when he and Lewis walked in, the room was a buzz of chit chat. They walked to the front and Lewis clapped his hands and the chattering died down. Addressing the team he said: 'Ok everybody, I have called you all together to bring you up to speed, we have it on good authority Thomas and his associates are coming in at an unspecified time by a privately owned chopper direct from Mexico. The chopper is registered to the main shareholder of a multi million pounds "IT" company—"It's The Solution". His name is Alex Francis Templeton, his personal and business financial accounts and phone records are being scrutinised as we speak.'

Lewis continued to relay all the latest events to his team. When he had finished he asked if anyone had anything to say, Di Barnes spoke up saying he had located an abandoned military airfield seven miles east of Chelsea. It hadn't been manned since the sixties and there is no static security there, but there is a mobile security crew who are supposed to visit four times a day but, I doubt very much that they do though. The runways are badly broken up and overgrown but, there are plenty of places a helicopter could land and the airfield is completely isolated. I requested the local boys check it out warning them Thomas and crew are probably armed.'Lewis shifted his feet and said: 'very good Barnes.'

While Barnes was speaking a detective constable came in the room and handed Lewis a piece of paper, he read it then told the team: 'Ok people listen up, I have fresh news on Thomas, Air traffic picked up an unidentified aircraft over the channel Islands just a few minutes ago on an unapproved flight path, unfortunately it disappeared almost as soon as it was spotted, possibly flying too low to be tracked. Air traffic assumes it will follow the coastline continuing to fly low, they say an experienced pilot would have the knowhow to keep below the radar. I think the chances are that now he will land in some remote spot and come in over land. As I said earlier all airports and airfields are on alert and traffic is being monitored. Lewis asked if anyone else had anything to add, nobody answered so he dismissed the meeting telling them to go back to their desks and look under every stone to find every likely landing spot within the twenty mile radius.

CHAPTER THIRTY FIVE

Thomas's helicopter had travelled undetected accept for the brief sighting by air traffic control. His plan was—as Lewis had suggested—to set down somewhere out of sight. He had chosen the edge of a marshland outside Chichester harbour intending to continue on by road. Templeton had arranged for a Range Rover to be discreetly hidden away for him at the landing spot.

All was not well however, Simpson and Nick's health had been slowly deteriorating since leaving Mexico. Simpson was the first to start showing the worst symptoms of sweating but at the same time feeling very cold and nauseous. Nick immediately said it was the curse, Thomas ridiculed him though saying he was as bad as those stupid Pedro's back in Mexico. Nick said: 'Look I've been thinking, what if someone had removed the original stone and replaced it with a fake one with poison in it, adding he had noticed when the glass broke it appeared powdery. He also said the effigy seemed to have been chipped away before and repaired. Thomas was furious Nick hadn't mentioning it before, he asked angrily: 'Why wait until we are virtually home to bring this up?' Nick however had only just thought to mention it because he had been suffering with pains in his stomach all of the way back. He told Thomas he would have to call for some medical help when they landed. Thomas turned to look at Nick and said: 'Oh yeah why not, let's have the whole ambulance service out while we are at it? 'You just don't get it do you? We can't call anyone, in fact the radio has to stay off all together or we will be traced. I told you, you haven't got anything serious, we will be home soon and then I'll figure something out, now stop winging you pair are like a couple of babies.'

Simpson however, was becoming worse as the flight went on he had come out in red rashes and was coughing up blood. Secretly Thomas was starting to worry himself. He suggested landing and kicking Simpson off, but Nick said: 'Yeah and I suppose I would be next? You can't just dispose of people like that, don't forget it was you who dragged us on this forsaken trip. You have connections, use the radio and call someone and have them waiting for us.'

Because Thomas himself was worried he gave in, he said: 'Ok but if we get caught you are dead.' Nick replied: 'Yeah well, if you don't call someone we could all be dead because you could have what we have, it just may not be showing yet.'

Thomas needed no more prompting he shouted to the pilot over the engine noise and asked him to patch him through to Templeton on the landline. Templeton came on the line and Thomas told him the two men were ill and needed medical treatment and about there being no priceless jewel. Templeton was not impressed in fact he was furious he had contacted him at all. Thomas explained they had a fortune in other gold and jewellery so there was still a lot of money at stake. Templeton said that may be the case but there was no chance of medical help, he told Thomas: 'The Police are all over my business as it is, somehow they have traced the Chopper to me and they know you are using it to get into the country. They're probably tapping my phones as I speak so I am hanging up, don't call this number again—call my mobile.' Templeton hung up and Thomas shouted: 'Shit shit.' Nick asked what was wrong and Thomas told him what Templeton had told him. The news depressed Nick even further, he paused and said: 'Great that's it then we're done for.'

'No were not he's in too deep, no, he'll help us somehow we'll just have to carry on for now.'

However Thomas was beginning to feel unwell but said nothing, he just said: 'You'll be alright just concentrate on what you are going to do with all that money.' Nick said no more, he felt too ill.

A short time after the pilot announced via the head phones that they would be landing in ten minutes. It was three twenty in the afternoon and Simpson was lying on the floor unconscious. Nick was becoming increasingly very ill, Thomas was concerned but not for their health he was more concerned they would get him caught. He was considering whether to dispose of them both but he didn't usually do his own dirty work although he kept thinking to himself "Desperate times desperate measures". Still not wanting to dirty his own hands though he made the decision to leave them on the chopper and offer the pilot a share of the treasure to dump them off somewhere.

When the pilot landed the helicopter Thomas told him that Templeton was paying him when he returned the chopper, he then approached the subject of Simpson and Nick, the pilot agreed. Thomas unloaded all the treasure and told the pilot to take his share, the pilot then returned to the chopper.

Before he went to find the Range Rover, Thomas sorted the kit bags making two bags out of the three. They were very heavy so he left them where they were and took a piece of paper from his pocket. It was a diagram of the area showing where the Range Rover would be hidden. He was aware the helicopter had not taken off yet but ignored it, however he had only taken one step when a voice came from behind, he turned to see Nick standing there bathed in sweat and physically shaking, he said in a weak voice: 'Not so fast, aren't you forgetting something?' Thomas was rooted to the spot and Nick hobbled towards him, he was carrying a large wrench he had taken from the chopper, Thomas tried to speak but couldn't summon up the words before Nick lunged at him waving the wrench above his head with both hands. He was so weak he struggled to lift the wrench but was able to strike Thomas but only on the left shoulder. He fell to the ground and Nick attempted to strike again but this time Thomas was able to grab the empty kit bag and shield himself with it. As soon as the wrench made contact with the bag Thomas pushed against it and Nick lost his balance falling sideways. Thomas quickly rose to his feet and grabbed the wrench from Nick's hand, he raised it to strike Nick but something struck him on the back of the head and he fell to the ground motionless. The pilot had changed his mind and come to Nick's rescue, hitting Thomas with a heavy gold Goblet which he took from the bag of treasure.

He quickly helped Nick to his feet and led him to a tree supporting him with his arm and lowered him down. He told Nick to hold on and went to the chopper to get his first aid bag as Nick had cut his head and face on the stony ground. He returned and cleaned the wounds and applied an antiseptic pad to the graze on his head and a deep cut above his eye. While he was attending to Nick he said: 'That man is a monster it is obvious he didn't care if you lived or died, I have radioed for help and gave them our position, so help will be here soon but I can't stay, I'm sure you understand.'

Nick put his hand on the Pilots arm and said: 'I understand and I'm grateful for what you've done, how is the other guy in the chopper?'

'I am sorry my friend he has gone, I will have to take him out of the chopper I'm afraid but I will cover him then I must go.'

Nick thanked him again and told him to take as much of the treasure as he wanted as it was no use to him anymore as he was going to die or go to jail, he assured the pilot he would not give him up to the Police.

After the helicopter had taken off Nick lay against the tree drifting in and out of consciousness. He was just coming around from one such moment when he saw through glazed eyes a movement, thinking it was the Police he said weakly: 'Thank God I need to get to a hospital quickly.' Unfortunately for Nick it wasn't the Police it was Thomas, he was knocked out for a while but had come around while Nick and the Pilot were talking. He knew the Police would soon be there and forced himself to his feet. He had waited until the helicopter took off as he didn't wish to tangle with the pilot again. He stood over Nick and said: 'I don't have time to deal with you but you will see me again, you can count on it.' He gave Nick a hard kick in the ribs and gathering as much of the treasure he could manage rushed off to find the Range Rover.

CHAPTER THIRTY SIX

Thomas was struggling to carry the two bags of treasure so he hid it in some bushes and went to get the car. He followed the directions on the small map and eventually found the Range Rover. It had been left in a gap between some high bushes and closed in with bracken and tree branches. He uncovered it and found the keys on top of the rear offside wheel. He started the engine and drove back to where he had hidden the treasure, by that time he had began sweating profusely and feeling faint. Fearing he had contacted the same illness as his men he hurriedly threw the treasure into the car and drove off at speed.

He took back roads to avoid traffic cameras but eventually he had to take the bypass, then the motorway. By now he was getting hot and cold spells and was drenched in perspiration so he pulled into a motorway services. When he had parked he called Templeton on his mobile, when Templeton answered he said: 'Templeton its Thomas, you have to send someone to help, I'm ill now and I am getting worse, I don't think I will last much longer without treatment. You have to send someone or you will not see any of the treasure.'

Templeton was busy shredding and burning everything that could incriminate him, he replied angrily: 'Don't you threaten me, because of you the cops are combing through my life, they are scrutinising all of mine and my families accounts as well as my business. Luckily for you however I do know someone who may be able to help you but not in public. Where are you now? What about the others?'

'I'm in a motorway services, tell me where to go and I'll get there, as for the others they're finished and I won't be far behind them if I don't get help, everything's gone to shit but you can't blame me, someone must of grassed on us.'

'Possibly, they have the registration of the chopper and they showed me photo's of you and your men. I think I have covered my back with my finances so there shouldn't be any connection to you, they don't know about this mobile, it's a pay and go. Anyway hang up and I'll call back in a few minutes with a location.'

"Templeton knew an ex doctor who was struck off being caught selling prescription drugs and putting them on patients records".

Templeton called the doctor and arranged for him to meet Thomas. He then called Thomas back and gave Thomas directions to a car park of a small supermarket. It was six pm and the store closed at five thirty so he said the car park should be empty by the time he got there. He then told Thomas: 'There is a doctor on his way, wait where you are until he contacts you. Don't leave the car because your face is all over the press and on TV. Once he has called you ditch the phone and destroy the SIM card. Don't contact me again until you are safely holed up with the treasure.'

By now Thomas was desperate to freshen up and use the toilet, totally against Templeton's warning not to leave the car he put his jungle cap on and went into the services. After his ablutions he felt a million times better although he was still ill.

He was hungry and thirsty so he delved in his back trouser pocket and took an envelope which contained a hundred pounds he'd stowed away for an emergency. He ordered steak and chips and a pot of coffee. Although he was hungry his condition prevented him from enjoying it, he could only eat half of the meal. He finished his coffee and bought a bottle of water to take with him and went outside. He was heading towards his car when a Police land Rover drove into the car park and parked right next to his car. He pulled the cap down over his eyes and returned to the building, he began to panic because he had left the mobile in the car and thought he would miss the doctor's call.

He stood inside the door watching but the Police remained in their car. Thomas continued watching but he was impeding people coming and going through the doors. He looked at his watch and saw that the doctor would be calling soon, if he hadn't done so already. Pulling the hat down over his eyes he bit the bullet and made his way towards his car. As he drew closer to the car the two front doors of the Police vehicle opened simultaneously and the officers got out. Fear began creeping into Thomas, his legs felt like concrete but he kept walking to his car. He tried to avoid looking at the officers but as he drew level with them one said: 'Excuse me sir but is this your car?' He froze on the spot then muttered: 'Y-Yes, is there a problem officer?' He had began sweating heavily again and was pale in the face. The officer noticed this and asked: 'Are you alright sir? You don't look very well at all.'

'Oh yes thank you, I've just got a stomach virus.'

'Well if you're sure sir, I was just going to tell you your tailgate is not shut properly. Didn't you notice it while you were driving?'

'No, no I opened it to get my coat from the back before I went in the services, I couldn't have shut it properly, thanks for telling me.'

'That's ok sir, well if you're sure you are alright we'll let you get on your way, are you driving far?'

'No only to Surrey.'

'Ok then sir have a good journey and take care of that stomach.' The officers touched the peaks of their hats and said goodnight.

Thomas was so weak he only just managed to open the car door and slide in onto the seat. He was still wearing his neckerchief from the jungle so he took it off and poured some water from the bottle on it and wiped his face and neck. He sat and recovered for a while then he started the engine and turned the air conditioning on. While he cooled down he checked his mobile to see if the doctor had called and was relieved to see he hadn't.

He relaxed and waited. Finally the call arrived earlier Templeton had told Thomas that the doctor's name was Sherwood, when Thomas's told him his symptoms, Sherwood said he wasn't sure from that information what he was suffering from without examining him. He gave Thomas directions how to find him and said he would wait in his car—a green Ford Fiesta. When the call was over Thomas ignored Templeton's order to destroy the mobile, he thought it may be a bargaining chip if Templeton tried a double cross.

When Thomas pulled into the car park at the back of the shop he spotted the doctor's car, but there was also another car parked a few spaces away. Thomas drove past the car but it was empty so he drove up to the doctor's car. He got out and the doctor moved to get out of his vehicle but Thomas pointed his gun at him and told him to stay where he was, he asked for some ID, the doctor said he only had his driving licence with him. Thomas told him to take the licence out of his jacket slowly and hand it to him. Templeton had told Thomas the doctor's name so he checked the licence, once he was satisfied he suggested the doctor treat him in the Range Rover as it was the larger car.

The doctor got out and took his bag from the boot of his car and with Thomas got in the back of the Range rover. Sherwood took Thomas's temperature and it was very high, higher than most viruses would cause, after further examinations he told Thomas: 'I have no idea what you are suffering from, the symptoms are similar to Malaria but I'm not sure that's what you have. I don't carry much in my bag other than normal pain killers and cold and flu medication, neither of those would help you I'm afraid. I have never come across anything like the symptoms you are showing.'

Thomas was not amused, he snarled: 'What sort of doctor are you, here give me that bag? Thomas snatched the bag and rooted through it, in his frustration he tipped the contents out on to the seat, there were pills and tablets and several small bottles of medicine. Thomas picked up handfuls of the contents and waved them under Sherwood's nose, he said still angry: 'There must be something here you can give me, stop the diagnosing and start the treatment.' Sherwood was worried, Thomas was showing signs of paranoia and he seemed unstable. He knew nothing he gave him would be any use but he had to appease him. He had a small phial of serum, he thought that might help bring his temperature down for a while, at least long enough for Thomas to get far enough away before he realises he hadn't really helped him. He told Thomas to pull his trousers and underpants down and lay on his side. Thomas was suspicious of this and said: 'Why do you need me to do that?'

'I have to inject you in the cheek of your behind the medication will enter the bloodstream quicker that way.' Thomas was still sceptical but did as the doctor asked anyway. Sherwood prepared the vaccine and inserted the needle in Thomas's buttock, Thomas yelled swearing at Sherwood, he said the needle must have been blunt but Sherwood ignored him and pushed it in all the way in. When the needle was withdrawn Thomas yelled again, he said he would kill Sherwood if he hurt him again. Sherwood told Thomas: 'You should wait an hour before you drive you may suffer from dizziness for a while. Sherwood then added as an afterthought: 'I will call you in an hour to see how you are.' Sherwood repacked his bag and said goodbye.

Thomas's original plan was to drive to the abandoned Military airfield to meet up with a small time fence, he was going to deal with any small items of jewellery and gold etc that Thomas may have brought back in addition to the giant stone. Now though he decided that he would get Elaine's company to handle the lot. So he decided to go straight to the house expecting to find Elaine and Clifford still held there.

Feeling better after just ten minutes he started the car and set off heading for the house, as he was driving he was trying to figure out what he was going to do with Bird and Palmer, after all the spoils were much smaller now and there was less to share. His condition even though he felt a little better was preventing him from thinking straight, so he thought he would just get there and play it by ear.

CHAPTER THIRTY SEVEN

The Police arrived just after Thomas drove away. A patrol car containing two uniformed officers was first to attend followed a few minutes later by an ambulance. Nick had passed out cold still propped up against the tree, one paramedic checked him out and the other went over to Simpson's body. He lifted the sheet and once he had established death he joined his colleague. The Police officer's asked if Nick was dying but at that time the medics couldn't say for sure but said it was probable.

The Police officers commenced processing the scene wearing forensic latex gloves. Firstly they checked Simpson's body and noticed how wet he was, they thought no more of it and replaced the cover and continued to look around. One officer checked close to where Nick was lying and found the wrench with blood on it. He picked it up and took it to the car, bagging it for evidence. He called the other officer and showed it to him and commented that the dead guy had no visible wounds so they went and looked at Nick. The attendant showed them the wound to his head and shoulder saying: 'Someone has treated him, his wounds were clean and his shoulder was strapped up very well, we have noticed though his clothes are soaking wet with perspiration and he has a rash virtually over the whole of his body.

The officer who looked at Simpson and said: 'That's odd because the dead guy is soaking wet as well.' The paramedic's looked at each other, one of them said: 'I'll check him over.' he went with the officers and unbuttoned Simpsons coat and shirt and saw he also had a large rash. He immediately told his colleague to leave Nick and come away, he said: 'I hope I am wrong but it looks as if we have something contagious here.' The officer that looked at Simpson said: 'God I touched him. What is it?' The medics looked at each other and one said: 'We don't know, this guy's wounds are not serious and shouldn't be causing his high temperature, its forty one degrees and rising and there's the rash. One officer immediately reported the situation to their control, as did the medic, the hospital told the paramedic not to touch the body or Nick anymore and get himself and everybody else away and the Infectious Diseases team would be there shortly.

The Police officers on the medic's advice got back in their car, the medics waited in the ambulance. They waited for over thirty minutes and it had become dark, then one of the officers saw flashing blue lights heading their way. Eventually two large vehicles arrived, their flashing lights lighting up the whole area. The minute the vehicles stopped men in white protective suits complete with hoods and masks jumped out. One—the man in charge approached the ambulance, the medics attempted to leave the ambulance but the man in the suit stopped them saying: 'Hello I am the head of the infectious diseases department, please stay in the vehicle and keep the doors and windows closed tight, someone will be over to speak with you soon. He then went and told the Police officers the same.

Meanwhile other suited personnel were inspecting Simpson's body and then Nick, one approached the ambulance and indicated to the driver to open the window, he asked the medic: 'What do you know about these two?' The medic told him that they were called out by local Police after an anonymous call but no other information was given. He told him how he had inspected the injured one and that he was bathed in sweat and had an extensive rash covering most of his torso. He then told him that Simpson's body showed the same symptoms, so they called it in. The man told him they had done the right thing but they would now have be taken to the hospital and put in isolation immediately, the man told him they would have to follow their vehicle and their families would be notified as to what was happening. The Police officers were told likewise and to follow the ambulance.

At that moment there was a roar of an engine and a bright lights coming from the sky as a Police helicopter swept in and landed. Lewis and Deacon had been informed of the situation and immediately ordered the chopper he had also alerted Armed Response. The Infectious Diseases team had begun loading Nick and Simpson onto their vehicles and were almost ready to leave.

Lewis and Deacon leapt out as soon as the chopper landed, the head man immediately went over to them and told them to stay by the helicopter until the two men were loaded on the vehicles. Lewis acknowledged him then introduced himself and Deacon.

The man related to Lewis the events, especially the mystery condition of Nick and Simpson. Lewis had the images of Thomas and crew with him and showed them to the man and asked if either of the men were in the pictures. He confirmed that they were the two men, pointing to Simpson's picture saying: 'He is the dead man.' He continued to tell Lewis that the other one was very ill and would probably not survive. He then asked Lewis: 'Do you know if they had been abroad recently?' Lewis said they had reason to believe they had just flown back from Mexico, to which the man replied: 'Ok that gives us something to go on, now if there's nothing more Superintendant we must get them into Isolation as quickly as possible.' Lewis said he understood and he would check in with him later. Lewis was just about to walk away when he enquired: '? What about the helicopter, when did that leave?'

The man replied: 'I'm sorry I know nothing about a helicopter. Is that how the men got here? If so we have to find the pilot and soon, he could be contagious.'

'Yes they did come in by chopper but we don't know exactly where they landed, we are doing everything we can to trace it I can assure you and when we do we will notify you.' The man then said: 'I forgot one of the Police officers handed me this.' He showed Lewis the bag containing the wrench, he continued: 'He thinks it was used to injure the live one, the strange thing is he was attended to before the ambulance arrived, someone had bound his shoulder quite professionally and cleaned the wound on his head.' Lewis thanked him for the information and went to take the wrench, the man however said he would need to take it to test the blood on it but Lewis could have it once it was processed. This didn't please Lewis but he had to accept it.

The infectious diseases team left and Lewis commenced looking around. Deacon shone his torch around and it picked up a reflection in the grass, he crouched down to see what it was then stood up and called Lewis over. Lewis joined Deacon asking: 'What have you got Inspector? Deacon shone his torch so Lewis could see, Lewis pulled gloves on then bent over and picked up a small solid gold band encrusted with large sparkling diamonds and rubies, he remarked at how heavy it was and said Karen would give anything for him to buy her a present like that. He continued to say that it confirmed the statements they had been given that Thomas had been to Mexico, he then added: 'Thomas was probably scared he would be infected and has disposed of his men, we must get this area searched, Holland could be around here somewhere, call a search team out and alert them to wear protective clothing, also put out a warning that it looks like Thomas is in the area but not to challenge him, he may not only be armed he could now be contagious, they are just to observe him and call it in, the same goes for Holland. Get SOCCO here as well.'

Deacon went to the helicopter and relayed Lewis's message then they continued to look around but, it was now too dark so Lewis said there wasn't anything else they could do but wait until SOCCO and the search team arrived, they would then go to the hospital.

When the search team and SOCCO finally appeared Lewis briefed them on the situation, he said if they find anything at all call his or Deacon's mobiles.

When they arrived at the hospital Nick was being examined by doctors specialised in Infectious Diseases. He was in an isolation ward enclosed in a clear sealed plastic of bubble. Lewis and Deacon were told that there wasn't a diagnosis as yet, they were running tests to try and establish the cause of his condition, but so far all the usual viruses and infections had been ruled out.

Lewis asked one of the doctors attending Nick if he had spoken at all, the doctor said he hadn't and he thought it was doubtful that he would in his condition. However he added that he had learned not to underestimate the human mind and would not rule it out. Lewis told the doctor that he and Deacon would wait around for a while just in case he should regain consciousness and could be questioned. Two hours later there was no change so Lewis called for uniformed officers to guard Nick's ward and returned to the station.

An hour or so later Lewis got a call saying that SOCCO had found more items of gold and jewellery spread around the area but nothing significant, however the search team had to give up until the next morning because it was too the dark to search properly.

Meanwhile Thomas was on a dual carriageway heading for the motorway, he started to get double vision and the sweats were starting up again causing him to swerve occasionally across lanes, luckily the traffic was light and no harm was done. He pulled off the road into a lay by, he was glad he had ignored Templeton's order to destroy the mobile because he needed to call the doctor again. Sherwood didn't answer right away, the call went to his voicemail; he was in the bathroom of a pub, he needed a drink after his meeting with Thomas.

His phone was in the pocket of his jacket which he had put over his stool, when he returned to the bar the barman told him that it had just rang. He reached in his pocket and retrieved the phone, he listened to the voice mail and he cringed when he heard Thomas's voice, he had hoped he had heard the last of him, however he dialled Thomas's number and Thomas recognised the number, he said: 'Look I am getting worse, that stuff you gave me was a waste of time, my eyes are going funny and the sweats are back.' The doctor tried to explain he had warned Thomas that this may happen and asked if he was still driving. Thomas said he was but he had pulled off the road and was in a lay by, adding it would be Sherwood's fault if he did kill someone as he had given him the wrong medication. He told Sherwood to get to the lay by immediately as he needed more medicine and the he—Sherwood—would have to drive the car. Sherwood said: 'No I'm not driving you, I am not getting involved in whatever you and Templeton are up to, I've done my bit now go away and leave me alone.' Thomas snapped screaming into the phone: 'Look if you don't come and drive me I'll find you and your family and I will kill all of you, I swear.' Templeton had warned Sherwood about Thomas and his rages and now he was really scared, he decided he had no option he told Thomas he would drive him but wanted nothing to do with anything else. Thomas told him he was already in up to his neck just by treating him, he told him to stop wailing and notify Templeton then get his ass over to the lay by.

Sherwood hung up and called Templeton, He was furious that Thomas hadn't destroyed the mobile and that he was involving Sherwood, up to that point he had managed only to involve a few people, the last thing he wanted was an unstable ex doctor hamming things up. However he also knew Thomas would keep his promise regarding Sherwood's family and things could get very messy if he didn't help. He advised Sherwood to go and drive Thomas where he wanted to go, but to use his own car then he could get out fast. He also told him to tell Thomas to get rid of the phone now or he would leave him high and dry with no more help.

Sherwood was very reluctant to concede to Thomas's orders and Templeton's decision but knew he was in a no win situation. He called Thomas back and said he would drive him in HIS car but as soon as he had dropped him wherever he was going he was off, he told him what Templeton had said regarding the mobile but Thomas ignored it.

It only took fifteen minutes for Sherwood to reach Thomas, he pulled in behind the Range Rover and Thomas opened the door and almost fell out, Sherwood got out and went to assist him but Thomas shrugged him off saying he was only after his treasure, it was obvious he was getting delusional.

He managed to calm Thomas down and get him into his car. He put him in the back seat as he didn't want to sit next to him. Thomas protested as best he could but Sherwood told him he was going to get his treasure and put it in the back with him then he could keep an eye on it, this appeased Thomas. Sherwood collected the two backpacks from Thomas's car. Thomas grabbed the bags from him as soon as he appeared with them telling him to keep his thieving hands off. Sherwood made sure Thomas had his seat belt on so the Police wouldn't have any reason to pull him over then shut the door. He got in the driver's seat and started the car. Sherwood asked where they were going and Thomas said he would guide him as they went along, Sherwood wondered if he would be in a fit state to do that but chose to say nothing.

CHAPTER THIRTY EIGHT

Lewis and Deacon were speeding homeward when they picked up a radio conversation saying that a helicopter had crashed, there had been a large explosion and a raging fire was sweeping through a carpet warehouse on the edge of Guildford. Deacon remarked that they were quite a distance from there but Lewis said: 'That's ok, let's go and see if we can be of assistance, it could be Thomas's chopper.' Lewis put his foot down and switched on his blue lights and headed for Guildford. As they drew close to the area a bright glow appeared in the sky. When they reached the scene pandemonium reigned with ten fire engines pumping water continuously onto the fire trying to extinguish it, there were Police cars and ambulances everywhere and Police officers trying to keep onlookers at bay. Lewis stopped the car and a uniformed officer came over, Lewis wound down the window and the officer informed Lewis: 'I'm sorry sir you will have to move on, you can't stop .... Lewis cut him short and showed him his ID card and told the officer: 'It's alright officer we're here in case we can help.' The officer apologised and Lewis asked what had happened. The officer told Lewis the chopper had come down about two hours or so ago on the rear of the building. Lewis asked if there were any survivor's and if anyone had got a good look at the chopper before it came down. The officer said he wouldn't think anyone had survived the crash and no one had witness the crash as it happened so quick. Lewis asked if they knew colour of the helicopter, the police officer said: 'Red, I think, but I can't be sure because no one has got close enough because of the heat of the fire sir.'

Lewis responded by saying: 'Not to worry constable, however the chopper could well be one we have been looking for in connection with an enquiry into a double kidnapping and murder case. I'd like to speak to whoever's in charge.' The officer said DCI Wright was the attending officer and went to fetch him.

A few minutes later the DCI came to the car. After introductions were complete, Lewis asked Wright: 'Can you ensure that every scrap of the chopper and its contents is collected carefully and delivered to Chelsea nick?' Tell anyone who questions that to contact the Chief Constable at Chelsea, he will sanction any request. Tell whoever delivers it to contact me or any member of my team. Finally If they do recover any bodies they must not be touched, instead contact the Infectious Diseases Department, they could be carrying a contagious virus.' DCI Wright said: 'Of course Superintendant I will pass it on to my team and my superiors.' Lewis thanked Wright for his understanding and bid him goodnight and left the scene.

Lewis and Deacon drove for a while then pulled into a pub, he said to Deacon: 'I thing we need a drink, what say you Inspector?' 'Deacon said: 'Good idea but I'll just have an orange juice because I don't drink alcohol you go ahead though, I'll drive the rest of the way.'

After they got their drinks they found a seat and sat down, Lewis sighed then said: 'What a mess, we don't know who was in the chopper and Thomas could be anywhere, if he is still alive that is, then there's this Holland guy, where is he?'

'I know Gov it wasn't long ago when we thought we were getting somewhere, now this. I vote we go home and get a good night's sleep in our own beds, maybe things will look a little better in the morning.' Lewis raised his glass and said: 'That's the best thing I've heard all day, cheers.' They sat and drunk their drinks contemplating the day's events before heading home.

Meanwhile Thomas had guided Sherwood to the lane leading to the kidnap house. Sherwood was approaching the lane when Thomas told him to slow down as he was feeling worse than ever. He still had double vision and was sweating profusely, the hot and cold spells were becoming more frequent and he noticed a small rash appearing on the back of his hands. He was lucid enough though to tell Sherwood to go just past the lane and pull up into the shadows of the trees.

When the car stopped Thomas opened his door and almost fell out and he saw the van had gone. Sherwood got out and helped him to his feet, Thomas said: 'Right get the bags from the car and help me up the lane.' Sherwood instantly refused saying he had fulfilled his part of the deal and he was on his own. Thomas pulled his gun from his pocket and forced the muzzle up against Sherwood's nose saying: 'You go when I say you go, now get those bags and get in front of me and be quiet.'

Nervously Sherwood took the bags from the car and Thomas told him to give him the car keys. They moved off towards the house but Sherwood struggled to carry the bags dropping them many times and Thomas blasted him each time. Eventually they came level with the house and Thomas whispered to Sherwood to find somewhere safe to hide the bags then come back.

Sherwood found an evergreen bush with thickly leaved branches that reached the ground, he lifted the branches and put the bags behind them and pulled the branches back down, he returned saying he had found a good hiding place. Thomas shoved Sherwood in front of him and they approached the house, when they reached the door Thomas noticed it was damaged but closed.

Thomas told Sherwood to knock on the door Sherwood though sensed trouble and refused. Thomas asked again this time waving the gun at him, Sherwood was powerless so he walked to the door and knocked lightly. Thomas said that was too soft and to knock again but harder, Sherwood conceded and knocked again with no response, Thomas told Sherwood to knock once more, this time Thomas had moved away warily because he knew if his men were still in there, they would have responded by then.

By the time Sherwood knocked a third time Thomas was on the path ready to make a quick exit, cautious in case Police were inside. A minute passed and then all hell broke loose as The Armed Response Team appeared from the back of the house screaming: "ARMED POLICE DROP YOUR WEAPONS AND GET ON THE GROUND NOW".

Sherwood jumped out of his skin and fell to the ground like a stone. Thomas had hid behind a bush and the second

Sherwood was ambushed he hobbled as fast as he could back to the car. He reached the car and opened the door and got in and drove off. His head was spinning and he was furious because not only had he lost the Jessop's he also had to leave his treasure behind.

Back at the house Sherwood was encircled by the ART and told to lie flat out on the ground. Detectives and plain clothed officers came out expecting to find Thomas, one of them—Detective Inspector Crane forced his way through the crowd of officers, he asked Sherwood where Thomas was, Sherwood was protesting he hadn't done anything, he was trembling but said he did not know where Thomas was, saying that he had been right behind him when he had knocked the door.

The DI despatched the ART to spread out and find him, Sherwood shouted: 'Watch out he has a gun, my car is down the lane and he has the keys, he may go for that.' Di Crane and a Detective Constable Hodges took Sherwood inside the house to question him further.

Lewis and Deacon were nearing the station when DI Crane called reporting the incident, Lewis cursed and asked Crane: 'Is he on foot?' Crane replied: 'No we think he is in a green Ford Fiesta.' He gave Lewis the registration number but said he didn't know the direction he had taken, Lewis said: I do! 'Ok get Sherwood to the station and have him questioned on tape and send the ART up to Templeton's mansion and surround it, tell them to keep a low profile with no lights or sirens, I'm on my way.' DCI Crane warned Lewis that Sherwood had said that Thomas was armed and very ill, adding though that Sherwood seemed fine.

Lewis called control and told them to send further armed backup to Templeton's house ordering them to stay out of sight, and to call out "Infectious Diseases." to attend. Lewis ended the call and told Deacon to turn the car around and head to Templeton's house but not to put the siren on.

CHAPTER THIRTY NINE

Thomas didn't go straight to Templeton's house, instead he went left towards the house Palmer and Bird abducted Joanne from, although he didn't know anything about that. His plan was to wait because he knew that as soon as the police discovered he had Taken Sherwood's car, they would leave the house and almost definitely head in the direction of Chelsea, thinking he would go back for the Jessop's.

He turned around and parked on the opposite side of the road just before a bend which hid him but he could still see the lane, he waited until all the Police drove away from the lane then waited a few more minutes, he then pulled out and drove up to the lane and parked. He hobbled up the lane to where Sherwood had hid his treasure. Franticly he looked under hedges and bushes until eventually finding his backpacks, he was sure that Sherwood wouldn't mention the treasure, planning to come back when the heat died down and take it for himself.

He managed to haul the two bags back to the car and heave them into the boot then drove off heading to Templeton's house. He knew that Templeton was his last chance of getting the treasure fenced. He planned to blackmail Templeton into agreeing to fence the jewels by threatening to name him as a co-conspirator if he was caught.

Templeton's mansion was set in private grounds enclosed by high walls and electronically operated gates. The ART had arrived before the backup, the leading officer strategically placed his men so the entrance was completely covered but they were out of sight. Lewis and Deacon arrived just after them.

Lewis's orders were to let Thomas arrive and enter the grounds, he was sure that Templeton would let him in knowing Thomas's capabilities. He then planned to wait until he considered it safe enough, the ART vehicle would then ram the gates and once they were clear all units could then converge on the house surprising both men, and hopefully arrest Thomas and Templeton.

Half an hour went by and Lewis remarked to Deacon that this was the night they have been waiting for then they would be able to sleep for a week. Deacon had replied telling him that he may have to wake him up in a minute if nothing kicked off soon. Lewis said he didn't understand why Thomas had not arrived but said they must be patient as he was sure he would come to Templeton's.

Ten minutes later the ART Sergeant who was scanning the area with night vision binoculars caught sight of a heat glow heading towards them. He watched for a couple of minutes then announced over the radio: "POSSIBLE TARGET APPROACHING DUE EAST, APPROXIMATELY FIVE HUNDRED YARDS AWAY". Lewis used his radio warning that no one was to make a move without his explicit order. After confirming it was indeed Thomas, the Sergeant followed Thomas's progress right up to the gates.

Thomas reached the gates and winding down the driver's window pushed the button on the intercom. Templeton's wife answered saying: 'Hello Who are you and what do you want?' Thomas in his normal sarcastic way answered: 'Hello Mrs Templeton? I wish to see your husband, tell him it's his old pal Darren, I have something he has been waiting for.' When Templeton came on he was very angry saying: 'Thomas; 'What the hell are you doing? I told you never to come here, for God's sake the Police will be watching, you moron.' Thomas told him it was not a nice way to talk as he had especially come to bring him a gift. Templeton had no option but to open the gates, Thomas drove in and followed the long drive to the house.

Templeton told his wife that he was going to be tied up for a while with a very important client and he was taking him into the study and he didn't wish to disturbed. She knew of his shady deals and how he treated people so she said nothing, pouring herself a large gin she turned and walked into the kitchen.

Thomas pulled up outside the door, Templeton was outside waiting. He let Thomas in, looking all around to make sure the coast was clear. Thomas didn't take the treasure in with him, he wanted to work a deal out with Templeton first.

Meanwhile Lewis had put the raid in motion, ART decided to pull the gates off their hinges instead of ramming them because the Sergeant said they looked too heavy and would damage the vehicle too much. Their vehicles were equipped with a winch below the rear bumper, two officers attached the clamps at the end of the wire to the gates and the winch was set in motion. Slowly the winch began turning. The gates were groaning as the cable tightened, until finally they gave way, once down they were lifted to one side and Lewis gave the order to "GO GO GO" and all units made their way slowly and quietly, up the drive towards the house.

Templeton had led Thomas to the study in silence, once they were in the study though he began a torrent of abuse and threats. Thomas stopped him and said: 'Look Just shut the steam tap off for a minute and listen, I had to come to you because the whole business is finished. The Jessop's have been found and my two men are missing, probably locked up. Not only that the three men that came with me to Mexico are dead, so calm down and think of a plan to get us out of this mess.'

Templeton sat in his leather chair and told Thomas to sit. Pouring two large Brandies and handing one to Thomas he told him he couldn't fence anything at the moment because the Police were watching his every move, they were scrutinising all his papers plus they had almost certainly bugged his phones and that is why he warned him not to call him, adding they had taken all of his private and business computers. He sipped his brandy then told Thomas there was possibly one person who may be able to help them, Thomas sat shivering while Templeton walked over to his bureau and took a small card from a hidden draw, he walked back and handed it to Thomas, He said: 'That's better, See what can be achieved with a little patience?' Templeton ignored him and asked if Sherwood had said anything about him to the Police, Thomas told him: 'Ooh I wouldn't know, but I wouldn't mind betting he is singing his little heart out to save his skin, I bet the old bill will soon be breaking your doors down, that is why we need to get the stuff moved and if I were you I'd get myself and my lovely wife away from here pronto.'

All the while Mrs Templeton had been listening outside the door, she was aware who Thomas was and of what he was saying, she suddenly thought of how she could get rid of Templeton and have Thomas arrested at the same time. She decided to call the Police to report that Thomas was in her house and what she had heard. She went back into the kitchen to make the call on her mobile, she called the emergency services number and they answered her call, they said that any calls concerning the investigation needed to be transferred to Chelsea.

The duty desk Sergeant at Chelsea took her call, immediately Mrs Templeton mentioned Thomas's name and about the murders he immediately asked her to hang on and called DI Barnes who was holding the fort while DCS Lewis and DI Deacon were out. The Sergeant briefed Barnes on the call then patched it through to him. Mrs Templeton repeated to him what she had told the Sergeant and Barnes said: 'Ok Mrs Templeton, thank you we do know all about your husband, I suggest you get yourself out of there as quickly and quietly as possible because we are about to raid your house with armed men.'

Mrs Templeton said: 'Oh my God!' Panicking she dropped her phone, while trying to catch the mobile she hit it with her hand, sending it flying out of the door and onto hall floor. Templeton and Thomas heard the commotion, Thomas shushed Templeton and opened the study door slightly, as he did he saw Mrs Templeton creeping along the hallway to retrieve the mobile. Acting swiftly he opened the door and grabbed the mobile, she froze on the spot then ran back into the kitchen locking the door. Thomas returned to the study and showed Templeton the phone number she had called, he said to Templeton: 'That damned wife of yours has shopped us the filth will be here any minute we've got to get out of here.' Templeton not wishing to go with Thomas reacted quickly, he was standing behind his chair which was on wheels, kicking out with his foot he shoved the chair at Thomas and it caught his leg. Thomas was so weak it knocked him sideways and he dropped the gun, Templeton quickly grabbed the gun and pointed it at Thomas. Thomas got to his feet slowly and attempted to lunge at Templeton He panicked and inadvertently pulled the trigger. The bullet entered the left side of Thomas's chest close to his heart and he dropped like a stone, blood pouring from the wound.

Just prior to that Lewis had received the message referring to Mrs Templeton's call and when the shot rang out from inside the house he told ART to bring the front door down he also called for an ambulance.

The main body of men took the front door and a smaller group went to the rear of the property. There front doors were constructed from heavy hard wood. Using battering rams the ART smashed into the doors but they didn't open, so they were hit once more. This time they gave way and the ART stormed in shouting: "ARMED POLICE STAY WHERE YOU ARE AND DROP YOUR WEAPONS." Before the two men could react, the door to the study burst open and armed officers poured in. Two officers leapt on Templeton grabbing the gun and forced him onto the floor, telling him to lay flat on his stomach and put his hands on his head. Other officers checked over the rest of the house and found Mrs Templeton cowering in the utility room.

The "all clear call" went out and Lewis and Deacon came into the study. Thomas was on his back with blood seeping from his wound, Lewis saw it was close to his heart and thinking he wouldn't have much time he knelt down ensuring he didn't touch him and asked: 'Where's John Holland?' Thomas was weak from the loss of blood and from the virus; he just looked at Lewis saying nothing. Lewis could see that he was dying so tried once more: 'Daren; I know who you are and what you have done, you are dying so why not do one good thing before you do, tell me where John is and how did you contract this illness?' Thomas was weak but answered in a whisper: 'Holland dead . . . . monster did for him . . . . virus . . . . the curse . . . with that he died.

Lewis overlooked the "Monster" part of Thomas's last word's assuming he wasn't in his right mind. He called the Infectious Diseases team in to deal with Thomas then went to see Templeton, he was sitting handcuffed, Lewis stated: "Alex Francis Templeton, I am arresting you on the suspicion of being an accomplice to murder and kidnapping, also for associating with and financing known criminals and perverting the course of justice." He then told Deacon to take him to a car before he did though

Lewis asked if he had touched Thomas, Templeton said he hadn't, Lewis said ok and told deacon to carry on.

Mrs Templeton was understandably distraught, she had been taken outside and placed in a car, Lewis attempted to question her but she was incoherent so he made the decision to send her to hospital to get checked over. Among the back up team were two WPC's, Lewis told one to take her to the waiting ambulance and go with her to hospital, he told her not to leave her side until someone relieved her, he then ordered the despatch of SOCCO and Forensics to process the house once Thomas's body had been removed by Infectious Diseases.

CHAPTER FOURTY

It was one twenty am when Lewis and Deacon finished at Templeton's house. They had found Thomas's treasure in Sherwood's car boot and were driving back to the station. Lewis was quiet despite the case being all but solved. After ten minutes Deacon broke the silence saying: 'Well Gov not the ending we expected.'

'No but I am not convinced it is over, theoretically there are only a couple of loose ends to tie up, and considering the felons involved in this case the Templeton's are small fry compared. No, we need to interview Alex Templeton ASAP I'm sure we have missed something.'

On their return to headquarters they headed straight for the coffee machine then to Lewis's office. As they both sat back in their chairs Lewis untied his shoe laces and slipped his shoes off, he looked at Deacon and said: 'Sorry, but I need to do this my bunion is killing me, I never seem to have five minutes these days to take these damn things off.' Deacon was diplomatic and said nothing. Lewis scrolled through his E-Mails and read one from Infectious Diseases informing him that Nick had lost his battle for life at ten minutes past midnight, it read: "All tests on the two victims revealed no obvious cause for their symptoms and no traces of the usual or rare viruses, infections or diseases were present in either victim" "Their bodies are being kept on ice for further tests and samples of their blood and tissue have been sent to University College London, one of the world's leading authorities in contagious and infectious diseases to be examined in the hope they could come up with something" The good news is the two police officers and the ambulance paramedics had so far shown no signs of being infected."

Another E-Mail was from the senior officer—DCI Wright from the helicopter crash site. The E-Mail was just to say that the helicopter was completely burnt out but the area search revealed several pieces of wreckage and gold and jewellery scattered around the site. He wanted Lewis to confirm whether the items were relevant to his enquiry. Lewis replied immediately telling Wright they were indeed relevant and to have them bagged separately and sent to him immediately, he then told Deacon: 'You go home and tell Barnes to go home as well. I'll see you in the morning. I'll stay and go over all the paperwork on the case and write up my report before I go home.

Lewis had dropped off in his chair while writing up his reports. When Deacon knocked on his office door the following morning he woke Lewis up. Lewis was not sure where he was at first but soon refocused and called for Deacon to go in. Deacon had stopped off at a cafe outside the station to buy himself and Lewis a "proper coffee". He handed one to Lewis, He half smiled in gratitude, he was shaving with an electric shaver and asked Deacon the time Deacon told him it was eight forty.

Lewis finished his shave and while he was putting his razor away his phone rang, it was the Commissioner, he told Lewis: 'Internal affairs have found the mole I hope you are sitting down.' Lewis waited for him to continue but was shell shocked when the commissioner announced the mole was Charles Price, the Chief Constable. He said he understood it was a shock to Lewis, as it was to everybody. He continued: 'I'm sorry Lewis but the evidence is clear, we have phone records from his home linking him to the mobile that Palmer had on him when he was arrested, and to Templeton's house, there was even a call to Price's landline from Palmer the night of the failed recapture of the Jessop's from the safe house.' The Commissioner went on to tell Lewis what else they had found.

Lewis hung up and sat with his mouth wide open trying to take in what he had just been told. Deacon saw that Lewis's face was almost white and asked: 'WHAT?' Lewis was unable to answer immediately, eventually he told him: 'That was the Commissioner. You know that Internal Affairs have been looking into how Palmer knew the whereabouts of the safe house? Well they've discovered calls to and from Palmer and Templeton on Chief Constable. There was even one from the mobile Thomas had made on the night of the woman's abduction.' Deacon was dumb founded. Lewis went on to say he tried telling the commissioner that there had to be an explanation but, he said the evidence was clear and that Special Branch was on their way to Prices house to arrest him at that moment.

Lewis thought to himself for a bit then said he would some digging around himself to satisfy his own mind. Deacon told him he would have to be careful as internal affairs did not like any interference in their enquiries.

He acknowledged Deacon's concerns then asked him to arrange an interview with Templeton.

Templeton's interview was set up for twelve thirty. He was handcuffed taken to an interview room and made to sit on a chair at a small table.

Minutes later Lewis entered and sat opposite Templeton, he switched on the tape recorder and opened a thick case file then asked: 'Mr Templeton, how did you get involved with Daren Thomas? You aren't exactly bankrupt are you? After all your business is worth millions, why risk it all for nothing?' Templeton remained silent for a few seconds then said: 'It wasn't supposed to be for nothing, all my money is tied up in my business, when Thomas was introduced to me by another business associate—whom I have no intention of revealing so don't ask me—he told me about his jungle idea and a few million in cash was too much of a temptation. I funded him by arranging the helicopter and pilot, I also booked the plane tickets.' Lewis said: 'Well your pilot crashed his helicopter last night near Guildford, we don't know why yet though because he perished in a blazing inferno. Although he may have died anyway as he was in contact with Thomas's men who died of an unknown disease. Right moving on, can you tell me how do you know Chief Constable Price?' Templeton paused before saying: 'I don't actually know him, you see my wife and I attend the odd charity event—you meet some influential people at them do's—I've said hello to him from time to time but I don't know him as such. I'd be rather stupid to do what I've done if I was linked with someone like him, what makes you think I would know him anyway?'

'It's just one of the lines of our enquiry. Now what about this Sherwood character, how does he fit into all this?' Templeton said he was just a means to an end when Thomas called saying he was ill and needed help. Templeton suddenly stopped talking and said he was not saying any more until he had a solicitor present. Lewis said there was no need as it was just an informal chat and he would be interviewed more formally later. Lewis went on to tell him that he and Thomas had caused people to lose their lives and, ruined those of other innocent people and that he hoped he was happy with himself. Templeton didn't reply he just looked away.

Lewis left Templeton and met up with Deacon. Lewis told him he was going to see Mrs Price later that morning to have a word about her husband's position. He suggested telling Bird and Palmer that Thomas and his backer had been found but, not to reveal the actual circumstances, if they do want to tell us anything else that may well be the prompt they needed.

CHAPTER FORTY ONE

Lewis waited until eleven thirty then called Helen Price. She answered his call but sounded distracted. Lewis was not surprised considering her life had just been torn apart.

He asked if she was up to him visiting her and she said it was ok, so he arranged to go at twelve thirty.

Lewis arrived at the house and Helen let him in taking him into the drawing room, they both sat down and Lewis said: 'I really don't know what to say Helen, I was so shocked when I heard, I'm not letting it rest though, I know Charles and he just would not be so stupid.'

Helen said she was still in shock saying they had taken his computer plus lots of other items away. Lewis asked where Special Branch had taken Charles, Helen said she had no idea and asked if Lewis would find out for her, adding she had been too shocked at the time to ask questions and she wanted to make sure Charles had the best solicitor possible. Helen went on to say Special Branch had just stormed in and took him at just after seven in the morning, dragging him out of bed. Lewis said: 'I'm so sorry Helen, but I must ask you this, have you seen or heard anything that may explain any of this, phone calls at odd hours or strange E-Mails perhaps?' Helen said she had not seen or heard anything and did not use the Charles's computer as she had her own, adding it was actually a laptop.

Lewis, thanking Helen, stood up to leave and said he would get to the bottom of it all and would be in touch.

He returned to his office and decided to call the Jessop's with the news about Thomas and his backer but, more so the CC, as Clifford was friends with the Charles. Clifford said that he could not believe that Charles would do such a stupid thing as not only would he throw his career away but his pension as well. He told Lewis that Charles had told him he was going to take early retirement next year so he could take Helen around the world on his yacht, which was something he and Helen had always dreamed of doing. Lewis asked him if he knew Alex Templeton. Clifford said he vaguely knew him from social events, he said the last time he saw him was at Helens birthday party, adding that Charles had introduced Elaine and him to them but they had not chatted. He added that he had noticed Mrs Templeton having a "serious" conversation with Helen in the hallway when he passed them on his way to the bathroom. He said whatever they were discussing it was not a friendly conversation, but he had not heard what they were talking about and they were gone back into the party by the time he came back.

Lewis apologised for springing the news on him over the phone but promised he would look into things himself.

Meanwhile Deacon had Palmer and Bird brought back from their cells so he could tell them the news. He had them put in separate rooms and in turn he informed them both that they had found Thomas and Templeton, they both reacted differently to the news, Palmer was nonchalant, Deacon asked him if it was a man or a woman who answered the mobile when he called to find the safe house. At first he said it was a woman then changed his mind and said it was a man.

Bird however was ecstatic that Thomas was not a threat to him anymore but, had nothing to add to his previous statement.

When Lewis returned from Helen's house Deacon told him about his talks to the two prisoners. Lewis said he was disappointed that they said nothing, but said they may change their tune as their trials loomed, for now though he wanted to concentrate on finding out who may have had a grudge or a motive to set Charles up, he said he was off to talk to Mrs Templeton at the hospital.

He left the office and was walking down the corridor when suddenly he stopped and shouted out loud "THAT'S IT, THE BLOODY COMPUTER." Deacon heard him and was about to come out of the office when Lewis rushed back in and blurted out: 'COMPUTER, SHE SAID SHE HAD HER OWN COMPUTER.' Deacon was puzzled and asked: 'Who? What computer?

What are you talking about?' Lewis had calmed down and said: 'Helen, Helen Price, when I asked her if she saw anything odd on Charles's computer, she said "no I never use his computer, I have my own" actually she said it was laptop. That's it don't you see?'

'No, not really Gov no, surely you don't suspect her do you?'

'Well I don't know her that well, actually I only really know her through Charles, hold on I just remembered Clifford Jessop told me something interesting earlier, but with everything that's happened lately it didn't really click. He said that Templeton's wife and Helen were in a conversation in the hallway during Helens birthday dinner, he didn't know what they were saying exactly, just that it didn't seem a friendly conversation. We will need to find out what they were talking about. Ok, change of plan, you go and question Mrs Templeton and I'll go back to see Helen and get her laptop. God I hope I'm wrong, I admit it will clear Charles but his life will still be ruined if I am right. Why do people have such a craving to be rich? I just don't get it.'

Lewis left and went back to the Prices house and Deacon headed to the hospital. Lewis arrived at the house and there was an old white MG Sports car in the drive and he parked his car next to it. He approached the front double doors but found they were half open. He pushed them open a little wider and called out: "HELLO, MRS PRICE ITS ME DCS LEWIS . . . . MRS PRICE . . . . There was no answer, so he went into the entrance hall and called out again. There was still no answer so Lewis cautiously began looking around. He went into the study which was the first room on the left and found that empty so he headed for the large lounge then the drawing room at the end of the hall but they were all empty. The kitchen was on the left and as he passed it he spotted saucepans and broken china on the floor. Lewis cautiously walked into the kitchen and saw a small patch of congealed blood on the edge of the work surface, there was also blood on the floor. He immediately called for backup.

Lewis walked back out into the hall way and after checking the lounge and drawing room again, he began to edge his way upstairs. He checked the bedrooms and he was surprised to discover that Helen slept in a separate room from Charles. He looked in the walk-in wardrobes and draws and found that all of Helens clothes seemed to be there. He then looked around the rest of the rooms upstairs but there was no sign of her or her laptop.

Lewis was on his way down the stairs when he heard a car pulling up in the drive. He went outside and two uniformed officers were getting out of a patrol car. He greeted the officers and briefed them on what he had found. Lewis then called the Commissioner to give him the news and also what he and Deacon had discussed earlier regarding Helen Price.

The commissioner told Lewis that Price had been interviewed several times and he hadn't wavered from professing his innocence, and was not acting like someone who has just flushed his career and marriage down the toilet. The Commissioner said he would discuss with his colleagues the latest events and what Lewis had told him especially concerning Helen's computer and her possible relationship with the Templeton's. Lewis hung up then told some other officers who had since arrived to go and knock on neighbours doors to ask whether anyone was seen at or near the house, he then went back into the house to have a more thorough for Helen's laptop, told the first two officers to stand guard until forensics and SOCCO arrived.

Lewis searched high and low downstairs but the laptop was nowhere to be seen. He went back upstairs and again looked in cupboards and drawers with no luck.

He was just about to leave Helen's room when he decided to look under the bed and low and behold there it was, he reached under the bed and retrieved the laptop. He went downstairs and handed it to an officer and told him to take it straight to the technical lab at the station and get it processed immediately.

Meanwhile Deacon had arrived at Mrs Templeton's ward and spoke to the ward clerk. He showed her his ID then asked if he could have a word with Mrs Templeton, the clerk called Staff Nurse Janet Wood over to help Deacon, she said it was ok but asked him not to stay too long as the doctor would be doing his rounds shortly and he would wish to see her.

The Nurse pointed to the end of the ward and said Mrs Templeton was in a single room on the left. He walked along the ward, a couple of patients called out to him thinking he was the doctor, Deacon ignored them and kept on walking until he reached the single room. There was no sign of the WPC outside the room, so he knocked the door but there was no answer, he tentatively opened the door and peered inside. The bed was empty so he walked in, he noticed the bathroom door was open and it was obvious she wasn't in there either. He called over a Nurse who had just finished attending to another patient and asked her if she knew where Mrs Templeton or the WPC could be. She told him to try the day room, she said the WPC and Mrs Templeton had been there about ten minutes earlier, if they weren't in the day room she advised him to go to the sister's office at the entrance of the ward and enquire there.

Deacon checked the day room and realising they weren't there went to the Sister's office but it was empty so he returned to the ward clerk, she told him to wait a minute while she called someone. After five minutes the Ward Sister appeared and asked if she could help. Deacon explained the situation the sister said she would check with her staff which she promptly did but with no joy. Deacon asked if he could use the phone and called Lewis's mobile, he was still at Helen's house when the call came through, Lewis was angry that the WPC and Mrs Templeton had just disappeared into thin air off a busy ward, he then told Deacon about Helen's disappearance. Deacon commented: 'I don't believe this Thomas is still hounding us even in death.' He added he would go to the hospital security office and check the CCTV images in case she left with someone. Lewis said that when he had done that go straight back to the station and cross reference Helen and Mrs Templeton on the computer and implement a search for Mrs Templeton and the WPC.

Lewis ended the call then rang the duty Sergeant at Chelsea asking him to check with Templeton if his wife had a car, and if so he was to get the registration number and details then call him back. The Sergeant returned Lewis's call confirming she did have a car and it was a Mercedes Benz convertible and should be in their garage, he then gave Lewis the details. Lewis headed straight over to Templeton's house in case the car was there but discovered it was missing from the garage so he put out an APB on the car.

Two hours later a call came in that Mrs Templeton's car was found abandoned in a country lane, both front doors were open and there was fresh blood on the rear seat, a sample of the blood had been sent to lab, SOCCO and Forensics had been dispatched to process the car.

When Lewis received the news he called Deacon, he was in the process of cross referencing Helen Price with Mrs Templeton, he told Lewis: 'There is no link between the two women under their married names, but they were both born in Worthing West Sussex and grew up together, living in the same street and going to the same schools. Helen Marie Price—then Helen Brent went to college before working as a Solicitor's secretary in Brighton, she later moved to Bayswater and at twenty nine married the CC in nineteen sixty four. Templeton—then Isobel Jane Harding never went to college and had several mundane jobs in the Worthing area before moving to Chelsea in nineteen eighty nine to live with Alex Templeton, two years later she married him in Barbados while on holiday.

There is no indication they have had any communication since they left school, accept for the charity events and of course Helen's party that you attended.' Lewis replied: 'It is obvious they have met at some time since and it seems there is bad blood between them, go and see Templeton and see what he can tell you and I'll go and see the CC and ask him if he knows anything further.

When questioned Templeton told Deacon that his wife had never mentioned knowing Helen, and he had never seen anything to suggest they knew each other. Meanwhile Lewis had gained permission to speak to the Chief Constable; he also said he never suspected the women new each other and could not recall seeing the two women talking at the party.

As soon as Lewis had finished with the CC he went straight to the scene of Isobel Templeton's abandoned car. Lewis met up with the Detective Constable heading the search of the area, he told Lewis there was drag marks leading from the car and a hole in the fence with blood on the fence post but, no signs of a body, he was waiting for a dog patrol as the bushes on the far side of the field were very dense and un-passable. The detective went on to explain that a woman's coat was found in the car . . . . At that moment Lewis received a call from Deacon to say that Alex Templeton had a change of heart and wanted to see Lewis, he also wanted his own solicitor present, Lewis told Deacon to get Templeton's Solicitor there immediately and he would return straight away.

On his arrival back at Head Quarters Deacon met Lewis at the entrance and said that the Solicitor was on his way in, but Templeton was happy to start speaking to Lewis before he arrived. Lewis rubbed his hands together and said: 'Here we go, come on let's see what he has to tell us.'

This time Templeton was taken into another interview room which had a two way mirror on one wall. Lewis told Deacon to watch from the next room and they would discuss matters afterwards but, if he thought of anything during the interview then to speak to him through the ear piece he was wearing.

Once they were sat down Lewis told Templeton that he would record the interview but, if he changed his mind and required his solicitor then he could stop and wait for him at any time. Templeton said that he wanted a deal because the information he had was vital to the case, Lewis said that once he had heard what he had to say he would do his best to arrange something but could not promise anything. Templeton nodded and cleared his throat then said: 'Well, I was lying when I said that Helen Price and Isobel did not know each other, in fact they grew up together but not as friends. They went to school together but after a few brief meetings in their teens they lost touch. However about five years before we married they met again at a school reunion, afterwards one of the former pupils held a party at his house, there was lots of booze and drugs and somehow they both got sucked in to taking the stuff. When they woke up the next morning they were both in bed naked, the host of the party was lying naked between them, but neither of them could remember much about the night before. They agreed never to talk about it to anyone and they both went their separate ways. Templeton told Lewis he never knew anything about the incident but one night they were at a charity fund raiser and Helen and Charles were there. They had been introduced but Isobel and Helen were both clearly uncomfortable at seeing each other, on their way home he asked her about it and after some persuasion she had told all. Templeton continued saying he had become crooked over the years and through greed and stupidity saw an opportunity to have a big wig in his pocket so to speak.

He said he persuaded Isobel to invite Helen for a drink one evening when they knew Charles was at a Police convention in London. They chatted awkwardly for a while but after a few wines Isobel prompted by Templeton brought up the subject of the party. Helen went white and said she ought to be going so he let her know Isobel had told him about the whole sordid thing, he said she almost died on the spot.

Templeton took a long pause clearing his throat, he then said: 'To cut a long story short I convinced her to be my eyes and ears whenever Charles made or received phone calls or visitors, she was to listen in on an extension in another room and inform me about the conversations. That's how Palmer knew the details of the safe house. If she refused I told her I would tell her secrets to everyone including her husband.'

When he had finished talking he asked about his deal and Lewis said he would see what he could do adding, it looked like Isobel had taken Helen hostage, possibly killing her.

Afterwards Lewis and Deacon met in the passageway outside and Deacon said that the dogs at scene of the abandoned car had lost the scent at the same spot the shrubbery had became impassable, he added that It appeared that someone had left a false trail, probably to buy extra time to get away. However they had found fresh tyre tracks in some loose gravel leading away from Isobel's car, he also told Lewis the WPC from the hospital had turned up. She had come back to the station because she had received a phone call from Mrs Price, she had apparently told the WPC that her husband the Chief Constable asked her to call and tell her that she could come back because Mrs Templeton was no longer under suspicion.

Lewis said to Deacon: 'Are we now to believe it is Helen that's taken Isobel? I don't know if I'm coming or going here Inspector.'

CHAPTER FORTY TWO

Lewis left Deacon and went to call the Commissioner and update him on recent events. He told him that Templeton had revealed a possible link between the missing women and the case. The Commissioner thanked Lewis and told him he was doing a great job, Lewis reminded him that it was a team effort and it was not over yet as they had to find the women. The Commissioner acknowledged Lewis's comment then said that Charles Price would be released imminently as there was clearly no point in holding him any longer.

As Lewis was hanging up the phone Deacon knocked his open door and went in, he told him that he had checked if Charles's car been impounded, he was told that it hadn't so it should be in the garage of the house. Deacon added that they could check the tyres against the treads at the scene of the abandon car and hopefully rule it out.

Lewis however said he had looked in the garage and the car was gone, he then called the DC at the search scene and told him to call off the search and send everyone in the direction the tyre tracks were heading, and check every building along the road including sheds, outhouses, garages and houses, if he needed warrants then get them. The Detective said he was already onto it and hung up. Lewis immediately put out an APB on Charles's car then called the Forensic lab to find out the results of the tests on the blood. He was told they had just got the results and it was Isobel's blood. Lewis told Deacon: 'Ok, so now it is definitely Helen that has taken Isobel, but what I can't fathom is why, or the reason she took her back to her own house, get Helen's car checked out, we assumed that Isobel took her so we left Helens car alone, by the way did the hospital security tapes give you anything?'

'No Gov, they only have one camera working at the moment and that only covers the gardens and the rear car park. The one that covers the front gates and the multi storey car park hasn't worked for over two weeks.'

'Very helpful that is, ok let's go and see if they have found anything on Helens laptop.'

At the tech lab the Technician that was working on the laptop told them that all the files had been erased professionally but, he was able to recapture some of them from the hard drive. There were E-Mails to and from Templeton—the ones to him were providing vital information on Police movements during the kidnappings and other cases, going back over a year. E-Mails from Templeton were requesting certain pieces of information he needed. He said: 'I still have some more information to download so I will be in touch when I have finished.'

Lewis and Deacon knew they could do nothing until Charles's car and—or the women had been found so they headed to the canteen. They discussed the case and were dumbfounded when they thought back to the beginning and how it all began with Sam Jessop's murder. Lewis commented: 'It's been a long, long journey and I am glad you have been in on it with me. If you had forecasted how this would pan out though I would seriously have had you sectioned. I only hope we can wrap this up soon without losing any more lives and who knows we may even get a medal.' They put their coffee cups together and Deacon said: 'Here—Here, I'll drink to that Gov.'

When Deacon and Lewis finished their break they went to Lewis's office, they each read through their notes and tried to figure out why Helen may have taken Isobel, but neither could think of a reason, after an hour Lewis told Deacon to go home and get some sleep, he said he would kip in his chair in case something came up. Deacon didn't protest and said goodnight. Lewis settled down in his chair to get forty winks while mulling things over and drifted off in to a fretful sleep thinking about the case.

At five minutes past three in the morning a woman walked into the Police station wearing a blue coat and white skirt, dark glasses and headscarf. She told the duty officer she was Mrs Templeton and wished to see her husband. The duty constable was new and not completely up to date with the case and said he would have to get permission. The constable made to pick up the phone but, the woman took a gun from her pocket and pointed it at him through the gap in the glass partition, telling him to take her to Templeton. She asked if there were many officers in the station, he said there weren't but there were two officers in the custody suite. She told him to open the door and stand back, she told him to move slow and quiet and to take her to the cells. He took her along the corridor and when they reached the custody suite she told him to open the door very, very slowly. Trembling, the PC opened the door, the two officers on duty were drowsy but when they heard the door open they leapt out of their chairs, the woman said: "Stop right where you are and put your hands in the air, I have a gun". They stopped dead in their tracks and obeyed her command. She told the PC to take their handcuffs and cuff them both to the radiator pipes. After he had done that she told him to gag them both using their socks. One of the officers had the cell keys chained to his belt, she told the young PC to fetch them and then look for her husband's cell.

He took the keys and shaking with fright found Templeton's cell, the woman told the PC to open up the cell then lye on the floor and put his hands behind his back. She took his handcuffs and cuffed him and shoved a hanky in his mouth.

The woman walked into Templeton's cell where he lay sleeping and shot him twice in the head, spraying blood and tissue up the wall and over the bed; she then turned and calmly walked out of the building.

CHAPTER FOURTY THREE

It was over two hours before the scene in the cells was discovered. The relief custody officers found the macabre scene and alerted Lewis. He rushed down to the cells, by then the young PC and the two officers had been set free. The younger PC, Robin Scot was in shock and slightly incoherent when question but, he tried his best to tell Lewis his version of events. Lewis asked if he could identify the woman. The PC wasn't sure but said he would do his best to describe her. Lewis then called the Pathologist to come and process the body, and SOCCO and Forensic to check the cell.

Lewis phoned his team telling them to come back into work, many were in bed sleeping and Lewis's calls were met with a few moans and groans. He then took PC Scott up to his office where he showed him photos of Isobel and Helen. The officer looked at the pictures but the woman's glasses had made it difficult to be sure the officer said he was sorry, Lewis said it was ok and told the officer to sit down and he would arrange for him to go to hospital and get checked over.

Lewis put out an immediate alert on the two women at all airports, train stations, and seaports, he then called an ambulance for PC Scott he also put out another APB on the car telling all mobile units to be on the lookout for the two women and said they were armed.

Lewis called Charles Price who had since been released but there was no answer. He left a message on the answer phone saying what had happened throughout the day and that Helen was now a suspect, he hoped Charles wasn't roaming the streets looking for her.

When Deacon arrived back at Head Quarters Lewis briefed him on events, Deacon thought for a while then asked: 'Well who was it Helen or Isobel?'

'Good question, there has been no sighting of Charles's car or the women. I'm hoping to view the tapes from outside the station, at the front desk and the custody suite.'

After a while the tech lab called saying the tapes were ready for viewing. Lewis said to Deacon: 'Let's go and look at these videos.'

They greeted the lab tech then Lewis asked him to run the tapes. They watched as the Jag arrived at the station, they saw the woman get out of the passenger door and walk up the steps to the front desk, but it was too dark to recognise her and she had her head down and turned away from the cameras.

The woman then approached the desk but again her back was to the camera. They watched her pull the gun and force the PC to take her to the custody area. The camera there picked her up and she was facing the camera but, she managed to keep her head down, so again they couldn't see who it was. It was the same story when she left the station, they watched her get in the car and she drove off, Lewis remarked: 'She knew how to avoid the cameras that's for sure.'

It took over half an hour to run the tape's, they thanked the technician for his help and left the lab.

Lewis and Deacon were walking back to Lewis's office when Lewis got a call from control, he was told that the jag had been spotted by a traffic camera, it was heading towards the area of the disused military airfield that Thomas was originally thought to have been heading for.

Lewis and Deacon rushed to Lewis's car and they sped off in the direction of the airfield, using the car radio Lewis alerted the ART.

When they reached the gates of the airfield they found the lock and chain had been forced off and the gates were wide open. Lewis drove in switching his lights off and they looked around. He drove on until they came across the old hangers and airfield buildings. They were surprised that there was no sign of a car or aircraft anywhere. He drove around the back of the buildings to the other end of the airfield, stopping and switched the engine off, he said to Deacon: 'I think we'll wait here, we have a good view of the whole of the airfield.' Deacon didn't answer he just nodded, Lewis noticed he looked a little uncomfortable but he shrugged it off, putting it down to the events of the last forty eight hours.

A few minutes later the ART notified Lewis they were approaching the airfield. Lewis told them to wait out of sight outside of the airfield and watch for the car and alert him the minute it arrived.

About fifteen minutes went by then suddenly there was a roar of an engine which appeared to be coming from above. Lewis looked up and saw the lights of a helicopter hovering above the airfield, eventually it come down and landed about thirty feet away from where they sat in their car. They watched but there was no movement from inside or outside of the helicopter.

Less than five minutes went by before they received a call from ART reporting that the jag was approaching the airfield, Lewis acknowledged the call and told them to stand by. He wandered why it had taken so long for the car to arrive but dismissed it.

That was when Lewis received the biggest shock of the whole investigation. He kept hold of the radio mike ready to call the ART in when he suddenly felt a dig in his side. He looked round and saw Deacon was holding a gun up against him. Deacon told Lewis to put the mike down. Lewis just stared at Deacon not able to come to terms with what was happening, he slowly replaced the mike and looked back at Deacon and the gun, then asked him: 'what; the hell are you doing Martin, have you lost your mind, for God's sake, why? What is this?'

'THIS is where you and I part company Gov, you never saw this one coming did you?'

Lewis agreed he had not suspected a thing telling him it was madness as they had been working together for seven years. He then asked: 'Why are you doing this? What's in it for you?'

'A fortune that's what's in it for me and no more working two or three days without a break for peanuts, getting called out at all times of the night and day. I am not wasting the rest of my life waiting for my pension. Look at your Chief Constable, over thirty years in the force and when he goes that will be that. He will be just another ex cop, I don't want that. When I leave here tonight I will be set up for the rest of my life.'

Lewis said: "I" isn't there a "we" what about Isobel and Helen aren't they in on this? How have you managed to keep all this so quiet? You have been in on the investigation all along even interviewing suspects, how long have you been planning it?'

Deacon couldn't look at Lewis, he just said: 'WE have been planning this for over a year, I met Isobel at a party and we hit it off straight away. Eventually she told me what Templeton was like and she asked me to do something, she obviously meant officially. I however managed to make her see it my way, so with my computer skills we have been milking him on a large scale and putting the money in an off shore account in the Cayman Islands, actually we have just over ten million now. As for Helen Price she was just an unwilling accomplice, Isobel recruited her at the dinner party you attended, that is what they were discussing when you saw them. We just cashed in on the hold Templeton had on her regarding her past.'

Lewis told him they were stupid and would never get away with it, adding: 'What about Helen's blood at her house, how did she get injured?'

'She didn't, Isobel just nicked her hand with a knife to get enough blood to throw you off the scent, I called Helen to make her call the hospital with the bogus message to tell the WPC to leave the room, Isobel then legged it. I went to the hospital and kicked up a fuss because Isobel was gone, we had you all fooled. Even that laptop you found at the Price's, that was Isobel's, we swapped them so you would think Helen was the mole, we had it planned down to the finest detail.'

As Deacon was talking the Jag arrived, Deacon said: 'Well this is where we say goodbye, get out slowly and go to the front of the car and get your handcuffs out.' Deacon got out simultaneously and went to the front of the car, Lewis said: 'Give this up Martin, we'll get you in the end, we always do.'

'I am prepared to take that risk, now turn around and face the car.' Deacon snapped. Lewis obeyed and as Deacon was fitting the cuffs Lewis said: 'Tell me where the Thomas fiasco fits into all this?' Deacon replied: 'Thomas was just an unexpected and welcome diversion, it allowed us to finalise our plans under the radar so to speak. As for Templeton, that wasn't planned, that was Isobel's decision. I knew nothing about it until the balloon went up I admit that has soured things a little, anyway that's enough chatter. Now walk towards the chopper and no tricks, I like you Andrew and do not wish to harm you but if I have to I will, I'm in too deep to stop now.'

Just as they were about to move away the ART Sergeant called: "DCS Lewis, Sergeant Walker ART, come in, is everything alright—over?' Lewis stopped but Deacon told him to ignore it and keep walking, Lewis said: 'If I ignore it they will come flooding in here knowing something's wrong.' Deacon thought then said: 'Ok but tell them we are alright.' Deacon unlocked the cuffs and Lewis lifted the mike and started to speak, but then suddenly he said aloud: "GET IN HERE FAST." Deacon went to snatch the mike from Lewis and to hit him with the gun, but Lewis hit him full in the face with his elbow sending Deacon off balance. Lewis went for the gun and they wrestled for it for several seconds but Deacon managed to twist Lewis's wrist, making him drop the gun. Deacon grabbed it just as the ART burst onto the scene and surrounded them both shouting at Deacon to drop the gun. Lewis got to his feet and saw Isobel get out of the Jag with two large bags and start to run towards the helicopter. He pointed at the helicopter and shouted out to Deacon: 'There goes your girlfriend and your money.' Deacon looked seeing Isobel heading for the chopper, he went to shoot at her but the ART responded and opened fire. Deacon dropped to the ground blood coming from his head and chest. Lewis fell to the ground and lifted Deacon's head onto his knee and said: 'Martin; you stupid man you had all your life before you, now look.' Deacon was fading fast but he managed to whisper: 'Helen in boot.' He lifted his arm and weakly pointed to the Jag he then went limp and gave out a last long gasp.

Some of the ART team rushed to the jag, Isobel seeing what was happening and hearing the gun fire didn't hang around, she boarded the chopper and it began to take off. The ART shot at the engine compartment and hit it several times but it flew away smoke trailing behind.

Lewis rushed to the boot of the Jag and found Helen, her hands and feet were bound with cable ties, she was barely conscious but managed to say: 'Charles .... shot .... home.' She was too weak to say anything else.

Lewis and an ART officer lifted her out onto the ground, Lewis ordered the officer to call an ambulance then ran back to his car and sped off to Charles's house, calling for armed back up and medical assistance.

On arrival at the Price's house he found the front door open and no lights on, he had only just arrived when in response to his call DI Barnes and two unmarked cars arrived containing two armed officers in plain clothes. Lewis told the officer's to go to the back of the house while he and Barnes went into the house from the front. Lewis called out: 'ARMED POLICE, STAY WHERE YOU ARE AND DROP YOUR WEAPONS.' There was no response so they went in and Lewis switched on the hall lights. As they ventured into the hallway, they heard a whimpering coming from the lounge. Barnes and Lewis stood either side of the lounge door and called out: 'ARMED POLICE COME ON OUT.' All was quiet so they edged their way into the room. Lewis switched on the lights and saw Charles lying on the floor in a pool of blood he had been shot in the chest. Meanwhile the paramedics had arrived; Lewis went and beckoned them in to see to Charles. He and Barnes then went and checked the rest of the house but it was all clear so they returned to the lounge.

Lewis asked how Charles was, one of the medics told Lewis it didn't look good he had lost a lot of blood and was in shock. He said they had administered adrenalin by injection and put up a saline drip plus given him oxygen.

Lewis stood back allowing the paramedics to lift Charles onto a trolley and take him out to the ambulance. The medics put Charles in the back and one stayed with him, the other medic shut the doors. Lewis gave him his mobile and office phone numbers asking him to call if there was any change, he explained who Charles was and that he was a personal friend. He also told the paramedic that Charles's wife was also being taken to hospital that evening. The medic assured Lewis that he would make enquiries regarding Helen and notify him of their condition he then boarded the ambulance and sped off with the siren and blue lights on.

Lewis and Barnes spent over an hour going over the house with the officers but found nothing untoward, other than Charles's blood in the lounge and overturned furniture. However he was duty bound to call SOCCO and Forensics to process the house. Leaving Barnes to oversee proceedings he said he was returning to the station. He was about five minutes into his journey when his mobile rang. He pulled over and pulling the mobile from his pocket he took the call, it was a doctor from the hospital. The medic had given them Lewis's number, he called to tell Lewis that unfortunately Charles had lost too much blood and was dead on arrival, there was no news of Helen at that time. Lewis thanked the doctor and sat with his head resting on his hands on the steering wheel. Suddenly it all got too much for him and he burst into tears, he sobbed for a while and then stopped and wiped his eyes. After a little while he called Karen, she answered and he said 'Hello darling, I'm on my way home.'

Lewis ended the call and then called DI Barnes and asked him to wind things up and he would see him in the morning.

Lewis didn't sleep at all that night so he got up at five thirty and went into work. He wrote up his reports on the previous days tragic events then sat staring at his computer screen. After ten minutes he decided he couldn't handle the job anymore, dealing with death, violence and grieving relatives left behind on a daily basis had all taken their toll over the years. Lewis thought it was time for someone else to take the reins. He picked up his pen and a sheet of official headed note paper and he sadly composed his resignation letter.

Addressing the envelope to the Chief Commissioner he placed it in his out tray. After gathering up his personal belongings Lewis walked out of his office, stopping outside Deacon's office to take one more look around. He murmured very quietly: 'GOODBYE MARTIN.'

EPILOGUE

Andrew Lewis spent the next few weeks trying to adjust to his new life, as usual Karen was his rock, not wishing to suffocate him but there for him when he needed her. He whiled away his time catching up on odd jobs around the house that he had long neglected, trying to divert his thoughts away from his recent losses.

Three weeks after his resignation Lewis and his wife had joined the large numbers of mourners at the highly attended funerals of Martin Deacon and Charles Price, despite what Deacon had done he had made many friends and they still respected him despite his recent uncharacteristic actions.

The evening of Charles Price's funeral Karen and Lewis were sat silently drinking a cup of tea when Lewis said: 'You ought to write to Sophie and ask her to send some details of properties in Canada.' Karen sat quiet not quite taking in what he had said. When it sunk in though she put her cup down and pulled him close to her smothering him with kisses, she jumped up and said she would write to Sophie immediately before he had a chance to change his mind.

The next morning at breakfast the phone rang and Karen answered it, Andrew was reading the morning newspaper and he heard her say: 'Ok I'll fetch him.' She came into the kitchen with a knowing look on her face and handed him the phone. It was the chief Commissioner, he said: 'Hello Andrew, how are you?'

'I'm getting there thanks, what can I do for you?'

'Well it's like this we have a serious situation on our hands, there has been a large explosion in a terraced house in west Chelsea with multiple deaths, we believe insurgents were constructing a large explosive device when it accidently exploded killing them and several innocent people, one was a small child.' Lewis was a little taken back that the Commissioner had called him, he asked: 'What's this got to do with me? I'm not a Police Officer anymore.' The Commissioner said: 'We know that Andrew and we understand but, the new DCS hasn't had time to get acclimatised and doesn't know the patch yet, plus he has been fast tracked, this is going to be big and you have more experience and you have useful contacts, if you could just come in and oversee proceedings while the investigation is ongoing you would be doing the force a great service. We could suspend your resignation for a couple of months and you will be on full pay.'

'Sorry sir but I can't I've promised Karen, we're going to Canada to live, she's my life now.' He apologised again and said goodbye.

Karen however instinctively knew the contents of the call, taking one look at her husband's face she went into the hallway and got his coat. Bringing it back into the kitchen she picked up the letter to Sophie and tore it in two. Lewis smiled at her and said: 'You are really amazing, you do know that don't you?'

He put on his shoes and coat and kissed her. She said: 'Goodbye darling see you when I see you.' Lewis was already half way down the drive . . . .

Printed in Great Britain
by Amazon.co.uk, Ltd.,
Marston Gate.